Wounds into Wisdom

By Kristie Higgins

Kristie Higgins/Allegro Publishing
406 Holly Rd
Glen Burnie, Maryland 21061
www.kristies223.wordpress.com

Wounds into Wisdom/ Kristie Higgins.
ISBN 978-0-9903715-1-9

Acknowledgements

To my alpha readers:
Debbie Layton
Dana Flanders Moritz
Cathie Brashear
Chrystal Vaughn
Kristi Lyerla

To my beta readers:
Melanie Maloney
Mary Hebda
Christina Kilpatrick
Ashley Singer-Falkner

To Brett Lyerla for his excellent cover art,

To Jill Miklosovic, my editor and friend,

To all of my friends and family who have encouraged me to publish my stories,

Lastly, to all those in the horse racing business who love and take care of their horses the way my characters do, and most importantly, to the early female jockeys who paved the way for many successful women in racing, who took punches and rolled, then got back up and won races,

Thank you!

Kristie

Turn your wounds into wisdom.

-Oprah Winfrey

Contents

Prologue

February 1969

"How despicably I have acted!" she cried; "I, who have prided myself on my discernment! I, who have valued myself on my abilities! who have often disdained the generous candour of my sister, and gratified my vanity in useless or blamable mistrust! How humiliating is this discovery! Yet, how just a humiliation! Had I been in love, I could not have been more wretchedly blind. But vanity, not love, has been my folly. Pleased with the preference of one, and offended by the neglect of the other, on the very beginning of our acquaintance, I have courted prepossession and ignorance, and driven reason away, where either were concerned. Till this moment I never knew myself."

"Love does silly things to people." Candy folded down the edge of the page, worn with excessive use. *Pride and*

Prejudice was one of her favorite books, though she had no idea why. She didn't believe in all that romance stuff, though she did sort of hope for it. One day. Maybe. Hopefully.

Longingly, she gazed at the poster of Bobby Darin on her wall. If only she could find someone as romantic as he. Musicians were the most romantic of all men. They were so deep. She suppressed a sigh of pining by pressing her lips together. Guys like that weren't real, but they sure were cute to look at. Candy fancied herself as an old-fashioned girl when it came to music. Darin's nine-year-old "Mack the Knife" was her favorite song of all time, and that record was always on her record player, ready to go.

Laughter from downstairs rang over the sound of the annoying rock music from the record player blasting in the living room. *Jimi Hendrix again.* He was her brother's hero as a drug-using guitarist. To Candy, the music was tinny and almost painful to listen to. It was wild, screeching, eerie almost, and loud. *That's not music.* The only reason her brother and friends could stand it was because they were high. The pungent smell of marijuana smoke slipped under her door in soft waves. Candy closed her eyes and let out a breath of air, hoping none of it got into her lungs. She was about to grab a towel from her hamper to cover the crack under the door when she heard shouting.

"Can Can!" It was her brother. "Get down here! Now!" The music stopped as someone dragged the needle across the record, scratching it. *Good.* She dropped her head into her hands and groaned. What could he possibly want from her? "Hey! Can!" She heard footsteps running up the stairs and her heart thumped as she anticipated his arrival. Any second now, there would be a loud bang as the door hit the wall behind it, sending the doorknob further into the gaping hole in the plaster.

She tensed. *Bang!* She jumped anyway. "What?" With her exclamation, her hands gripped the side of her bed, her long, ginger hair shaking from her frustration.

"Rachel's on TV!"

"What?" Candy stood. A glimmer of hope shone in her eyes. Did they have a stakes winner today? On her day off, too. Ugh, how frustrating that she wasn't there to see it.

"It's bad, Can. Come on!"

Her hope vanished in an instant. The two ran down the stairs together in a rush that might have been the scene on a Christmas morning in any other house. Not theirs. That thought was the furthest thing from her mind, though, as she turned her head so she could see the television as she ran. Once at the bottom, she pushed Don out of the way and sprinted to the television. One of Don's friends slapped the side of it and the black and white picture became clearer.

"She was wearing a dark blue pea coat and mittens, jeans, and a green blouse. And b-boots." The woman on the screen paused to compose herself as a man rubbed her back in encouragement. After a moment, she was able to continue. "We are offering a reward of two thousand dollars for any information…"

It was Rachel's mother. Candy's skin crawled with fear, and every hair stood straight up on her arms. Her bony hands covered her mouth as she noted a small picture in the corner of the screen, Rachel's eleventh grade yearbook photo.

Julia, Rachel's mother, had her arms wrapped around a notebook as it covered her chest like a shield. This woman, also Candy's boss at Belmont Park, was the strongest woman she had ever known, but now, she was a mess. Candy could almost see her quivering with fear despite the blurred black and white picture. To see Julia this way, someone who had always been dauntless in Candy's eyes, scared her to death.

"No," she whispered, her voice husky with emotion. Fortunately, the others in the room let her watch the rest of the story. When it was over, the talking head went on, speaking as if the world had not ended. It certainly had. "No. No," she continued with tears drizzling down her face and over her cold hands. The warmth of her tears did little for that chill. Nothing could. Nothing ever would.

"Can, you went to the movies with her last night, didn't you?"

She almost didn't hear her brother's question as she continued to stare at the television. Now the reporter was talking about the Beatles, but she didn't hear a word of it. The question finally registered with her and she nodded.

"Oh, my God," she whispered.

"Didn't you walk her to the station? Did she get on the train?" Don's voice rose with every word.

With balled fists, she turned from the television and screamed at her brother. "I don't know!" Candy couldn't take another question from him and ran back up to her room. She slammed the door behind her and paced the floor in her small room.

Fortunately, there wasn't much furniture in her way – only a twin bed and a small dresser. One of the drawers had no handles and was crooked and unable to close all the way. The dresser was the same shade of wood as the paneled walls of her attic bedroom. The orange carpet remnant was worn, so thin in places that she could almost see the wood floors. She almost tripped over one wrinkle, but didn't because she knew where it was without thinking, as it had been there for so long.

"What do I do?" she asked herself, but had no answer. Only seconds later, it hit her. *Look for her.* It was cold, February, and icy. She had to get to her quickly. If Rachel were outside somewhere, maybe in an alley, still in Queens, Candy knew she could find her. She knew this borough like the back of her hand. It was noon, so the sun was up lighting the way, maybe melting some of the ice that had formed overnight. Maybe it was warm enough for Rachel to survive. If she were out there somewhere, Candy would find her.

She grabbed her coat and tossed it on as she ran down the stairs.

"Where you going?" Don shouted as she barreled through the front door. Her brother's demand for answers was her last concern. She had to find Rachel. Rachel was her best friend, her only friend, her rock.

Every alley was an opportunity to Candy. She thoroughly searched behind trash bins, cans, bags, kicked aside rats as she asked them where her friend was. They weren't telling, the filthy beasts. Behind every trash can, in every corner, she positively knew she would see her friend lying there, half frozen. Despite that, she would still be alive, and Candy would take her home, warm her up, give her some soup – well, if she had any soup. She probably didn't. The house was usually void of food. They didn't even have mice because there was never anything for them to forage. They had all gone next door. One good thing about being poor.

Once she had thoroughly searched all the alleyways between her house and the subway station, she ventured on to other alleys. Just in case. Maybe Rachel had gone a different way. Why would she do that? Didn't matter. If there was a remote chance of finding Rachel, Candy was going to take it.

Her adrenaline, along with her hope, faded over the next three hours. With each step, her shoulders sagged a little more, her head drooped, and finally, she stopped. Her heart burned as she turned around in a full circle for one more look.

She had to admit the truth. Her friend had vanished.

Chapter One

"A little late to be hitchhiking, ain't it?"

"I guess. I need a ride. Can you help me out?"

"That depends. What you got in exchange?"

Traffic whizzed by and she prayed no one would hit them as she stood on the shoulder with this strange man's car half in a lane and half on the shoulder. Candy made out two dark eyes peering out at her. The streetlights burning brightly overhead made it impossible to see much else, but it was obvious he was practically drooling as he ogled her through the passenger side window. She knew what he wanted, and there was no way she was about to start using her body to get rides.

"Nothin'." She continued walking, hoping he would move on. Thankfully, he did.

At that point, she realized how dangerous this was. Rachel had walked only a block from her house on her way to the train station and was abducted. *If I'm taken, too, at least I'll know what poor Rachel went through. Besides, nothing to live for now anyway.*

She had given up her job as a groom at Belmont Park after seeing Rachel's story on the news. There was no way Candy was going back to the track to be reminded of Rachel's absence. Besides, she couldn't face Rachel's mother.

It was all Candy's fault. She knew she should not have let her friend walk on her own. Rachel had walked that walk many times before from her house to the subway in Queens. Still, you never know what can happen these days. Candy was the older and wiser one and might have been able to protect her. Her throat constricted as she tried desperately not to cry, but it was to no avail. Tears puddled in her eyes, reflecting the bright lights from the street lamps above and blinding her until they fell. Despite her sorrow, she kept walking.

A horn blaring from behind her scared her as a car sped up and approached, then stopped with screeching tires next to her. "Ooo!" She jumped away from the road. Once she recovered, she got a good look at the car. It was her parents' old car, and that meant Don was driving. With a groan, she closed her eyes and shook her head, then walked away as a heavy car door slammed.

She heard stomping grow closer behind her, and he yanked her arm. "Where do you think you're going?" he bellowed like a father. He was sort of her father, as their parents had been dead for three years now after a car accident. They had both been high, and now Don was probably high, too.

His drug of choice was heroin, and in between, it was pot. Now, noting his attitude and anger, she wondered if he had found coke. That's all they needed, to lose more money on drugs for him. She rolled her eyes as she ripped her arm from his grip and walked away again.

"Get back here!"

"Go home, Don. Come back when you're sober." Lowering her voice, she mumbled, "Like that'll ever happen."

"I am sober," he insisted. "Come on, Can. We gotta find jobs. You ruined everything leaving that job at Belmont. Now what are we gonna do? Huh?"

"I know what I'm going to do. I'm going to get away from you and your stupid drugs, and I'm going to earn my own money for my own place. I'm going to buy my own food and my own clothes. And I'm not paying for you to kill yourself with drugs like Mom and Dad."

Cursing at her, he pushed her down, spilling her backpack contents onto the shoulder of the road. He kicked a small, plain wooden box under the guardrail and into the long grass laced with snow. She screamed as she chased after it, then landed on her knees with a whimper. Clawing at the grass, she ripped out stalks by the handfuls. Finally, she found her box, then looked up to yell at her brother.

He was already speeding away.

Swiping her tears, she stormed back to her backpack, fell to her knees again, and picked up her things. Once everything was safe and sound, she cradled her wooden box. It had a crack now, which released a tidal wave of emotion. She leaned over, wracked with sobs, her body bouncing with each cry of sorrow.

Chapter Two

Her feet were killing her. After walking all night, with her steps gradually slowing, Candy finally stopped to rest. It wasn't that she wanted to stop. Her feet protested and simply refused to do what she wanted them to do. Cursing her feet, though they were thankfully covered with warm boots, she plopped down onto a bench.

Pulling her hat further over her head with her mitten-clad fingers, she shivered and wrapped her coat tighter around her slight figure. She was glad she had left her long ginger hair down and straight, as it was keeping her neck warm.

None of the familiar sirens wailed, which was eerie to her. There was no traffic, no people. Nothing moved. The only sounds were the rustle of frozen leaves in the young trees seemingly growing from the sidewalks. She took note of her surroundings. Where was she, anyway? Still in the city, of course. She figured it might take her days to walk out of the city limits.

This place was nothing like Queens. Despite her depression-induced brain fog, she remembered going over a bridge. Which one was it? She had no idea which borough she had landed in. It was clean, proper, and orderly, that much she could see. She would love to live here. As she gazed up at a fourth-floor apartment, a light came on. *Probably someone getting up early for work, hoping to beat the traffic through the city.* The light almost warmed her frozen nose as she imagined herself inside that place.

She could almost feel it. It would be warm; she would have a fire going and keep it going all night. She would cuddle herself in her down comforter, lay her head on a feather pillow, and sleep all night, every muscle relaxed and warm. As she stared, she felt her body rising and floating up and into the window. A man stood in the window now, sporting a naked but hairy chest. He scratched his chest for a few seconds, paused, then with a jerk, ripped the curtain over the window, blocking her from the room.

With a pronounced frown, she dropped her gaze to the ground again. People like her didn't live in places like that. A daughter of two drug addicts, most likely the result of an accidental pregnancy, she grew up taking care of her parents instead of the other way around. Then when Don started down the same path, she had to take care of him, too. She knew that sort of life wasn't normal. All the other kids had parents who took them places like the park or the zoo. Even the grocery store would have been nice from time to time.

When police arrived at the door the night their mom and dad died and coldly informed them that they had lost both parents, Don and Candy stood with their eyes wide open and jaws practically on the floor, but said nothing. When police asked if Don was over eighteen, he only nodded. They informed him that he was Candy's guardian now and left. Candy tried to be sad. Instead, she was relieved.

Dealing with Don alone would be much easier than dealing with two forty-something-year-old druggies. Who does drugs at that age, anyway? According to television and movies, only teenagers did that stuff. Not her. Other than inhaling leftover smoke from their joints, bongs, and other paraphernalia, she had never touched it. However, Don did. He almost jumped for joy when he learned that his deceased parents had left behind a stash.

When that was gone, he tried to get work around town, but many times overslept and was fired for not showing up. Candy, however, was the responsible one who always worked, and worked hard. Despite that, now that her parents were gone, she was barely able to make the rent. There was no food in the house, so she ate whatever she found lying around at the track. That's where she spent most of her time.

And that's where she had met her best friend, Rachel. She was cute, but not stuck up about it, like so many other girls. The two of them were like peas in a pod and swore to each other that they would one day become famous jockeys. Candy had ridden only a little, thanks to Rachel giving her a few lessons, and her next goal had been to become a pony girl, someone who helps take the horses to and from the track. *So much for that.*

Her best friend, all she had left in this world, was gone.

"Ma'am?" A male voice resounded from somewhere behind her.

With a jerk, she twisted in her seat. No one was there. She glanced left, right, behind, but there was no one.

"Ma'am?" It was coming from above. A man was perched on a balcony donning a purple robe with a little design on the pocket. It might have been a monogram, but she was unable to see it clearly. Smoke billowed from a pipe in his hand.

"Yes?" She pushed her hair back from her face.

"You best be moving on. They walk the beat around here, you know." He dismissively waved his pipe at her.

As if she didn't belong here... Well, she didn't, but how did he know that? Was it her ratty coat and hat? Her worn backpack? The fact that she was wearing jeans? Jeans were for the working class. Lowering her eyes again, she tightened her jaw to keep from crying, stood, and continued on despite her aching feet.

Submitting to the cold, she finally descended the stairs to a subway station. She hadn't wanted to use any of the five dollars she had, but she was so cold, she was forced to do something to get out of the elements. Taking her time, she read the signs, pretending to decide where to go, using up as much time as possible until the train started running again. As she watched the clock above the turnstiles, she tried to make it go faster, but it was of no use. She had an hour to go until five.

A subway worker eyed her as he approached his booth. His obvious glares told her she was unwelcomed at this hour. She wasn't about to leave unless he told her to because she was finally starting to be able to feel her fingers again. When he didn't approach her, and instead went into his booth, she relaxed. Just in case, she made her way out of his line of sight and closer to the stairs. With her partially thawed hands, she covered her face and backed against the wall. Then she slid down, finally letting go of the sobs that had been trying to overtake her.

She thought she heard people talking softly, murmuring, shuffling feet, the squeaky brakes of the subway. *Subway?* Candy woke with a start, her eyes suddenly wide open as she drew in a quick breath of air. Crowds of people were coming down the stairs dressed in rich overcoats, designer shoes, hats, and expensive purses. No one looked at her. Was she worthy of their attention? As she searched the eyes of the people who were seemingly office workers of some sort, she found them focused on getting to the turnstiles and then the train, and not on her. One man, though, glanced her way, and then shot his gaze away quickly.

She chuckled once. They thought of her as a threat and were trying to ignore her. Rolling her eyes, she took her hat off and ran her fingers through her hair. The horrible taste in her mouth reminded her that she hadn't brushed her teeth since yesterday and hadn't eaten much. Her only meal had come from a trash can.

Almost sardonically trying to play the part of a homeless person, she had eagerly watched a man throw away something after wrapping it in the paper it had come in. She had waited until he was gone, then ran to the trash can and pulled it out. It was an entire half of a Reuben sandwich. It was gone within seconds as she practically shoved the entire thing in her mouth at once.

Her stomach growled as she remembered the taste of that morsel. *Oh, it was so good.* Reaching under her coat, she touched her stomach, pressing against the ache of hunger, and then ran her fingers up the bumps that were her ribs. Being thin was in these days, but she was too thin. She was always hungry; she knew that much. The constant hunger pangs and growling noises had always been part of her life. Rachel used to slip her leftovers from home and the track kitchen, which helped. It was the only time her hunger had stopped.

Rachel would be here for her now if she knew where she was and what she was going through. If only. Then there was old familiar burning in her nose and behind her eyes as tears tried to escape. Covering her face, she refused to let the sadness rear its ugly head. Besides, she had to maintain her threatening appearance so she could enjoy the frightened looks on the white-collar workers' faces.

One woman stood out among the crowd. Silently, Candy cheered for her, imagining the woman was some sort of CEO or manager. She could not have been a secretary, not with those clothes and coat. The woman stood tall with her head held high, her nose slightly in the air as she clip-clopped her way past Candy. Before she reached the turnstile, she shuffled over to her right a bit, out of the way of the herding mob behind her. She stood there for several long seconds, still facing the turnstiles. As Candy knit her eyebrows at the sight, the woman turned and stared straight at her.

Candy's heart almost stopped for a second as her blue eyes met the woman's hazel eyes. She had on way too much makeup, Candy noticed. Her cheekbones were prominent and not a hair was out of place. As Candy noticed that she had been staring, she realized the other woman had been staring, too. Why? Candy almost found the strength to tear her eyes away.

Then, with her heels clacking on the tile floor, the woman with her strong, authoritative aura stepped over to Candy. Was this woman going to talk to her? If so, she should be eye to eye. Right? Or at least close to it. Was it rude to stay seated on the floor? It seemed this woman was at least two feet taller than she was. Candy thought it best to be as tall as possible.

Using the wall for help, Candy stood on two shaky legs while grasping her hat in her left hand like a security blanket. Her backpack still sat on the floor behind her, and in case someone tried to steal it, she made sure to hook the strap around her leg. The woman glanced down at Candy's feet, watching her guard her only possessions left in the world. Finally, the woman stopped, and they were face to face.

"Hi," Candy croaked. She cleared her throat and then repeated her greeting, making sure to keep her chin down so the woman wouldn't smell her morning breath.

She was almost glaring at Candy with one eyebrow raised. Would she yell at Candy for being in the wrong neighborhood? After all, that's how people were around here. Finally, she spoke. "You have a nice face. Good bone structure."

Candy was stunned, and words froze in her mouth. Finally, she found her manners, manners she had learned from other people in the world, not her parents. "Uh...Th-Thanks. Thank you."

The woman looked her over for a few seconds. "Open your coat."

"Um."

"Trust me," she added, blinking slowly. Candy met her eyes again, fear overtaking her now, as she was unable to decide whether to let this woman order her around like this, or run, or what. However, the woman's expression was lighter now, not so harsh. Maybe it would be all right. So she allowed her coat, one that was obviously two sizes too large, to open. Candy lowered her eyes to her ratty brown sweater and blushed at the obvious difference between the two of them.

The woman then reached for her sweater. As she tried to lift the sweater, Candy swatted her hand away purely on instinct. "Sorry," she said to the woman, but she wasn't sorry. Who did she think she was, anyway? The woman dropped her hand and thus also the idea of looking under Candy's sweater.

"You have good cheekbones. Thick hair. Pretty color. Your eyes tell a story, one of hardship. Your body is thin, but you are a little short to be a model."

Model? "Um, what? I mean, how tall are models?"

"My height. At least five foot ten. How tall are you?"

"Five nine." Candy stood up straight and tall.

The woman narrowed her eyes and scrutinized Candy again from head to toe. "What are you doing here?"

"I um, I had to leave. I mean, I have no one left."
As hard as she tried, she was unable to stop the tears as the
words pierced her heart. Saying it aloud hurt severely. She
dropped her head into her hands, hiding from this confident
woman who probably never cried a day in her life.

Candy heard the woman shuffling, but not leaving
as she expected. Candy lifted her head to find the woman
pulling out a business card. The woman handed it to her.
Candy paused and then took it.

"Give me a call if you decide you'd like to try it. If
you can't call, there's the address. But I wouldn't wear
what you're wearing. Do you have anything nicer?"

Candy stared down at her backpack. Jeans and a
few shirts, all worn, faded and stained from her hard work
at the track. She shook her head, admitting defeat.

The woman glanced in both directions and pulled
money from her purse as she shielded it from passersby.
She leaned in. "Listen to me. You cannot spend this on
anything but clothes. Do you hear me? You have to buy
something nice, or they won't even let you in. Buy blouses,
skirts, pants, dresses, whatever. Make sure it's nice. Do you
understand?"

Wide eyed, Candy nodded. Was she dreaming? Was
she still asleep on the floor at the bottom of the stairs? She
started to reach for the money, but the woman pulled it
away slightly again.

"Clothes, young lady. This could determine your
career. Do you promise me you'll do this? Otherwise, I
can't give you this money knowing it will go to waste on
drugs or something."

Candy's eyes suddenly filled with anger. "I don't do drugs," she growled. "I will *never* do drugs."

Candy's anger took the woman by surprise, and her aging eyes opened more widely. The two stood staring at each other, almost in a standoff. Finally, with one eye slightly closed, the woman relented and handed over the money, folded enough so that Candy couldn't tell how much it was. She hoped it was enough to buy clothes *and* food.

"Thank you." Candy was calmer now that her anger at the mere mention of the hellish lifestyle that destroyed her family finally dissipated.

Then, with a nod, the woman walked away. Candy scanned the area for anyone who might have seen the exchange of money and might try to take it from her. No one was paying attention, much to her relief. So she lifted her backpack onto her shoulder and shoved the money into her jeans pocket. Finding energy from somewhere deep within, she bounded up the stairs, which were empty on her side since everyone was on the other side going down.

For the first time in many months, she was encouraged. Her big chance to become a famous model! Talk about the story of a lifetime – *Homeless girl becomes supermodel after being discovered in the subway station.* She pictured herself hobnobbing with movie stars and… *Oh no.* Where would she take a shower for this meeting? By the time she made it to wherever this studio was, she knew she was going to be reeking of body odor. It didn't help that she had no idea where she was. As she took in her surroundings, with the morning sun illuminating the sides of buildings, shadowing others, she figured she had to be near or in Manhattan or the Upper East Side. She found herself on a corner and read the street signs. *Sixty-first* and *Lexington.*

There were stores everywhere. *Clothes. Shoes. Hair salons. Perfect.* Then she spotted a sausage cart with a red umbrella, and her stomach growled again as it begged for sustenance. There were a few men standing around it, each waiting their turn, and she stood behind them with wide eyes, eagerly trying to decide what she might want on her sausage. She closed her mouth so she wouldn't drool as she took in the marvelous aroma laced with the spice of mustard and relish.

As one by one the men bought their breakfast sausages, she should have been making her way closer to the cart but was instead pushed away as more men showed up. *How rude. Do they have no manners at all? Don't they know I'm a woman? A starving woman at that.* Her hat was stuffed into her coat pocket, so it was clear she was female, since her long strawberry hair flowed almost to her waist. But they didn't seem to care at all.

She began to push her way in, and when they tried to push her back, she stood her ground. As weak as she was, she was even more desperate for something to eat. Finally, she reached the front. The vendor glanced at her, then turned to another man and asked him what he wanted.

"Excuse me," Candy bellowed. "I'd like two sausages, please."

Everything stopped. It was silent, as if all of New York City had stopped to stare at her. Without moving her head, she darted her eyes from side to side, taking in the sight of all the grown men around her. Acting like a mother she had seen on television, she glared at each man, then at the vendor with a look that said, "You should be ashamed of yourselves." They seemed to agree. She decided to roll with it and play the part, lifting her chin a bit to reinforce her authority.

"Thank you." They lowered their heads in submission, with only a few nodding in acknowledgment of her words.

As she turned back, the vendor was holding two small sausages in buns in one hand. Her mouth watered. Then, as she was about to reach for the money the woman had given her, one of the men shoved a dollar in front of her. "On me," he said simply.

With her mouth agape, she stared at him as the vendor took the money and handed the sausages to her. Distracted by the whole exchange, she had forgotten to ask for toppings. But it didn't matter. It was food. And it was free.

"Thank you." Joy bubbled from her. The man only nodded and then left.

As Candy cherished her free food, guarding it with her whole body, she shuffled herself closer to a building and ate her breakfast. Both sausages were gone within seconds, and energy coursed through her veins. She almost sighed with relief at the rush. She was now strong, encouraged, and ready to take on the day and go shopping.

First, she had to know how much the woman had given her so she could budget her money. However, she couldn't let anybody see the money, so she ducked closer to a set of concrete stairs, hiding off to one side, shielding her windfall. Cautiously, she searched for muggers first but saw none. Everybody was too busy heading to work or wherever they go around here. She reached into her pocket and pulled out the folded bills. After scanning the area for danger one last time, she unfolded them.

Silently hunched over, she stared at a twenty-dollar bill. She couldn't believe that woman had given her one. A total stranger, too. Then, fully expecting a bunch of ones behind it, she found more twenties. Her jaw dropped as she checked each one, not believing her eyes. "One, two, three, four…," she counted, and eventually found ten twenty-dollar bills. *Two hundred dollars?* Her eyes popped with surprise. What did this woman think she was going to spend all of that on, anyway? With only two or three of those twenties, she could buy a whole wardrobe at the Queens Fashion Store.

Nevertheless, the woman had said her clothes had to be good enough to impress the people in the studio. Her stomach rolled with nervousness as she pictured herself in one of these expensive designer stores dressed as she was right now. She hadn't even brushed her teeth today. Glancing around, she tried to find a place that might have a bathroom. Nothing around her looked promising. She was going to have to walk somewhere and find one, so she shoved her money back into her pocket and set out on her quest.

The sun was up now, the air was slightly warmer, but her breath still fogged in front of her mouth as she walked. It was amazing to her how many people were out walking. Among the crowd, there was a petite young girl about her age with long, dark, curly hair and green eyes. *Rachel.* With her mouth open in amazement, she jogged closer to her through the crowd, and just when she was about to call Rachel's name, Candy realized it wasn't her. She stopped dead in her tracks and stared, her heart breaking all over again. People continued walking around her, some bumping her as they passed.

What was Rachel going through? Was she even alive? Did someone hurt her? Had someone killed her? A sob tried to escape, but she stopped it with her hand as she attempted to appear brave amid the scores of white collars. She couldn't think about that now. Her tears might freeze to her face.

So she kept walking. From her vantage point, she saw the faint silhouette of the Empire State Building. How far was it? She knew Macy's was near there. Was it possible to walk all that way without collapsing? Her legs were exhausted. Well, she had the money. *Might as well take a taxi.*

She stood on the curb, watching the traffic crawl by her inch by inch, and knew she could probably get there faster if she walked. However, inside the cab would be warm. But they were going so slowly that it might cost her half her money by the time they got there. She had no idea how much taxis charged, as she had used only the subway. The taxis appeared to all be full anyway, and none were stopping for her. Besides, maybe there were better stores along the way. So she pressed on toward Macy's.

On the next block, she found a store that seemed more in her price range. It was bigger than the designer boutiques, maybe more affordable, and maybe with a bathroom inside. She walked in.

Touching a few shirts, she shopped for something pretty. Then, curiosity overcame her, and she wanted desperately to check the price. She didn't want to appear concerned about it, though. People who shopped in a store like this weren't concerned with the cost. Nonchalantly, she glanced back and forth for prying eyes and saw none, so she pulled the shirt out enough to see the price tag.

Forty dollars. For a shirt? She knew with certainty that those people at the modeling agency were going to know how much she spent on clothes in an instant. She had to look rich. So she picked it up and hung the shirt over her arm.

"May I help you?" she heard from behind her. With a sharp breath, she turned and saw an elderly woman dressed in a black Katherine Hepburn-style suit behind her.

"Oh. I'm just looking for an outfit. I don't need any help yet. Thank you, though." She hoped to sound mature and sophisticated. She may have even heard a hint of an English accent in her own voice.

The woman in the suit eyed Candy from head to toe and crossed her arms. Candy wrinkled her brow at her for a second and then headed for another rack with pants. The woman followed. Candy glanced at her but knew instantly what the woman thought. Candy knew she probably smelled to high heaven, and she was dressed like a bum. Maybe if she explained herself.

"Look. This lady gave me her card and told me I could be a model. She told me to go buy some clothes, and she gave me some money." Candy pulled the mangled stack of twenties from her jeans pocket, then put it back in. "See? I have money. Okay?"

"Where did you get that money?" Candy thought she saw the woman's foot tapping the floor beneath her wide-legged pants.

"From the lady." Candy reached into her coat pocket and pulled out the business card, then showed it to her. The woman snatched it from Candy's hand and walked away. "Hey!" Candy rushed after her. When she caught up, she tried to take the card back, but the woman tightened her fist around it.

"We'll give her a call, then." The woman sneered, then picked up the phone. Candy shook her head, crossed her arms, and huffed.

"Give me the card," she tried, though she knew it was futile.

"Yes, I'd like to report a robbery."

Candy gasped. "What? No! You bitch! Give me my card back. She stole it from me," she shouted into the phone, hoping the police, or whoever was on the other end, heard her.

"Yes. Thank you," the woman said, and then hung up the phone.

"I can't believe you would do this to me! I finally get my big break, and you ruin it. How could you do this to me? Give me that card back!"

"You will keep your voice down, or I will remove you from my store."

Something inside her snapped, and she narrowed her eyes and leaned over the counter. "You will give me that card back, or I will knock you over and take it back." The woman didn't budge. Somewhere in the back of her mind, she heard fingers snapping and the song about the Jets from *West Side Story.* She was about to become a Jet.

Dropping the shirt she had been holding, she sprinted to the other side of the counter and grabbed at the woman's hand. As they fought, another customer came over to help. The thin, frail customer only screamed, "Stop! Stop!" as she waved her hands on either side of her face. Candy was determined and strong from her sausages this morning. Finally, she was able to pin down the woman's arm on the floor. She then pried the elderly, bony fingers open and shook the woman's hand until she dropped it. Candy snatched up the mangled card and sprinted her fastest out the door and into the street, bumping into several people on the way out.

After hurrying away for a block, she finally slowed her steps and turned to see if anyone was following her, namely, the police. Was she now a wanted woman? Would she wind up in jail for simply shopping? Thankfully, though, no one was coming.

Opening her fist, she studied the remnants of the business card. Thankfully, the address was still legible. Her shoulders sagged, and she looked up with relief, then carefully slipped the card into her pocket next to her money. Well, it was apparent buying designer clothes wouldn't work.

Pulling her hair back, she twisted it into a bun and shoved it into her hat, then pulled the hat down snugly over her head. This was her disguise.

By now, her bladder was screaming at her, and she knew she had to find a restroom or explode. They'd never allow her in a store or restaurant looking like this, but she had to find something. *Central Park.* She was only a few blocks from there. Through her pain, she jogged to the Park and finally found a public restroom.

She wrapped her coat around her backpack and stood at the sink with the pack on the floor between her legs. Despite some funny glances from other women, she took her toothbrush and toothpaste out of her backpack and began brushing her teeth. She used the soap in the dispenser to wash her face while desperately wishing for a shower.

As she dried her face with brown paper towels, she sensed someone watching her, so she raised her eyes to find an elderly lady in cat-eyed, dark-rimmed glasses standing next to her. A black camera hung from her neck. *Tourist.* Candy faked a polite smile, knowing the woman wasn't going to try to ruin her like the last old lady she'd had to deal with. A younger woman came out of the stall, and without washing her hands, she grabbed the older woman's arm and pulled her from the room while the aged woman continued to stare at Candy.

Candy squinted at the door as it closed. Was that younger woman afraid of her? Why? She was only a kid. Or was she? Inspecting herself in the mirror, she then saw what the woman at the train station had seen. Her sunken and shadowed eyes told a story, one of hardship. Her cheekbones were very prominent, reminding her that she was hungry again. Her clothes were a mess.

She had a decision to make – find clothes and go to the modeling agency, or use that money for food. Maybe even shelter. Hotels around here were too expensive. She had to find something cheaper, and with a shower. And heat, of course. Then again, if she were clean, she could go shopping for a few things and still go for that modeling job. *Hmm.* She found herself back around to the beginning again, and it seemed buying clothes for modeling was her best choice.

As much as she hated the idea, she knew exactly where to go in her old neighborhood for a motel. She also knew where to find nice clothes – at the store near her house. It was going to have to do because there was no way she was taking another chance on trying to buy designer clothes.

Standing up straight, she nodded at herself in the mirror and was encouraged. She put on her coat, swung her backpack onto her shoulders, and walked out with her head held high.

Chapter Three

"Well, I made it real far," Candy said aloud as she closed the motel room door behind her. She went right for the heater, turning it to its hottest setting. Her muscles relaxed as warm air drifted around her. After relishing and appreciating it for a moment, she tossed her backpack onto the bed and opened it to find clean clothes. She laid them on the bed, then stripped off her dirty clothes and headed for the shower.

Finally clean again, she put on her best outfit, which consisted of a blue blouse, some clean underwear, jeans that she used for work at the track, and a different sweater. That was all she had been able to fit into her backpack. Well, after today, she was going to have more. She reminded herself she'd have to buy a bigger bag to put all of her nice new clothes in as well.

Making sure she had her key, she tossed on her coat, mittens, and hat and walked to her favorite store – The Queens Fashion Store.

"Excuse me. I'd like to try these on, please."

The clerk was taken aback by all of the clothes piled in Candy's arms. Candy's bright blue eyes crinkled and shone over the mound like a sunrise. "You can only take in three at a time. Here, I will help you."

"Thanks."

The clerk, a young woman with a long dark mane, led her to a dressing room, where she helped Candy by handing her clothes and taking away things she rejected. After spending several minutes with the kind and helpful clerk, Candy felt comfortable enough to tell her about her big break.

"Are you kidding me? You're kidding me. Right?"

"No. I swear. She gave me money to buy nice stuff and told me to go to the agency. I'm going to find the nicest clothes I can and go there. Hopefully today."

"I bet you'd have to make an appointment for that."

"Oh. Really?"

"Yeah. My guess is, from what I've seen in movies, usually people who walk in have those headshots and other pictures and they hand them over to the secretary and never hear from the agency again. If I were you, I'd make an appointment to see that woman you mentioned."

"Oh, all right. That's a good idea. Thanks." Then, she handed a shirt over the door, dressed again, and continued her shopping spree. Making sure to save enough for the motel for a few nights and some food, she spent only eighty dollars. At ten dollars a night, the roach motel wasn't much, but it meant a bed and a hot shower. The other hundred she had would surely be more than enough for miscellaneous, food, and subway fare to Manhattan for her big meeting.

With her new rolling suitcase, she trudged down the icy sidewalks and back to her motel to make the big phone call to the agency.

"Local calls ten cents," she read on the phone before picking it up. With a quiet groan, she straightened out her mangled business card and tried to read the phone number. One number was right in a crease and impossible to read. *Well, I'll try every number then. At the most, it will cost me a dollar.* She didn't like spending anything at all, as she had wanted to save it for more important things. However, she justified it by telling herself she might be a millionaire soon and not have to worry about things like this.

"Sorry, wrong number," she heard four times. Finally, the number five worked, and the secretary at the modeling agency picked up the phone.

"Hi. I'd like to make an appointment with Madeline Karn, please. She gave me her card and told me to call her." Candy tried to hide the slight quiver in her voice.

Unfortunately, she wasn't able to get an appointment until the next day. So she left again to find some cheap food to keep in her room. Canned food and a can opener were going to have to do for now. She also bought a loaf of bread and some peanut butter. She wasn't sure if she had gone overboard, and before leaving the store, she had almost put the bread and peanut butter back. Still, her entire shopping bill was less than three dollars, and she had two full bags of groceries to carry inside. It was the most food she had ever had in her possession at one time. She wouldn't dare bring this much into her house with Don and his friends around. The food would be gone within minutes.

As she opened a can of spaghetti, she took in the tangy tomato aroma, and then stopped. No silverware. Shaking her head, amused with herself, she boldly decided to dump the almost liquefied spaghetti into her mouth. By the time she had finished her can, she had tomato sauce all over her face. By some miracle, she had kept it from her clothes. When she stood and caught a glimpse of herself in the mirror, she laughed at the sight and was unable to stop.

"Rachel," she croaked as she finally recovered. "You'd think this was funny, I bet. Can you believe this? Rachel? Are you there?" Clamping her mouth shut, she told herself she was being silly trying to talk to her possibly dead friend. Was she dead?

Candy wished there were a television in the room for updates on the news. Then again, she wouldn't want to hear about her friend's death on television. It would kill her, too. She decided that she would know in her heart if Rachel were still alive because that's how it is in movies. Close family members always know. Though they weren't totally family, she was close enough.

As she finally found the strength to clean her face, she tried to decide how she felt. Was Rachel dead? Or alive?

"Candy," she heard. With a jerk, towel still in hand, she turned around to see no one. She had heard Rachel's voice behind her. She was sure of it.

"Are you okay?" After waiting for an answer and receiving none, Candy sobbed into her scratchy white hand towel and fell to the hard floor on her knees. "Please be okay, Rach," she cried repeatedly as her words muffled into the towel. "Please be okay."

That night, she decided she couldn't take the suspense anymore and called Rachel's house. It didn't matter what anyone felt about her asking about Rachel. It didn't matter if she reminded them about Rachel's absence. She had to know.

As she picked up the phone, it hit her that she hardly knew Rachel's home number. She'd rarely called her since they saw each other so often at the track. "Come on, brain," she told herself as she bounced her knee. Eventually it came to her, she dialed, and the phone rang.

Candy's heart jumped as she heard Julia's voice. Candy hadn't been to work since hearing about Rachel's disappearance and knew Julia would be wondering where she was, too. Besides that, she probably had questions for her, since she was the last one to see Rachel.

"Candy, where…are you okay? Where's Rachel?" Julia could not get her words out quickly enough.

Candy sniffed, then spoke through tears. "I don't know where she is. We walked to my house, and then she was on her way to the subway. That was the last I saw her. I should have walked with her, Julia. I'm so sorry. It's all my fault."

"No, honey. No, it's not your fault. She's walked that way plenty of times. How could you have known?"

"It's only a block."

"I know. I know."

"I looked." Candy sucked in a stuttering breath. "I tried. I looked in every alley in Queens."

"Me, too."

"I'm so sorry."

"Honey, it's not your fault. Nobody can blame you. I don't."

"Thank you."

"You're welcome. Are you coming to work tomorrow?"

"I don't know if I can."

"I can use all the help I can get, Candy."

"I know."

"Will I see you there?"

Candy paused. "I guess."

"See you tomorrow, then."

Candy hung up, but she knew there would be no way she could handle seeing the track without Rachel. Julia would find help. She knew the backstretch community at Belmont was close, like one big family, and they were probably all doing everything they could to help take care of the horses.

So why couldn't Candy bring herself to help, too? As tears slipped down her face, she thought about all of the loss she had dealt with in her life. It hit her. She was so afraid of another loss that she ran. She had to separate herself further. Maybe even leave New York. She had to start over.

Chapter Four

She begged the desk clerk to call her at ten to make sure she was up. She wasn't up, and she answered the phone with a groggy voice. It was as if she hadn't slept in a week, she was so tired.

As she looked in the mirror, she found those familiar black circles under her eyes. Was it because she was fair skinned or because she was so tired? Exhausted, more like it. It almost hurt to breathe. She managed to drag herself in and out of the shower, put on her best outfit of a plain blue blouse, low cut bell-bottoms, a wide belt, and a new purse. She shoved some money inside the purse. *Wait. What if someone mugs me?* She took her money back out of her tiny purse and put it in her pocket, leaving the purse empty.

Paranoid about losing a part of her outfit, she strapped the purse across herself and put her old, ratty coat on over it. *Oh no. The coat.* She had forgotten to buy a coat.

With a glance at the little round clock on the nightstand, she saw that it was eleven, and her appointment wasn't until one. But she wasn't sure how long it was going to take to get there. Haphazardly, she made herself a peanut butter sandwich with a plastic knife she had stolen from the motel lobby and washed it down with a cup of the motel's finest tap water. She shoved her key in her other pants pocket and made sure she had the address to the agency. After taking one final look around the room, she closed the door behind her.

First, she made her way to the subway to figure out how long it was going to take to get to Manhattan. She figured she had time to buy the coat and get back to the subway, but only if she hurried, and only if nothing went wrong. *Oh, boy. Something always goes wrong. But if I show up in this coat...* She had to stop wasting time, so she turned off her thoughts and headed for her favorite store to pick out a coat. Fortunately, no one else was in the store, and the same clerk was there. She made sure to update her on the latest in her progress toward becoming a famous model.

"You'll have to walk in heels, too, you know," the clerk added as she rang up a brand new gray pea coat.

"Yeah. I think I'll be all right. I've never worn them. But it can't be all that bad, right?"

"You've never worn heels? Oh, we have to practice."

"I don't know if I have time."

"It'll only take a second." Without arguing any further, she motioned for Candy to follow her to the shoe section, and they picked out the highest heels on the racks.

"Be sure not to walk on your toes. Go heel, toe, but take small steps."

Candy scrunched her face.

"Okay. Here. Give it a try." The clerk handed Candy the pair of purple stilettos.

With fumbling hands, she put the shoes on over her socks and stood. She felt ten feet tall as she checked her reflection in the mirror. She held in a snicker.

"First, you walk like this." The clerk demonstrated how to walk in a straight line and stand up straight.

"How do you know all this?"

"I don't know. TV? Give it a shot."

"Okay." Candy gingerly stepped forward, finding her balance for the first few steps. As her confidence grew, she walked a little faster and more comfortably.

"Make like a string on the top of your head. Pull the string up."

Candy stood straighter and taller.

"Yeah."

As she watched herself in the mirror, she tried her best to walk like a runway model. *It isn't as easy as it looks*, she thought. But she didn't have time to learn. "I really need to go. I'm going to be late."

"Well, at least you got a little practice in."

"Think I should buy the shoes?"

"They'll probably give you some shoes and clothes. But it's good that you look nice going in."

"You're right. Thanks so much for your help." Candy ripped the heels off and shoved her feet back into her old brown boots.

"You'll have to come back and tell me how it went."

"I will. I'll be back this afternoon." In a hurry, Candy left, but not so hurried as to forget anything. She prided herself for being the responsible one in the family, what little family she'd had in the past, and gave herself a mental pat on the back for not forgetting her purse or her new coat. She left the old coat with the clerk to hold until she got back and hurried from the store as the clerk waved like a parent sending her child off to school.

It was frigid, but she refused to wear her hat because she didn't want to mess up her hair. Her moist breath froze to her face as she hurried down the sidewalk to her subway station. This was her train, the one she always took to the track. Not anymore.

"Never look back," she told herself as she found an empty seat. "Right, Rachel? Move ahead. Be strong. It's the way women are these days. Strong. They get their own jobs and make their own money."

"We're getting there," Rachel replied from somewhere in her mind. Candy peeked around for people watching her, embarrassed that she had been talking to herself. Aloud, too. Only one man seemed to notice, though. At least she was never going to see him again.

The subway dumped her in the middle of Manhattan, and she had no idea where to go from here. There was a diner across the street, so she went in and found the hostess. The kind woman gave her directions and even drew her a map on a napkin. Candy thanked her profusely and left.

Things were going her way today. It was a big switch from yesterday. She had gotten up on time, she had food to eat, she had money to buy a new coat, and she was going to make it on time to her appointment. She almost cried as her heart wanted to overflow with joy, which was also a huge difference from yesterday. Everything had gone wrong, and she had been so depressed. Not today. Today she was going to start her new life. She couldn't wait.

Finally, she made it to the agency and was fifteen minutes early, another good sign and also something that might impress Ms. Karn. After checking the directory by the elevator, she made her way up to the fourth floor. As the elevator doors opened, she found a bright, open, and airy office bustling with activity. She stepped out right before the doors closed again and froze in place.

"May I help you?" A nasally voice pierced her ear.

With wide eyes, she glanced over to find an older woman in a beehive hairdo eying her up and down like the mean old lady had done yesterday. But today, she was meant to be here. She had an appointment. New clothes, too. So she mirrored the woman's sneers, sending them right back to her. The woman widened her eyes for a second as Candy stepped toward her, and it made Candy swell with pride. "I'm here to meet Ms. Karn. I have an appointment. My name is Candace O'Neil."

The woman looked her up and down with an obvious inspection, then paused. Candy did not waver. Seconds ticked by. Finally, the secretary checked her book. "Have a seat. You're early."

"I know. Thank you." Candy pointed her nose in the air, then made her way to a nearby chair. She sat up as straight and tall as humanly possible and crossed her legs. The weight of her heavy snow boots pulled on her leg, and she couldn't stand it for more than a few seconds. So she uncrossed her legs and tried to stuff her feet under the chair so people wouldn't see the ugly boots. She wished she had brought those heels with her but she would have had to carry her boots around. She mentally rolled her eyes, making sure not to actually do it. Distinguished people didn't roll their eyes like bratty kids.

A tall, thin woman raised an eyebrow at her as she glided by in four-inch heels. Candy thought the woman looked ridiculous in those shoes. Nevertheless, Candy knew she might have to wear them soon, too. She didn't like that idea much and hoped to get a job as a catalog model so she could wear regular clothes. That would only be the start, though. Then, she would be on the runway, modeling the latest fashions. Then, in magazines. Then, on to France.

The secretary rose to peek over her tall desk. "Ms. Karn will see you now." Candy stood tall and proud and marched into the office behind the woman.

"Hello again." Candy offered her hand.

Ms. Karn stood, looking pleased. "You look much better today, young lady."

"Thank you." Candy explained her lack of designer clothes and told her how she had bought some nicer things at a store she knew from her old neighborhood, and about how happy she was to have enough money to buy food for a change. Ms. Karn didn't reply, and Candy mentally slapped herself for being so honest. She was talking too much. So she clamped her mouth shut and lowered her head at the now stern woman across from her.

Ms. Karn organized a quick photo shoot for her, with new clothes and shoes. Candy loved the clothes and wished they would give them to her, but they told her she had to give them back at the end. *No matter*, she thought. *I'll be wearing things like this soon enough.*

Though she had no idea what she was doing, she did her best to act like a model while having a photographer help pose her. She especially loved when they turned a fan on her, making her hair billow in the breeze. Naturally, a smile or two happened, but the photographer told her to look sad. She had to appear distressed but that was hard when she was having fun and things were going her way.

After she had finished and changed, she met with Ms. Karn. "Where can I reach you once we make a decision?" Ms. Karn shuffled papers around her desk.

"Oh. Um. I...um..."

"You're homeless," she stated as she stopped her shuffling and looked up from her papers. "Is there a shelter or –,"

"Well, no. I'm in a motel right now." She clasped her hands behind her back. At least she wasn't completely homeless.

With her head tilted and one eyebrow raised, Ms. Karn stared at Candy for a few seconds, and then picked up a pen and paper. "What's the name of this...*motel?*"

"Queens Motel."

"Queens Motel," she repeated with a sharp tone to her voice as she wrote it down. "Very nice. Well, Candy, I will get back to you soon."

"Soon? How long? I mean, I need to know how long to stay there."

"Give me a day or two. I'll call you with a decision. I'm assuming you gave them your name at the front desk? They'll know which room you're in?"

"Of course."

"Thank you for stopping by, Candy. It was a pleasure." Ms. Karn filled with false graciousness as she stood and waved her hand at the door behind Candy.

Puzzled at her attitude, Candy turned and left, making sure not to leave anything behind. Why was Ms. Karn so nasty to her? Why was the secretary nasty? The other model who walked by? Was it her lack of designer clothes? It almost made her not want to be in this business if that's the way people acted.

Besides, Candy wasn't refined and proper. After all, she was living in a motel now and hadn't had money to buy food yesterday. There was no way someone like that would fit in in the modeling world. Candy's heart sank.

As she walked back to the subway, she second-guessed her decision to spend that money on clothes. The wiser option might have been to save it for food and travel. Travel where? Where was she going to go, anyway? She didn't care. She would hitchhike her way across the country like a hippy. Maybe go to San Francisco. Well, she had heard it wasn't so great there anymore, as crime and drugs had blanketed the city. *No San Francisco, then. Maybe Los*

Angeles. Or maybe even Miami. There were a lot of models in those cities. If only there were a way to get to Paris.

The suspense was killing her. Still no word about Rachel. But how was she to know for sure? Could she try calling Julia again? If she called Rachel's mother to ask if there was any word yet, she'd have to explain why she wasn't at work. She swallowed her pride, formulated an excuse for skipping work, and called Rachel's house.

This time, Rachel's younger brother Billy answered, his teen voice squeaking. He cleared his throat and repeated his greeting, lower this time.

"Hey, Billy." Candy's voice cracked now, but for a different reason.

"Candy?"

"Yeah."

"Have you seen Rachel?"

Candy's heart broke for Rachel's little brother. He had recently turned fifteen, but the tone of his voice when he asked her that question made him sound like an innocent little child, unsure of the world. She lowered her head into one hand while the other still held the phone. "No," she was finally able to say. It was silent for a few moments. "I'm so sorry, Billy. I was calling to see if you had found her yet."

"No. People are looking, though. Have you seen the news? Mom's been asking…" He paused as he desperately tried to keep from crying. "…for um…for her back. And a reward. There's a reward, too."

Candy sniffed and grabbed some rough tissues from the little box on the nightstand. "I saw your mom. On TV."

"Okay." His voice was so shaky now that she knew he wanted desperately to get off the phone. It wasn't cool to cry in front of girls. So she decided to be merciful and let him go.

"I'll see you around, Billy."

"Okay. Bye."

Candy remembered hearing someone say that if they don't find kidnapped people within twenty-four hours, they're likely never to be found. Her heart burned with pain at the thought of what Rachel might be dealing with, if she were even alive. She wished desperately to trade places. Rachel was the one with the potential. Not her.

That night, her pillow soaked up tears for hours, as she had nothing there to distract her but a Gideon Bible, which she refused to read. She didn't trust God now. This wasn't fair. Her only faith now was in herself and her pillow.

Chapter Five

"Hello?" Candy asked as she yanked the phone up to her ear at the same time.

"Miss O'Neil, I presume?"

"Yes?"

"Hello. I am calling at the request of Madeline Karn. We don't normally do this, but she said you did not have a permanent address, and we could not mail anything to you."

"Yes."

"We're sorry to inform you that we have looked over your...portfolio, and we have decided not to take you on as one of our models. We appreciate your interest, and don't give up on your dreams. Thank you for your time."

It was almost as if the woman had read her statement from a cue card. Despite Candy's parched and thick throat, she found the strength to say good-bye.

Oh well. Only a few days ago, I would never have even considered this anyway. It only put me back a few days. That's all. Was worth a shot. Time to move on now and make sure Don doesn't find me, or he'll drag me back home and sell me into slavery or something. Yes. It's time to leave.

After her photo shoot two days ago, she had gone to the Fashion Store to get her other coat and had told the clerk how it went, and how she wasn't hopeful because of their attitudes. Despite that, deep down inside, she had hoped to be chosen. It might have been a great life with all that money and fame and new clothes. Then again, if she turned out like those other women, it would be impossible to forgive herself. *This was for the best,* she told herself.

"Now what?"

She was excited to have her rolling suitcase full of clothes as well as her backpack, but it was a lot to carry around with her. The suitcase was small enough that she was able to carry it, so instead of ruining the wheels on the rough road surface, she decided to do her best to carry it as she made her way to the main road. Besides, if she looked weighed down, it might increase her chances of being picked up. She held out her thumb and hoped for the best. No one stopped, surprisingly, and she decided to get back on the highway she had taken her first night away from home.

As she walked along the highway, she passed another person who had been hitchhiking but was taking a rest by sitting on the guardrail. The older man looked scary to her, as he was covered with facial hair and layers and layers of torn clothes. A red mangled hat completed his outfit like a cherry on top of a melted sundae. She hoped he was warm enough and wanted to ask him where he stayed at night. Not so much as to check on him, but as to make plans for herself. She wasn't sure what to do. *Were there homeless shelters around here?*

It didn't matter. She hoped to be out of the city by dawn. Maybe even before, if she found a way to get out of here.

She hadn't wanted to waste any of the money she had left on subway fare, though it would have gotten her out earlier. Then again, if she had ridden the subway, she wouldn't have had as much opportunity to find a free ride somewhere. *Oh. Free?* She hoped someone wouldn't ask for money or anything for compensation.

BEEEEEE. The high-pitched wail of a Volkswagen horn sounded behind her, getting closer with each passing second. Oddly, the horn wasn't stopping. Curiosity got to her, and she turned around. The Volkswagen bus coming into view was covered in peace symbols and different-colored swirls of paint. BEEEEEE. The horn continued. *What in the world?* As it increased in volume and drew closer, she was amused as other drivers glared over occasionally and honked their own horns in anger.

The high-pitched horn continued even as the old van pulled over to the side of the road and stopped in front of her. She knew the horn had to be stuck. It was further confirmed when they turned off the van, and the sound fizzled to a stop, dropping in pitch as it died a slow, painful death. Inside, a few people were waving at her and laughing as if having the time of their lives. They encouraged her to join them, so she hurried her steps and made her way to the side of the van, where the door opened.

Her happy face mirrored theirs as they greeted her.

"Ahoy there, matey," one man greeted.

"Let me take those." A slight, pale young lady reached for Candy's bags as she jumped out of the van.

Candy pulled back. "Um, I don't know. Where are you guys going?"

"Going to D.C. right now."

"D.C.? Why?"

"Protest."

"The war?"

"Nixon's taking things to a whole new level. We have to get rid of that fascist pig. We gotta convince the government to impeach him."

Candy couldn't care less about politics. But she did hate the war and what it did to people. She'd seen more wheelchairs in the last five years than she had in her whole life. Young men with their pants folded under half of a leg, shirt sleeves pinned to their sides, haggard, drawn, pained looks on their faces. It was a horrible time to be a young man.

"Come on in. It's cold out there. Where you headed?" the driver asked as Candy stood in the doorway pondering her decision. The girl that had hopped out waited patiently. Candy knew she had to have been cold dressed in her lightweight cotton skirt and tunic. She had no coat.

"Um, I, I don't know, really."

"Sounds like you'd fit in perfectly. Come on," a man about her age encouraged with his arm outstretched toward her. He waved his hand a few times, as he tried to pull her in without touching her. They seemed so nice. Harmless.

"All right," she finally decided, and hopped in, prompting cheers from the others. Her bags were tossed in the back and on top of their other things, so she headed for the back row of seats. She sat next to a girl dressed in full-fledged hippy attire – multi-colored tunic, bell bottoms, sandals *(how did the girl get around in snow?)*, a hemp weaved headband, and purple-tinted glasses that sat low on her nose.

"Name's Autumn." The girl reached out for Candy, and they shook hands briefly. The girl's handshake was weak, as she almost didn't touch Candy's hand. It was a far cry from Rachel's handshakes, as she had always tried to grip as strongly as possible to prove her strength. Rachel even arm wrestled some of the others at the track, guys included, to prove she had muscle from all those years of riding thoroughbreds. Many times, she won.

Candy shook her head to get rid of thoughts about Rachel and keep the tears at bay and finally spoke. "Nice to meet you."

At that point, the driver started up the van again, and the horn resumed. The three passengers grinned in her direction. "What is with that horn?"

"It's stuck." The driver pushed a red button repeatedly, then threw up one hand as it had no effect on the horn. Candy cackled loudly, prompting everyone in the van to join her. He put the van into gear and merged back onto the road.

"Look. He's ticked." The guy in the front passenger seat pointed to another driver on the road. The driver's face was full of anger as he occasionally glanced at the van. Suddenly, the man in the car floored it; his car sped away, leaving every one of them screaming with laughter.

Candy had tears running down her face, as did the others. She was having so much fun that she hadn't even thought about how long it had been since she laughed like that.

Finally, the jokes subsided as they grew tired of their game of making fun of angry people. But the horn continued, and as they talked, she occasionally giggled for no apparent reason. They understood her outbursts, as it had happened to them as well.

"Okay. So, you're Roody," she yelled over the horn, pointing to the driver, who nodded. "You're Christian." She pointed to the passenger side, then to the girl in the row in front of her. "You're...um…"

"Opal. Like the gem." She reminded Candy of Grace Kelly, so she pictured the princess wearing opal.

"Opal. And Autumn." Candy continued her attempts at remembering names.

"You haven't told us your name, yet," she heard from the front. *Christian,* she reminded herself.

"Oh." Candy's cheeks flushed. "Candy."

"Candy. Beautiful name for a beautiful girl." Opal slapped his arm, and he snapped out of his trance.

"What do you guys do for money?" Candy asked in a conversation lull. "How do you pay for gas and food and stuff?"

"We have a little from odd jobs when we lived up north. But I guess we'll figure it out as we go along."

Candy knew she would have to contribute toward gas and food, too, and that was okay with her. It was only fair. As her stomach growled, she remembered the food she had bought for her motel room. She still had a few things left. "Hey, um, I have a little food leftover if you guys are hungry."

"Hungry?" Everyone spoke at once, making Candy jump. They were practically drooling at the mere mention of it.

"Yeah. I found a plastic knife, and I have some peanut butter and bread. Anybody for a sandwich?" Candy reached for her backpack. Her question was met with four eager faces and shouts of approval. It seemed they were as hungry as she had been most of her life. It only seemed right to share the food with them, and she hurriedly did her best with her plastic knife, thick peanut butter, and white bread.

They didn't care what the sandwiches looked like, or if the bread had torn under the pressure of trying to spread the peanut butter. It was food.

"I wish I had milk, but I don't have anything to wash it down. Sorry." Candy's words were muffled by the peanut butter. But the others were too busy shoving the food into their mouths to notice.

"Oh. We have water," Roody mumbled with a full mouth as he pulled out two canteens. The others, with their mouths also sealed shut by the peanut butter, nodded in approval, and reached out to take the canteens. They took turns drinking from the canteens, which mortified Candy. They seemed to share everything, even germs. *Gross.* By the time one of the canteens had reached her, there were remnants of the others' sandwiches on the canteen's opening. She wiped it off with her shirt and was relieved when they didn't say anything about it.

As she tilted the dark green canteen and poured water into her mouth, she noticed how thirsty she was and couldn't stop herself from drinking more than her fair share. Someone ripped it from her hand, prompting a yelp. She reached up to wipe spilled water from her face. "Sorry. I'm thirsty."

Their anger dissipated quickly as she apologized, much to her relief. "It's all right." Opal screwed the cap back on. "But we gotta make it last until we can find somewhere else to fill up, okay?"

Candy nodded as her cheeks flushed.

As they passed through Philadelphia on I-95, she gazed out at the dark asphalt road behind the van and thought about all the miles she had put between herself and her old life, between herself and Don, between herself and her job as a groom that she now sorely missed, and between herself and Rachel.

The tears would not be denied this time. As she stared out the back window, she prayed desperately for her friend to be all right. She hoped Rachel wasn't suffering at least. Sobs wracked her body, and she hid her face in the crook of her arm as it rested on the seat back. Autumn put her hand on Candy's back, showing that someone cared, which made her cry even harder because it had been so long since anyone besides Rachel had cared about her.

"What's wrong?"

Candy tried to calm herself enough to answer, but it wasn't working. The tears fell, soaking into her coat sleeve as they dripped from her eyes more and more with each passing moment. Still unable to speak, shook her head in reply as Autumn continued to rub her back.

Minutes later, with Autumn still there for her, Candy was finally able to stop the waterworks and wiped her face with her hands, then dried them on her jeans. For several seconds, she fought within herself. *Look back or look forward?* She couldn't bring herself to face the life outside the back window again, though it was all she had ever known. With eyes closed as she turned, she finally faced front and looked ahead, only to find the other three with concerned faces for her. She tried to laugh any remaining tears away.

They seemed to understand and didn't ask her about it any further. Maybe they had been through the same process of leaving behind their old lives. She was grateful there were no questions. She didn't want to talk about it. She had to forget about it. Move on. Though she had brought some of her past with her.

The little wooden box still sat in the bottom of her backpack, and she hadn't been able to bring herself to face it since she left home the night Don had kicked it from her and cracked it. That box had been her mother's, and when she was little, she used to love going into her mother's room when she wasn't around to check the contents. Every time she opened the box, something different was inside. She didn't know what those things were, but later she learned they were for shooting up. But those bad things weren't always in there. Sometimes they were gone, and she found jewelry or other trinkets inside. She always wondered why Mom put those things in there. Was she hiding them from her dad? Sometimes Dad pawned things for money. Maybe that's what it was. Sometimes pictures were there, sometimes things that might have been her dad's. She couldn't tell what they were. But the most exciting part was that it was different each time. It was like a game to her, and she wondered if her mother knew the joy it gave her to find new things each time.

As she grew, she continued to check the box periodically but never found the courage to ask her mother about it. It might have been a game, but Candy wasn't sure. Her mother rarely played games with her, and only for a short time. Candyland, her favorite of course, or other board games had to last less than ten minutes because that was about how long her mother's attention span seemed to be. Those ten minutes were the happiest time of the day, especially since those times were so few and far between. She learned quickly to appreciate every second. But when she was about ten, her mom decided to throw away the games, proclaiming Candy was too old for them now. Mom never played with her again, as this was about the time things started to get worse. Her parents were using more and more every day.

After learning of her parents' death several years later, she went right to the hiding place of the box, under the bed, and opened it to find nothing. There was absolutely nothing left inside, strangely symbolic of her own life.

As bizarre as it sounded, she wondered if she left the box alone long enough, would something else appear inside? She had been resisting the urge each day to peek inside for years. Would she be disappointed to find nothing inside again? That was ridiculous. Of course, nothing was inside. Mom wasn't around to put anything in there. It wasn't as if it were a magic box. Though when she was little, she often thought it was.

For a fleeting second, she considered throwing the box away but quickly dismissed it, unable to part with the only thing from her childhood that was even remotely happy.

She hoped one day to get married and have kids, and maybe make the box into a game. Of course, she would also.play other games with her kids. She was going to pay attention to them, letting them know that she loved them, that she cared, and that she would always be there for them. She was going to be the best mom ever. Not that she knew how, aside from watching her friends' parents and watching moms on television.

Chapter Six

"You sure do smell good for someone who's homeless." Opal had leaned over the second bench seat to sniff Candy.

"I had a motel room for a few days, until…well, until I was sure my life in New York was over."

"Over? What do you mean?"

"This lady... Oh, never mind. You're going to think I'm crazy."

Each of them insisted so vehemently that they were going to believe whatever she said, that she finally told the story of the woman in the subway station who might have given her her big chance at being a model. "It would have been a great story to tell my kids. That's for sure."

"It still is a great story. Doesn't matter if you're Twiggy or nobody. You should still tell your kids."

Candy agreed with a nod that somehow ended in tears again. She was so tired of crying.

"What's wrong?" Opal and Autumn asked in unison.

Candy shook her head but managed to stop her tears before they became as ridiculous as they had earlier. She knew she should learn better self-control. *Grow up.* "It's nothing, really."

"You wanted to be a model like Twiggy?"

"No. Ha." Candy relented, knowing these two were going to drive her crazy until she told them something: "My mom would have never told me a story like that. She hardly ever talked to me." One tear escaped, but she angrily swiped it away as it touched her sharp cheekbone.

"My mom was the same. Autumn's too. And Roody and Christian, though they will never admit it." Opal's voice was low enough to hide in the constant blaring of the horn.

Candy peered closely into Opal's brown eyes, and something hit her. "I'm so selfish. Here I am feeling sorry for myself, and you guys have been through the same. Or maybe even worse."

The girls were silent for several seconds, each lost in their own thoughts, and Candy thought the conversation had ended. Autumn spoke next in her soft-spoken, gentle, and innocent voice. "My dad did some awful things to me. He was a monster. I hated him. And my mom, well, she knew and did nothing about it. Why? Why didn't she tell him to stop? What kind of mother lets their kids suffer like that?"

"She was probably scared to death of him, Autumn." Opal touched Autumn's arm.

Autumn had clamped her lips together in a thin line, but her jaw quivered and tears rolled down her bony face. She was as thin as Candy but appeared rougher with her small features and thin eyebrows. Thin wasn't always beautiful, and though Autumn wasn't ugly, she wasn't pretty either. But she seemed like such a sweet and innocent person that Candy couldn't help but want to protect her.

Candy was grateful that she hadn't been abused like Autumn. At least she had that much. But she didn't dare say a word about that. Candy put her hand on Autumn's shoulder in a show of support, as Autumn had supported her earlier.

"You're such a strong person, Autumn. I mean, I don't know you very well yet, but so far, I can tell that you are strong. You're going to be like me, aren't you? You're going to do the opposite of whatever your parents did. Maybe sometimes having bad parents isn't the worst thing. At least we know what *not* to do now."

Autumn sniffed and did her best to giggle her tears away while Opal lowered her gaze. Autumn and Candy touched Opal's shoulders in support. "Opal, what's your story? How were your parents awful?" Candy asked.

"My parents didn't do anything like that. In fact, they didn't touch me at all. They didn't love me. I don't understand how parents cannot love their kids."

"I bet they did. They just didn't know how to show it," Autumn offered.

Opal shook her head as she picked fuzz balls from the matted blue cloth covering her bench seat. "No. They sent me away to special schools my whole life. Kept telling me I was a genius and that I had to have the best education. Meanwhile, they were off touring Europe or going on an African safari. I've never even been out of the country. And when I'd go home during summer break, they'd send me to camp after camp, some lasting a whole month or more. On holidays like Christmas, they were always busy with adults and never talked to me. They would shove me aside, tell me to go read a book or practice the piano. There were never any other kids to play with or talk to. So, holidays were the worst." She snorted. "My name's not even Opal. I changed it because that's my birthstone, and I wanted to start over with a new life, a new name."

"What's your real name?"

"Brenda. Ha. I hate that name." She shook her head. "Well, Brenda's gone now, and now I get to do whatever I want while my parents think I'm away at Radcliffe."

Candy and Autumn dropped their jaws at the same time, then covered their mouths, which seemed to amuse Opal.

"So, where did you guys meet?" Candy asked.

"Just like you. Roody was driving, picked us up off the side of the road. I've been with them for a couple of months now, and Autumn was with these two before me."

"Yeah. He picked me up six months ago or so. Last summer. Up in Connecticut. We hung out and whatnot. Worked here and there to save up our money so we could go to California. So, here we are."

"Where did you work?" Candy asked Autumn.

"Fast food joints, a drive-in, a diner. We worked together whenever we could and lived in a motel. That's no life. We want the good life where we won't need money. We won't need to work. We'll live off the land as God intended. We'll live like Adam and Eve once we get to San Francisco, you'll see. We'll all love each other, and there will be no jealousy or ill will towards each other. Just the way God meant it to be."

"But with clothes?" Candy was unable to stop her seemingly silly question in time. The others laughed, and she joined in for a second. She expected and waited for an answer, but they never said another word about it.

"What did you do before this, Candy?" Opal asked. Candy now understood where Opal's demeanor and perfect posture came from. She had been groomed from the very beginning, inside and out, to fit into high society. Like it or not, some poorer teens labeled her as a "soc," short for socialite, a stuck-up rich kid. She was trying hard to overcome and destroy that label, but Candy was sure it wasn't easy. Probably no easier than banishing any label. Rich kid, poor kid, groom or hotwalker, waitress or fry cook… they wanted to do away with all labels and start over. Candy was excited about that prospect.

"For a job? I was a groom, mostly. At Belmont Park. Have you heard of it?"

Autumn lit up like the sun. "I love horses," she crooned. "You got to touch them and be with them all day? Oh, what a fun job that would be."

Candy nodded, though solemnly. "It was. It was the best job ever. My friend, Rachel, was a gallop girl, an exercise rider in the mornings. Also, she helped in her mom's barn all afternoon, taking the horses to and from the paddock or walking them, or whatever. Her mom's a trainer there. We were so happy, and yes, it was a fun job, though hard."

"Why'd you leave it, then?"

"Rachel was kidnapped and I couldn't go back there without her." Candy set her jaw, hoping for a way to avoid crying about it again, and she managed not to this time. The others expressed their sympathy by frowning, but said nothing, so she kept talking. "Besides, my brother is a drug addict, and I wanted to get away from him, too. I have nothing left in New York. It was time to move on. Start over."

"You'll see. Where we're going, you won't have to worry about abuse, or people getting kidnapped, or any other crime." Opal placed her hand on Candy's arm.

"Except drugs," Autumn added with a shrug. Candy panicked. She wasn't sure how she had forgotten about hippies and their drug use. Her heart beat faster as she eyed the door. She wanted out. Now. But Autumn reassured her. "They won't make you do anything, Candy. If you want to be with people who don't do drugs, then you can be with people who don't do drugs."

"What about you guys? Do you do it?"

"Just smoke pot. Pot's harmless. But we'll never get into the hard stuff, you know, like LSD."

"How do you know pot's harmless? Certainly doesn't seem that way to me."

"Because it makes people happy, yet calm and relaxed. We can all sit around a fire and sing songs together as a family. It's better than alcohol because you won't get sick. You'll only want to eat," Autumn joked, and Opal agreed.

Candy didn't even want to try it.

Chapter Seven

"Washington, DC, five miles!" Roody announced as they passed a road sign.

Everyone cheered and peered eagerly out the windows.

"I don't see a skyline," Autumn mused.

"There's not much of one in DC. Height restrictions. Some believe no buildings can be taller than the Capitol dome, while others say it has to do with the width of the street in front of it," Opal answered.

"What?" Candy curled her mouth in a sneer.

"I don't know. Some rule they made," Roody interjected, turning his head toward them so it was easier to hear him over the horn.

"Politicians." Opal shook her head. The others groaned in agreement and glanced at her, then pressed their noses against the windows again. "They must have been bored one day and said, 'Hey, let's change the building codes'." Everyone nodded and murmured their agreement.

Florida Avenue became more and more crowded, the houses became older, and corner stores were filled with people. Graffiti decorated the sides of buildings, and traffic stopped them dead in the road. Cars were completely snarled as far as the eye could see, which wasn't all that far – several blocks or so. They were going nowhere fast, but as their horn continued on its own, other drivers shook their heads at the group. Everyone seemed to think they were impatiently honking at the traffic, which Candy found hilarious.

"Where's this protest? What part of the city?" Candy raised her voice, calling out over the horn.

"It's on the Mall, where they all are. That's where Martin Luther King's speech was, too. You'll get to be where he stood, and where it all happened." Opal waved her hand across the window.

They finally found their way to the Mall, the long stretch of land containing several Smithsonian museums, the Washington Monument, and the Capitol building. On the other side of the Washington Monument were the reflecting pool and the Lincoln Memorial, where Dr. King stood and gave his most famous speech in 1963.

They drove along the entire length of Independence Avenue and wound up on Constitution Avenue on the other side before finally finding a small parking spot near what appeared to be office buildings.

Candy grabbed her backpack, the others grabbed their bags and a blanket, and they set out to find a place to sit. Candy was glad when Opal finally put on a winter coat because, while it was a bit warmer than New York, it was still frightfully cold.

As they walked, Roody grabbed Autumn's hand, and Christian grabbed Opal's hand. *Nothing like being a fifth wheel*, Candy thought. It didn't help much when Autumn reached out for Candy's hand. Candy took it, though, thankful to have friends around her now. It wasn't time to shop for a boyfriend, as she wasn't anywhere permanent yet.

Soon, the sun fell upon them, warming them slightly as the trees and buildings gave way to a vast, open area of grass. A few trees spotted the brown grassy areas, with park benches on either side facing the grass, not the roads. To her left was the Washington Monument.

"Watch. Wherever you go, it follows you." Opal enjoyed acting as their tour guide, having been there several times on field trips. As they walked, the monument seemed to lean toward them, and they began running to get away from it, but they couldn't. Finally, they stopped and caught their breath.

Candy was curious about something. "Did they bury him there?"

"What?" Opal laughed. The others didn't, as they had wondered the same thing.

"Of course not, silly. Did you guys think that, too?" she asked, facing each person. They nodded with their heads lowered, as if being scolded by the teacher. "He's buried at Mount Vernon, his home in Virginia. I guess you guys have never been here, have you?"

"Nope," they all answered at once.

"Well, ask me anything. I know this city like the back of my hand," Opal announced with her nose in the air.

"When does the protest start?" Candy asked.

Opal did not reply, but instead gaped at Candy with a blank stare.

Roody answered for her. "Tomorrow. I guess we'll sleep in the van, or if someone we meet has a tent they'll let us share, we can do that." Then threw up one hand, frustrated with himself. "I know, I know. I should have brought a tent."

Judging from the expressions on the others' faces, they had discussed this before and did not want to bring it up again. No one said anything else about it, though, and they kept walking.

Other people milled around, some already claiming their spots in the grass, some on blankets, some not. Police occasionally mingled in and around the crowds, probably checking for drugs.

Candy covered her mouth. "Do you guys have...you know...drugs on you?"

"Of course."

Candy was scared she was going to be arrested and wind up in jail for something she was totally against. *Oh, the irony.* Christian noticed her concern and peered around Autumn. "Hey, it's okay. The fuzz don't care none. Pot's perfectly fine in their eyes. Hell, they smoke it, too. Just you watch. You'll find people offering hits to the cops, and they'll take 'em."

Autumn interrupted. "Ha. Yeah, then five minutes later pepper spray your face, put handcuffs on you, and take you to jail."

"Are you speaking from experience?" Candy's face blanched.

"Not exactly. It's what I've seen, that's all. Even saw one guy get beat up for standing there doing nothing."

"Oh, no. Guys, I don't like this. I don't want to go to jail. And I don't want to get beat up." Candy's heart beat faster and faster.

"No, no, Candy. It's okay. Plus, you're a girl. They don't touch girls. You'll be fine. You don't have drugs on you, anyway. And we'll protect you if a fight breaks out, okay? Don't worry," Christian offered.

Candy covered her mouth with her hand, then bit a fingernail. She didn't have much of a choice. She was with these people now in a strange and new city. She had no idea where things were or how to get around. She had to stay with them.

They decided to splurge on hot dogs and soda for their next meal, taking advantage of a short line at a food truck. Then, they found a good spot and spread their blanket, huddling together to keep themselves warm.

As night fell, more and more people crowded the area, and they found another group of men and women their age huddling together to keep warm. They decided to huddle with them for more warmth. They stood, picked up their things, and walked to the nearby group.

"You guys up for some company?" Christian asked as they approached.

"Absolutely, my brother," one of the young men called as he waved his hand for them to come closer. Christian and his friends spread their blanket next to the one already on the ground and sat down.

"Christian." He held out his hand toward one man.

"Sebastian."

"Charity.

"Autumn."

"Rayne."

"Candy."

"Hanna."

"Dylan."

"Too many names to remember," Candy joked, and the others agreed. She sat nearest the last man to speak. "Dylan, right?"

"Dylan, yes."

"Only one I can remember right now," she murmured under her breath as she leaned toward him. He grinned at her, looked away for a second, then narrowed his eyes at Candy. She glanced up at him, smiled politely, and he finally looked away. Was he staring? She hoped not.

Roody asked the others, "What about you guys? Anybody been drafted yet?"

"No. Not yet. I have a college waiver," Rayne answered.

"I make sure I don't have an address. They can't draft me if they can't find me," Roody said.

"I signed up for college as well." Dylan's voice rose. "Didn't need it, but I wasn't about to go over there and…" He shook his head as he could not finish his statement.

Sebastian leaned closer to Candy. "His brother…you know."

Dylan frowned and looked away.

Candy and her friends saw Dylan's reaction and knew right away what had happened.

"I'm so sorry," Candy offered him.

Dylan ripped brown, matted grass from the ground and shook it in his fist. "What can you do? These bastards are forcing people to go over there and fight a war we don't belong in." He shook his head and threw the grass.

"I agree. The war is pointless. All it does is kill people or bring them back home maimed and scared."

Rayne muttered under his breath, cursing the president. "He needs to go over there and see what it's like. Maybe he'll wise up."

"He watches the news, I'm sure," Opal said.

Rayne pursed his lips. "Doubt it. If he does, he obviously doesn't care how many of us are dying. Every night, they list names. He probably turns it off so he doesn't have to see it. If he even watches."

It was silent for several seconds as a cloud of anger hovered over them.

"Well, this is why we're here, guys." Sebastian pointed one finger toward the Capitol building. "We're here to protest. We're here to show our support for the safety of American men and to show support for Dylan and others who have lost someone."

"Here, here," they agreed in unison.

"Get out that guitar," Charity suggested, hoping to lighten the mood. They sang a few songs as they sat in a circle. It grew colder as the night progressed and they began to shiver.

"Let's get closer." Sebastian winked, and then pulled on Hanna's hand. Hanna scooted under his arm, and he wrapped his arm around her shoulders. Candy watched them, smirked, and then diverted her gaze. *More couples. Great.*

"I know. Let's lie on one blanket, and then put the other over all of us," Dylan suggested, to which everyone scoffed.

Roody snickered, then spoke. "So, you want to put eight people on one blanket the size of a twin bed, and put the other blanket on top? How? Like a tent? Or do we get to stick our heads out to breathe?" The expression on his face let the others know he was being facetious, but Dylan wasn't laughing.

"All right. I'll show you. Let's lie down lined up here like sardines, then cover up with the blanket."

The others thought it was silly but agreed anyway. "Okay. Let's do this."

Giggling, the eight of them squished themselves together to be as close as possible. Christian and Sebastian were on the outside and barely on the blanket.

"This is the way penguins keep warm." Dylan's head popped up from the middle and he looked back and forth.

"What?"

"Yeah, they gather up like this to keep warm."

"What about the penguins on the outside? Won't they freeze?"

"No, they switch every so often."

"Well, then we're switching too."

Candy giggled at the exchange between Dylan and Sebastian. Sebastian poked his head up and looked at Candy. "He's a nature freak. He watches those shows on PBS."

Dylan reached over and slugged Sebastian's arm.

The girls snuggled with their boyfriends, while Candy, who was in the middle and next to Dylan, felt extremely uncomfortable. But she was warm, which she appreciated greatly.

Dylan was getting a little too close for comfort. All the others had someone except for them. She knew what Dylan was thinking, and she wanted no part of it, despite the constant reminders that she was essentially alone.

As they lay on the ground gazing up at the white starless sky, he offered his arm as a pillow for her, which she accepted only because her too-large coat made it difficult to lie flat. Besides, he was warm.

"Your legs cold?" He was too close to her ear and she pulled away.

"No, I'm fine." This was a bit much for her. Not only was she among a pile of hippies who seemingly hadn't showered for a week, but this guy she hardly knew was all over her. She found herself pulling his hand from inside her coat several times and was becoming annoyed.

"Sorry," he said for the umpteenth time. Her angry scowl sent him the message to back off. So he did. And finally, she fell asleep, warm and comfortable.

A few times during the night, as people moved to more comfortable and warmer positions, Candy woke up and found herself hoping morning was soon around the corner. It seemed they were doomed to be in that warm, yet cold and crowded, night forever.

"You asleep?" Dylan asked her, barely above a whisper.

"Not really. Keep waking up." *No thanks to you.*

"Me too. You comfortable?"

"I'm fine, I guess. You?"

"Yeah." It was silent for several seconds. Candy hoped that was the end of the conversation, as she desperately wanted to fall asleep again. Unfortunately, he spoke again. "Where are you from?"

"New York." She didn't ask him where he was from, hoping he'd picked up on her hint.

"Oh. That's cool. I'm from here. Maryland, anyway."

"Oh. That's nice." Was she going to have to be blunt and tell him she was tired?

"You know, I can't help but notice. I bet you're a model, aren't you?"

"What?" She turned her head toward him, finding herself face to face with him. He wasn't bad looking.

"Are you? Are you a model?"

"Well, no. But I tried. I mean, this lady gave me her number and said to come by her studio, and I did. Had some pictures taken, but they looked at them and decided I wasn't good enough."

"Not good enough? That's ridiculous. You've got the face."

She sat up to lean on one elbow. "Huh? I mean, how would you know?"

"I'm a photographer. I work for an agency in Northwest. Did you bring your portfolio with you?"

"No. They never gave me the pictures they took."

"Oh. Well, maybe you could come by my place and I'll shoot you."

"Shoot me?" She raised an eyebrow.

"Yeah. Shoot." Making the sound of a gun, he stuck his finger into her ribs, tickling her. As she squirmed to the ground again, the others woke up and protested with groans and moans. Candy and Dylan covered their mouths and squelched their laughter.

Funny how things work out. She knew this was fate. It had to be. The other modeling agency didn't work, but someone else noticed her now? Someone else in the business? It had to be. She knew she only had to keep trying, that's all.

When the sun finally came up, they woke up and took turns going to the port-a-potty while saving their spot on the grass. The reflection pool wasn't far, and they might have seen it from where they were, but the crowd had surrounded it and now had also covered much of the grassy area. They knew not too many more people were going to fit here safely. Then again, the more people there were, the warmer it was.

As they settled, they shared what was left of Candy's peanut butter and bread for breakfast.

Candy wiped her plastic knife with a napkin. "What will we do for lunch?"

"Don't worry. We'll figure something out. I'm sure someone will bring enough to share." Roody stood and pounded grass from his khaki bellbottoms.

Candy wasn't sure how it was possible to bring enough food for tens of thousands of hungry people. Finally, later, someone did bring food. Someone had stolen food from a grocery store delivery truck, and a group of people carried boxes to a spot on the ground nearby. Candy watched as people fought the urge to rush the group, eager to find sustenance. She was surprised to find the crowd still in control.

"This is what happens when everybody decides on a peaceful solution over the way the rest of the world works. This is how it is supposed to be." Dylan had noticed Candy's surprise.

Candy nodded as she watched a line form. "Well, should we go get in line?"

"Candy and I will go, guys," Dylan announced. When the others expressed approval, he took Candy's hand and led her to the back of the line. Candy was a little surprised that they were holding hands already, but she figured he was a hippy and that's what hippies do.

"Think there will be any left?" Candy whispered as they stopped behind an extremely hairy man. Did he really need the dirty and worn coat he was wearing?

Dylan nodded. "If not, there will be more later."

They lost sight of their friends while standing in line, moving up slightly every few minutes. Candy thought it might take all day to make it up there.

"So, do you think your agency would pick me?" Candy leaned in toward Dylan's arm. It seemed to be a big arm with lots of muscle. She also noticed his hair was messy, but a sexy kind of messy, like how the Beatles wore their hair.

He peered down from several inches above and inspected her face. When he reached for her, she almost pulled away but told herself he was safe. Hopefully. He touched her so lightly it felt almost like a feather. She blushed slightly as he drifted his fingers across a sharp cheekbone, down her jaw line, then down her neck to her shoulder blade. His finger traced the prominent collarbone visible between the collar of her blouse. She couldn't believe she was allowing this stranger to touch her like this. And when he opened her coat, she even let him move his gentle touch from her shoulder to her chest as he traced the shape of her small bosom. By the time he had made his way to her ribs, he had moved on from his fingers to his whole hand, and he ran his hand from her stomach around to her back.

His eyes had followed every move of his hand, dilating, widening as he discovered her. Candy swallowed a lump in her throat. "Absolutely," he answered, finally catching her gaze. By then, she was lost in his delicate touch and unaware of the crowd around her, until the people behind them pushed the couple forward in line, causing them to both stumble with nervous laughter.

They were quiet as they waited but still held hands. His eager and rough movements last night had infuriated her, but today, the way he touched her drove her crazy inside, and she fought now to control herself and resist the urge to rip his clothes off and devour him. In trying to resist, her desires grew. As their gazes connected again, she knew he felt the same.

Finally, they reached the front of the line, and a man shoved a few cans of Spam into Candy's arms, and a loaf of bread and a six-pack of soda into Dylan's arms. They were pushed aside, stunned. When they were a safe distance from the line, they stopped and eyed the cans. "I've never had Spam," Candy declared finally.

"Neither have I. Looks disgusting." Dylan made a face that made Candy howl at him as she doubled over, nearly dropping one of the cans.

As they started back for their group, they heard shouting as a crowd ran toward one spot. "Come on," Dylan shouted and then did his best to hurry Candy along as they carried their armfuls of food.

"Don't lose me," Candy shouted as she was almost separated from him. He stopped and thought for a second. He then held the soda and bread with one hand while holding her around the waist with his other arm. Why were they headed into the thick of things? But then she realized that it was right where their blanket was, and where their group was supposed to be.

Candy tried to stay calm, but was failing. She not only worried for her new friends, she worried for her backpack. Her stuff. Her magic box. What if people were trampling it? She began to sob, her bottom lip protruding like a toddler's as she worried her only decent memory of her childhood might be destroyed. Dylan pulled her into his chest, then reached down, and buried his chin into her hair for a second. She wasn't sure, but he may have kissed her, too.

As they grew closer and closer to the commotion, they also moved more and more slowly until they were forced to stop. The crowd was too dense, making it impossible to get to their blanket. Their friends were gone, too. "Do you see them?" Candy craned her head and shouted over the crowd noise.

"No." Dylan also craned his head.

"Oh no. What is going on? Where are they?" But Candy knew he had no answers for those questions. Then, surprising her, he pulled her away from the crowd. "What are you doing? We have to get to them."

"It's safer if we wait until the crowd clears. Otherwise, we might lose the food and possibly get hurt. So we'll stay here for a few minutes, okay?"

However, when the police stormed into the crowd, throwing people aside to their left and right, Dylan and Candy knew it was bad. Dylan muttered a curse word under his breath, and Candy glanced up at him. It was obvious he had seen something. She was almost afraid to ask. For several seconds, she stared at him, watching him attempt to observe the activity over the crowd.

"What is it?"

Dylan groaned. "They've got Sebastian."

"What?" Candy jumped a few times but couldn't tell what was happening. "Why?"

"He is a hot head and starts fights with people. Dammit, I knew I shouldn't have brought him here. Too big of a crowd. Too much temptation for him."

"What? Is he a boxer or something?"

"Something like that. Yeah." At that point, they watched his friend and another man being led away by police.

Finally, after what seemed like an hour, the crowd dispersed, and they were able to find their way back to their blanket.

Candy dropped her Spam and dove for her backpack. It had been kicked around, she noticed, and she hoped and prayed her box wasn't broken. As Dylan set the rest of the food down, she dug into the bag, then pulled out the little brown stained box. *Whew.* It was fine.

"What's that?" Dylan asked.

Hmm. "Magic Box" didn't sound right. "It was my mom's," she said instead, then shoved it back inside, making sure it was wrapped in one of her sweaters.

They finally relaxed and scanned the area. "Where are the others?"

Candy helped search but was unable to find anyone in the crowd. "I don't know. I don't see them. They weren't arrested, too, were they?"

"I don't think so. I only saw Seb. Well, maybe they'll be back. Maybe they ran away, worried they'd be arrested, too."

"Yeah. That's probably it."

"Well, let's try this...Spam...stuff." He made that same disgusted face, which Candy still found hilarious.

"Looks like Army food or something." Candy watched Dylan open the can.

As he wrinkled his nose at a gelatinous goo on top of the meat, Candy laughed again. "Actually, they did serve this stuff to the guys in the war."

"Which war?"

"World War Two." He then dumped the meat onto a slice of bread. As the meat slipped from the can, they heard a suctioning sound. Then, with a pop as it escaped, a can-shaped lump landed on the bread, smashing it as it fell. Candy doubled over and fell onto the ground laughing as Dylan pushed her. "Stop it." He tickled her and pushed her from the blanket.

"No, no, I'll freeze to death." She crawled back to the warmth of their blanket. There she found Dylan sitting on his knees holding a slice of bread, staring at the lump. It sat on the partially flattened slice of white bread as he pondered how to make a sandwich out of it. Candy couldn't breathe. She wanted to make a suggestion but was unable to stop laughing long enough to speak.

"What?" Dylan gingerly balanced the other piece of bread on top of the lump, making Candy cackle even harder. She wiped tears from her face as she lay on the ground on her back. "How are we supposed to eat this crap?"

Candy took some deep breaths and regained a bit of control. "Break it into parts, silly."

"Oh," he said, as if he hadn't been able to come up with that solution on his own. She crossed her arms, then slapped his coat-clad arm, and he answered her with a smile that warmed her entire body.

As they watched the people around them carrying signs and shouting from time to time, they wondered about the others. Hours went by, and they never came back. They had disappeared into thin air, it seemed, leaving behind their possessions.

That afternoon, they started to consider that they might have to go to the police station and bail them out. But Dylan maintained that he never saw the others being arrested. As far as Sebastian went, Dylan was sure his parents were going to bail him out. They always did.

"Should we go check the van I came in? Maybe they got lost or something," Candy suggested.

"I'm not sure."

"Where did you guys park?"

"Took a bus."

"Oh."

It was silent for several seconds as they considered their options. Candy only wanted to check for the van. She hoped and prayed they hadn't left her here. Her clothes were in there as well. Her brand-new nice clothes.

"You want to check, don't you?"

Candy nodded, and felt even worse when Dylan shook his head. She felt his frustration. "Sorry. Never mind." She touched the matted yellow blanket beneath her. It was so worn that it was almost see-through. Brown grass poked through one hole.

"No. I guess I agree. We ought to see. Then we'll come back and wait again. All right?"

"Maybe I had better go by myself."

"I don't want to take a chance at losing you."

Candy's heart jumped as she thought about Rachel, and then she quickly dismissed her picture.

"Candy, I mean I don't want you to lose me either. If you lose your friends, then lose me, you're on your own. At least with me, I can...help. Sort of."

"Sort of?"

"Well, I mean… Well, um, never mind. Let's go check." Dylan stood. They folded their blankets, stacked the others' bags over their shoulders, and set out for their parking place. Only she had no idea where it was.

She only knew they were near the limestone buildings. There were so many of them! With every step they took, she felt the tension rising. Dylan was becoming more and more frustrated. With a quick sniff, she turned her head away from Dylan so he wouldn't notice her tears.

Finally, things started to seem familiar. "Wait." She stopped. He took a few steps, then turned back around toward her. She wiped away a stray tear.

"You crying?" His voice was rough as he stepped toward her. A jolt of fear hit her and she pushed it away before he noticed.

"No. Just the cold." Her voice quivered as she sought to stay in control. "I'm cold. That's all. Here." She pointed one shaky finger toward the empty curb. The space between two cars – perfectly sized for a Volkswagen van. Panic set in as she rushed back and forth, hoping she was wrong. But she knew deep down that she wasn't wrong. "Why'd they leave me? They took my clothes. My new clothes."

Dylan stood dumbfounded, staring at the sidewalk. "You sure?"

"I'm sure. This is the spot." Candy held her forehead.

"Well…" He paced back and forth while running his fingers through his hair. Silently she pleaded to him, hoping he had answers, but he didn't seem to know what to do either.

Hiding her face with both hands now, she finally let go and broke down, sobbing. What little hope she had found in that van earlier was now gone, as were her friends and her new clothes. It was over. She was trapped in DC, far from home.

When she felt Dylan's warm and strong arms around her again, she couldn't help but relent and sink into his warmth. She buried her face in his coat as he squeezed her and rocked her back and forth.

Chapter Eight

     She didn't care what happened to her anymore. Dylan might have left her there on the cold streets of DC, and it wouldn't have mattered. She had no more tears. Maybe they had frozen in the cold February air. Maybe she ran out, since she had cried so often this last week. Maybe the human body could only come up with so many tears, and then you wouldn't have to worry about them anymore.

     As she stared out of the bus window, she watched herself leave the city and go... where? She had no idea. Somewhere in Maryland, that's all she knew. It didn't really matter, anyway. She barely remembered getting on the bus, but she knew Dylan was leading her with wordless motions. Like a shadow, she did whatever he did as she was powerless to do anything but go with him.

     "It's not the end of the world, you know," she heard.

     Was he finally talking to her? Dare she look his way? "I guess," she conceded, then gazed outside again. Ahead of her were trees, houses, and a wide avenue, but behind her was the country's capital. *So much for seeing the history of it all. Oh well. At least I can say I have been*

there. 'Oh, yes. I've been to DC. It is such a beautiful city,'
she might say as she did her best to impress someone at a
black-tie event. That would be the kind of party she would
go to as a model. Standing around on high heels, trying to
appear rich and sophisticated, speaking with a hint of a
European flair, tittering politely at her date's jokes. Her
date? She nonchalantly peeked up at Dylan.

His perfectly chiseled face and crisp, clean clothes
led her to believe he might do well as her sophisticated
date. The two of them might look good together. And
maybe he could help her rise to the next level – from the
Sears catalog to the runway and then on to Paris. Maybe
she would be on a billboard one day or on television, like
Twiggy.

Still, she had to start somewhere. "So, you're a
photographer," Candy mused aloud.

He glanced her way, then faced front again. "Yes."

"You said maybe we could do some pictures."

"I can shoot some of you. Yes."

"When?"

"When we get back to my place."

His place? Well, then again, where else would she
be going? She hardly knew the guy, though. Maybe he had
an extra bedroom so she wouldn't be forced to sleep in his
bed. *With him.* Although it might not be so bad. *Does he
have notches in his bedpost?* A hunk of a guy like that
probably got any girl he wanted, whenever he wanted.

Did he already have a girlfriend? Would she be
there? Would she come visit, find Candy there, and then
start a fight? What then? Where would she go with her
eighty dollars? How long was that supposed to last? She

felt fortunate to have her money, if she couldn't have her clothes. She wished she hadn't spent all that money on clothes now, though.

Why would they leave her there? Why would they take her suitcase and drive away without looking for her? They knew where she was. She was getting food for them. Were they trying to ditch her?

She shot a quick glance up at Dylan. Might he do the same? As he adjusted the blanket and backpack on his lap, she wondered if he was going to take her picture, then throw her out onto the street. Where was she supposed to go? *How do the homeless stay warm around here? Well, does it matter?* Maybe if she slept on the sidewalk, she would eventually fall asleep from hypothermia and then die. Didn't seem like such a bad chain of events now. Her heart ached, but she had no tears left to cry.

Miles and miles rolled under the bus as they sat in silence under piles of their friends' bags and blankets. It was getting warm in the bus, and the dirty sneaker smell was making her nauseated. At each traffic light, she hoped the doors might open to let in a bit of fresh air. Finally, every few blocks, the doors did open, and she eagerly sucked in every ounce of clean air possible before they closed again. With each bus stop, she also hoped to be able to stand up and leave the bus. And with each stop, other people got off, leaving them soon with only a few people left. *It figures he would live at the last stop.*

The sun was already going down by the time they made it to their destination, wherever that was. The driver yelled, "Fenton," and Dylan stood, then gathered his bags and slung them over his shoulders. Candy stood also, hoping he wasn't going to leave her there without telling her anything. As she threw her backpack over her shoulder and picked up another bag, the bus stopped. She kept a close watch on Dylan, searching him for signs of a possible dismissal. Fortunately, she never saw any, so she eagerly followed him from the bus and into the street.

After checking for cars, they crossed the street and headed for a neighborhood of homes. As they walked along the sidewalk, she hoped he lived in a nice house like these. They were brick, well taken care of, and clean. She imagined that when it snowed here, people were the type to quickly clean their sidewalks and driveways and make neat pathways for people to walk. This was nothing like home, where no one cared. But how long was he going to keep her until he kicked her to the curb? Before he told her she was no longer welcome?

They weren't far from the bus stop when Candy followed him up a few brick steps to a front door under a covered porch. There was even a porch swing. *So cute*, she couldn't help but think. *He is doing very well for himself as a photographer.*

Shuffling with his packs, he found his key and then opened the door. He pushed it open and waited for her to walk inside. She admired the clean wood floors, perfectly white walls, arched doorways, and clean-cut furniture. It was bright, open, airy, and surprisingly clean. Did he live with his parents?

He watched as she took it all in, step by step, inspecting the home. "It's beautiful." Oddly beautiful. She wanted to ask if he lived with his parents but thought it might be too nosy.

He waved his hand toward the back of the house, past a kitchen, and down a hall. She set her things down in the front room, a living room, and headed down the hall to the back of the house. There, in a room that spanned the whole width of the house, was a bright, white room full of cameras, lights, umbrellas, backdrops, screens, everything a photographer needed for a studio.

"Is this where you take your pictures? I thought you worked for a modeling agency."

"I do. I have a studio at work, and I have one here for me, to shoot people such as yourself or the mom down the street who wants pictures of her baby. Things like that."

"Oh, I get it. You work here and at the agency."

"Yup." He began moving things around, fiddling with equipment. Immediately she noticed a distinct change in his demeanor. His face had brightened, as bright as the house, and he moved eagerly with a set goal in mind. What it was, she had no idea, so she stood still, shuffling her feet and leaning against a wall as he worked at a feverish pace.

Finally, he gazed up at her with big blue eyes and a toothy smile, the same one he had shown her when they first met, not when he was annoyed with having to bring home a lost little girl. He was happy again, and she knew it was because he was in his element. This was home, in more ways than one. His sudden change was a little silly to her. He had changed like Dr. Jekyll and Mr. Hyde.

"Oh. What will you wear? Hm." He stopped to think for a second, then resumed his frantic movements. Pulling back a curtain, he uncovered a closet full of women's clothing.

Women's clothing?

"No, it's not what you're thinking," he stated as he saw her expression.

With her hands over her mouth, she couldn't hold in the laughter any longer, prompting him to shake his head before resuming his search. After shoving hangers and clothes back and forth, he finally found what he was searching for. A strapless, little black dress.

It was obviously too small for her and was too short. "How am I supposed to fit into *that?*"

"Take off your coat. I can't tell what size you are."

"Six. Or eight."

He tilted his head. "You are not a six. More like a zero."

"Do they even make a zero? Zero? Are you serious?" She slid her coat off from her arms, letting it puddle onto the floor. As she put her hands on her hips, her long fingers nearly touched in front.

As he eyed her body, she blushed heavily and ducked her head. He walked toward her and turned her around, making it possible to observe her from all angles. "Dylan," she scolded.

"Shh." Then he went back to the closet and pulled out a dark blue mini-dress with straps. She eyed it and hoped it fit. She loved it. "Did you bring makeup?"

"Oh. Um, no. I don't usually–,"

"No matter. I have some."

"What are you doing with women's clothes and makeup?"

He waved his arm around the room and declared, "I'm a photographer, my dear, and a damned good one. I pride myself on being prepared for any situation, even one such as this."

"And how often do you find lost girls in the city and bring them back here promising a modeling career?" she joked with her chin in the air.

He approached her, the joy now vanishing from his face. Her heart beat faster. "Never. But for you, I will make an exception." He gently brushed her nose with his finger and then walked away.

Raising one eyebrow for a second, she froze in place and decided not to joke about anything else unless he did.

In the bottom of his closet, he found a small blue makeup case with a handle on top, picked it up, and handed it to her along with the dress. "No blue eye shadow. Only dark colors. I might shoot you in black and white, anyway. Just in case, make your eyes dark and mysterious. That's the look for you." With a nod, he went back to his equipment. "Go on." His back was to her now.

"Um, where –,"

"Oh. Sorry." He took her arm and led her to the powder room in the hall. "Here you go."

"Thanks."

The bathroom was small and crowded, with only a sink and a commode, but at least was clean. She sat on the fuzzy blue toilet cover and began undressing. After taking the dress from the hanger, she slipped it on and tried to zip it in back, but couldn't get it all the way. She went back out to ask for help.

"You're not wearing a bra." There was a hint of awe in his voice.

"Well, no. It would show. And I don't have a strapless."

"I like it." Candy could tell he was visualizing her without the dress. She crossed her arms over her body, and her dress sagged from her shoulders, reminding her of her zipper issue.

"Um, I need help with the zipper. Can you zip it for me?" She pulled up her hair and turned around, hoping to hide her now reddened face.

"Mm-hm," he moaned, then began pulling the zipper bit by bit while running the backs of his fingers up her spine. She couldn't help the goose bumps on her arms and hoped he didn't notice. He did. He placed his hands on her upper arms as she let go of her hair, then ran them down her arms and back up, seemingly enjoying every inch. "Okay," he whispered into her ear. She almost shivered but was able to stop it before it happened.

"Thanks." She felt the strength leaving her body. She managed to get herself back into the bathroom and took a second to compose herself after closing the door. Desperately, she hoped he didn't expect her to sleep with him. *Although how bad could it be?*

As she lifted the lid on the makeup case, it unfolded itself to display two levels of trays full of every kind of makeup imaginable. She pulled out foundation, powder, eyeliner, mascara, blush, dark grey eye shadow, eyebrow pencil, lipstick, tweezers, tiny scissors, and several makeup brushes. Then, she touched her equipment, one piece at a time, not knowing where to begin.

Using a makeup sponge, she dabbed on foundation and spread it around. It was too dark. Pursing her pale lips, she searched the bathroom and found a washcloth. She washed off the makeup after tying up her hair with an elastic band. Then, she tried a lighter shade and decided it would work. Then she moved on to the rest, hoping she wouldn't look like a kid playing in her mother's makeup. When she was done, she didn't look like herself, and as she surveyed her work, she wasn't even sure that this was how makeup was supposed to be. Finally, she let her hair down and brushed it with a small brush she found inside the case. Despite not being satisfied, smacking her rosy lipstick-clad lips, she left the bathroom, now twenty minutes later.

Dylan was in the kitchen across from the bathroom, sitting on the counter with a glass of ice in his hand. His eyes danced as he saw her. He hopped down and set his glass on the counter behind him, making the ice clink as it settled in the bottom.

"Did I do it right? I'm not used to this."

He approached her and inspected her face with his fingers. Then he took her hand and led her back into the bathroom. Taking the washcloth she had used earlier, he seemed to smear the makeup all over her eyes, which horrified her, knowing how much time she had put into her work. When he was done, she frowned and knit her eyebrows at him. "What?"

"I um, I don't know. Is it supposed to be smeared like this?"

He turned her toward the mirror. What she saw nearly scared her. There was a skeleton with blue eyes.

As she saw his reflection in the mirror, he was smiling, surprisingly. "This is how they –?" she started.

"Yup," he interrupted, then took her hand again and led her back into his studio.

Now, he seemed even more excited as he guided her toward the marbled gray backdrop. As she stood waiting for him to go back to his camera and fiddle with more equipment, she tried to remember how they had posed her up in New York earlier that week. She had not seen the pictures, didn't know how they turned out, and didn't know if she had done anything right. She hoped he would teach her how to do this.

"All right." He picked up his camera, finally, and pointed it her way. "Let's pretend you're in, say, Paris, and there's a cute guy, and you're flirting with him."

Shouldn't be too hard, considering there's a cute guy on the other side of the camera, she thought with a flirty guise. The camera snapped, surprising her. No wasting time with him. She did her best, though she wasn't sure what to do. But it became much easier when he told her to stop smiling and pretend she was a lonely homeless girl on the street. *Wearing a gorgeous dress like this? Whatever.* At least she felt more in tune with this personality.

She sat on a box covered with a sheet, putting her knees together with her feet far apart. As she leaned over, he told her she was doing great, his first positive words during their photo shoot. Now a little more encouraged, she thought about her first night away from home, feeling unwanted, unloved, in the way, like a piece of trash. Her thoughts nearly brought her to tears, but when she was about to go over the edge, she found control as she forced her thoughts to happier times, like yesterday in the van when they had laughed at the sound of the horn.

But they had left her, which made her sad again. Then there was Dylan, who was now hopefully helping her get into modeling, which made her happy again. The entire routine was exhausting her as her emotions swung wildly back and forth, almost making her dizzy.

Finally, a half hour later, he put the camera down and studied her as if he had finished a painting and was surveying his work.

"Now what?" Where would she go if he threw her out now? Her heart beat faster and now the tears almost did come as she knew she had nowhere else to go.

But before the first tear fell, he had his arms around her, picking her up, forcing her to wrap her long legs around him to hold on. As he grabbed her lips with his, he backed her up onto a table and set her down, freeing his hands. Before she knew it, the zipper was down again, and he had pulled the dress over her head and tossed it onto the floor. She tugged his shirt over his head while he freed himself of the rest of his clothes. He moaned as he tasted her neck, her shoulder, her chest, and landed solidly on one nipple. She held his head as she cried out loudly and arched into his mouth. She hooked her legs around his hips and drew him closer, begging for him, and he eagerly obliged.

They lay in his bed; it had gotten dark, and she was sure he wouldn't throw her out now. Besides, every hour or two, they woke up and made love again. She knew at the very least that if she could keep him happy, she would stay warm. Not that she didn't enjoy herself, too. He was good.

Damned good. It was amazing how good. Her body felt like Gumby's now, warm, soft, pliable, able to take any shape. She closed her eyes in total bliss and exhaled any residual stress away.

As the sun came up, they slept like spoons with Dylan's arm draped over her. She was so warm. She hadn't been that warm since, well, she had nothing to compare it to. One thin ray of light beamed through the side of the shade, illuminating his dresser. She found it cute that he had so many "man things" around the room like a lava lamp, a strange abstract painting, a few bottles of cologne, a comb, and a jewelry box. *What kind of jewelry does a man wear?* None of the guys at the track wore jewelry, other than wedding rings. Even those didn't last long sometimes.

He sucked in a lungful of air, and she knew he was awake now. With a rumbling moan, he pulled her closer, and she felt him ready for her again. The frequency of their lovemaking amazed her, but she wasn't about to argue. She had never been more satisfied in her life. Not that it had been a long life of having sex. It had only been a few years.

Roger was her last boyfriend, and there was another before him, briefly – Danny. He was her first, and neither he nor she had known what they were doing. They had sneaked off, mostly in his car, and she had only been there, it seemed, to satisfy him. He didn't care about her one bit. But when Roger came along, she knew how it was supposed to be. Until she met Dylan…and *now*, she knew how it was really supposed to be – mind-blowing. It was as if he had read her mind, knowing exactly what she wanted or needed.

"I'm so sore," he moaned as he rubbed his rounded backside. "I'm not used to this."

Candy ran her fingers through his chest hair. "How long has it been?"

He thought for a moment. "Six months. Record time for me, I think."

Candy sat up and peered down at him as she opened her mouth in an O, but then lay down again as it hit her that it had been the same for her. When she admitted that fact, he gasped in mock surprise, and tickled her until she had rolled off the bed. When she tried to climb back in, he playfully stopped her. But she was able to get the better hand and pushed him off the bed, laughing at him the whole while. He stood from his position on the floor and went toward his closet, poking her first, then moving out of reach.

She figured out he didn't live with his parents when she didn't hear anybody else in the house that morning. He didn't even have a roommate, which she thought was strange for someone his age. *How old was he, anyway? Should I ask? Is that rude? Is it too... Oh, hell. I slept with the man. Might as well find out.* "How old are you?" She watched him pull out a t-shirt for her, and one for himself.

His answer was impish. "Guess."

"Twenty-one."

"Nope."

She continued on, and with each passing and rising guess, her eyes became wider and wider until it seemed they might fall out of her head and onto the floor. He tickled her when she got to twenty-eight, and she knew. He was nine years older? *Oh, God.*

When he asked how old she was, she was still stunned from the surprise, and now with fear as she wondered if he was going to throw her out for being too young for him. She touched her chin. Should she lie about her age? Maybe if she told him that she was twenty, it might not seem so bad. Or would he find out? Did it matter? *Was nineteen too –*

"Twenty." How had that slipped out so quickly?

"Oh, wow." She could tell he was not upset, thankfully. He was dressed now, although only in his boxers and a t-shirt, and she slipped her shirt over her head. The shirt wasn't long enough, as she was so tall, and he knew what she needed, but was not offering.

"Um, can I have some shorts or sweatpants or something?" She sat her hands on her hips.

"No. I think you look better without them."

"Dylan!" She threw a pillow at him, which he caught and threw back.

"Help yourself." He waved his arm toward his dresser.

"I don't want to go through your stuff."

Pressing his lips together, he marched to his dresser and pulled out a pair of sweatpants for her. Candy could tell he was annoyed, but what could she do about it?

After putting them on, she tightened the drawstring around her waist. She tugged at them, making them wider, like clown pants. Peeking through her eyelashes, she glanced at Dylan, who was trying his hardest not to laugh. "Don't you like them?"

"They're perfect." Dylan swept his arm around her and led her back downstairs to the kitchen.

As they made breakfast, she felt uncomfortable for more reasons than one. She'd never made breakfast at home. She either didn't eat or found something at the track, and it had been that way for several years now. Even when her parents were alive, she didn't cook. If she were lucky enough, they had a box of cereal and milk at the same time. They never had eggs or bacon, or any of those things mothers made on television. And waffles? Forget it.

Dylan whipped up so much food that she wasn't sure what to eat first, and she definitely could not eat all of it. She wanted to eat so much more, but it was impossible.

"Come on, Skinny Minnie. Look at those ribs. I know you're hungry. Eat," he insisted as he pointed to her nearly full plate with his fork.

"I can't. I swear, I can't. I am so full."

"Oh, come on. Girls always say that."

"I'm serious. I'm not used to eating like this. I mean, I'm lucky if I get a leftover hot dog for breakfast back home. I've never even seen a spread like this in real life."

As he chewed his waffle, he stared at her with no expression, and suddenly she felt exposed, as if she had said too much. Maybe he didn't care to know that much about her. Maybe it didn't matter. Maybe he only wanted her for sex. This was the perfect opportunity for a place to stay and a possible job, though. She was going to have to put up with his idiosyncrasies to get a chance at launching her career.

He took a bite of his eggs and then spoke once he had finished that bite. "You grow up poor?"

She nodded as she considered how to save the food for later. Should she bother to store it up for when he kicked her out?

"Oh. Sorry." He dug his fork into his eggs again.

"I take it you didn't?" If he asked about her growing up poor, he shouldn't be offended if she asked him the same question.

"Nah. I mean, middle class, I guess. Not rich or anything."

"Did you buy this house yourself?"

"Yup. Like it?"

"Love it. It's beautiful. So bright and warm and... clean."

Begrudgingly, he admitted he hired a cleaning lady once a week. She wondered how he could afford that and afford this house. The modeling business must be lucrative for more than the models.

After breakfast, as they stood together at the kitchen sink, she watched her entire plate full of food fall into the sink, going to waste.

"There's more where that came from, Candy," he said softly. She glanced up at him like a child caught stealing something. It was as if he knew her thoughts about saving it, and she was ashamed. Her heart burned with sadness, but she was out of tears. She had used up a year's worth of tears in the last week.

One week. How had so much changed in only one week? However, as long as Dylan let her stay here, she felt as though she had somehow climbed up a rung on the ladder of life. She wasn't on the ground anymore, being trampled by the world.

Chapter Nine

Candy watched a game show rerun on television while Dylan developed his pictures. It was Sunday, and she knew that tomorrow, it was time to get back to work. Still, she was afraid to ask about staying. She hoped that if she didn't say anything, and the subject weren't brought up, that he might assume she was staying.

As she sat wrapped in a crocheted blanket, she listened to the noises coming from his dark room in the basement. The thought of him, the mad scientist, working on his experiments in the dark laboratory was hilarious to her. The feeling was short-lived, though, as a commercial for a real estate broker appeared on the color television in front of her, jolting her back to reality. Real estate. Housing. What about her housing? What would she do?

Finally, she heard his bare feet slipping their way up the wooden staircase. The door creaked as he opened it, he came through, and then closed it. When she saw his face, any doubt in her mind instantly vanished.

He leaned down so he was close to her. "They…look…unbelievable." Then he sat down next to her.

"Can I see?" She bounced like a child in her seat.

"Not yet. They're not done. Soon. Patience, my pet. What are we watching?"

"The Dating Game."

"Oh." His demeanor soured in an instant as he sank back into the couch.

"You don't like that show?"

"Not really."

"Well, I don't care. We can watch something else. What do you normally watch?"

"I don't know," he groaned as he stood again and walked to the television to change the station. He turned the dial a few times to change the channel, finding some stations coming in better than others. Finally, he found a documentary on a PBS station that came in with a double picture with blue and red streaks. Candy thought she saw a polar bear walking around on the snow or ice. Contented, Dylan came back to the couch and slumped into the soft cushions. "Here we go. Something quiet and relaxing."

Candy offered half of her blanket, and he accepted. He lifted his arm until she fell into place on his chest. It didn't take long for her to fall asleep.

She woke up again as he was trying to slide out from underneath her. As she sat up, she rubbed her face. "Oh. I fell asleep."

"Uh huh." By now, he was standing and headed for the basement door. She wanted to follow him, but didn't want to get in the way or mess up the pictures somehow by going down there. So she waited. And waited. Finally, she decided to get up and change the channel back to the game shows she had been watching. *Much more entertaining than watching animal documentaries.*

Some time later, he returned with a stack of pictures and spread them out on his coffee table. Candy was mesmerized by pictures of a woman that looked nothing like her. Or at least she thought not. With her jaw dropped, she inspected them one by one. "Is this me?" It was the same dress. It was her hair.

The way he had developed them made her face appear soft and smooth, not caked with powder or blush. Most pictures were in black and white, but the color ones resembled paintings with thick and vivid colors. Her eyes were bluer than the ocean, her hair a golden ginger shade of red.

"That's you, gorgeous."

"Only because you made me look that way. Wow, Dylan. I can't believe these. Do you think your studio will like them?"

"I think so."

"You going to take them tomorrow?"

"I'll take them in, but I can't promise anything. But I know they will look at them soon, especially if I put this one on top." He pulled one of the photos from the pile. The eight-by-ten color photo seemed to tell a story of a girl who had been left behind, possibly after a party. Her haunted eyes were dark and shadowed, yet her blue irises shone with a bit of hope as she gazed into the camera and wordlessly asked, "Will you help me?"

Shaking her head slightly, she studied herself in the photo, and then faced Dylan with amazement. "You're good."

"I know." He leaned back into the couch again, clasping his hands behind his head.

As the lazy afternoon wore on, they found themselves without their clothes again on the couch. Hours later, several times later, he pushed her from his lap and stood. "We should go get dinner."

She felt alone for a second but decided to negate that feeling with humor. She eyed his naked body up and down, and then reached out for him, but he pulled away. "Don't touch me, woman!" She stood to come after him, but he rushed away, and she chased him around the house, bringing laughter with them into every room.

"I'm going to take a shower," he announced as they finally made it to the bedroom. Without waiting for a response, he went into his bathroom and shut the door.

"Okay." With one eyebrow raised, she stopped in her tracks, then spun on her heels to face the other direction. She searched around the room for clothes, wondering what to wear. Her only clothes were grungy and worn, aside from a new blouse she had thrown in the bag the other day. She pulled the wrinkled blue mess from her backpack along with the jeans she had worn several times now. They were dirty with dead grass and mud and smelled of three-day-old sweat. Ashamed, she laid them on the bed and tried to smooth out the wrinkles. She knew he was going to come out of the shower and probably suggest some nice restaurant. She was going to look ridiculous in her worn, dirty clothes.

She thought about searching the other bags they had brought back from the city, but she didn't want to use somebody else's clothes, especially if they were already dirty.

Oh. The clothes downstairs in the closet. For a second, she considered asking him before running down to choose something, but she decided instead to run down and find something first. Something not too dressy, not too casual, since she didn't know where they were going to eat. As she descended the stairs and made her way into his studio again, she realized she didn't have the proper manners for such a place. This place certainly would have real plates and silverware, and crystal glasses that sang when you wet the rims and ran your finger around them. It would have, of course, a waiter in a black tuxedo, with a cloth draped over his arm. Maybe he would offer a bottle of wine. She had never had wine before.

As she uncovered the closet full of gorgeous things any girl would love, she felt like a child of good parents on Christmas. She wanted to wear them all and began trying on a few dresses. They fit but were too dressy. She was sure he was not going to take her to anything too fancy yet. He knew she grew up poor. He must have known she didn't have proper etiquette for eating in a nice restaurant. *Right*?

Instead of a dress, she found a pair of navy blue bell bottoms, very low cut with wide belt buckle openings. Then, she found a white belt and white blouse, so she pulled them out to wear with the pants. With frantic fingers, she began putting on her new clothes. A colorful scarf beckoned her from the top shelf in the closet. She would grab that for her neck as soon as she had her blouse buttoned.

"What are you doing?"

She stopped mid-button, her face turning white. "Um, I don't have, um, clothes. They took them." Her voice became softer with every word.

"Can't leave the house with those." He pointed toward her and looked her up and down. "I need those."

"Can I, um, borrow, and um, pay you back or something?"

"Ha. You'd never make enough to pay for those, honey." He strode toward her and unbuttoned her blouse again. She stood still, hoping at least he would get turned on and forget about this. But after taking off her blouse, he hung it up and walked toward the door again. "Come on up. Maybe I have something upstairs you can wear."

"Okay," she heard herself answer.

Now, wearing nothing, she padded across the parquet flooring to the stairs, then up to his room. He was already searching through his things and pulling out shirts.

"Maybe I should do some laundry."

"Yeah. Later. Here. Put this on." He handed her a paisley shirt on a hanger and a t-shirt draped over his arm. She found her bra, put it on first, then the shirts.

"I look like a man."

"Women dress like this these days. It's got a pattern. No one will know."

"What will I do for pants?" She was trying her hardest to stay strong as she felt she might cry any second.

"I guess you should wear those jeans again."

"They smell." She wrinkled her nose in disgust.

He scratched his head as he thought again for several seconds. "Try mine, I guess."

She pulled them on, buttoned them, then let go and watched them fall to the ground, folding like an accordion. She frowned at the crumpled pants. He chuckled and shook his head, then scanned his room again for something else.

"I'm sorry. If only I had my suitcase."

"I know, my pet. Don't worry."

If only, honestly, he felt that way.

With a groan, he finally gave in and led her back downstairs and gave her the exact outfit she had picked out earlier. She wanted to squeal with delight but managed to keep it to a tiny squeak and one hop. He chuckled as he shook his head at her. "Women." He helped her dress into her outfit again.

She stood back to admire herself in the mirror. She wiggled her toes as they stuck out from beneath the bell bottoms. She didn't have socks, let alone shoes. There were several pairs of socks in her suitcase, now gone with those hippies. "Shoes?"

Where did they go, anyway? Why would they leave her there? Why would Dylan's friends leave, too? Sebastian was probably out of jail by now, but the others? Where were they?

She came back to the present when she found Dylan on his hands and knees holding up a pair of shoes for her. He might have been a man proposing to a woman, and her lips curled into a devious grin. After running her fingers over the shoes, she swung her arms around his neck and pretended to cry. "Yes! Yes!"

"Didn't think you'd like them that much." He stood, breaking from her arms in the process. *Oh well.* The shoes were so cute that she quickly forgot about her botched joke and snatched them from his hands. Then, she brought them with her to the bench she had sat on the day before for her photo shoot and slipped them on.

"Perfect fit. Like Cinderella."

"Mi-lady." He bowed and extended his hand.

Blushing, she took his hand and then stood. His hair was still wet from the shower, reminding her that she had to take a shower, too. "Oh, um, this princess needs a shower, too. I don't want to go out in public smelling like sex. I mean, we must have done it like four hundred times already."

"Ha!" His loud exclamation made her jump, but his expression stayed jovial. "Four *hundred?* That's a bit high, don't you think?"

With her hand on her chin, she studied the ceiling. "No. I think it was…four hundred twenty-three. Yes. That's it."

As she heard his laughter, her heart soared with joy, as she felt completely safe and secure with him again. He was such a sweet guy, letting her wear his prop clothes like this, also taking her in, letting her sleep with him… not that he didn't benefit from it, too. He had fed her and let her relax on the soft couch with a blanket and watch television. Those things were never possible back home in Queens.

Back at home, she was always peeking over her shoulder for Don or his drugged-up friends. They made passes at her, and she felt no shame when she slapped them or hit them with something. She had even learned to punch like a boxer, and she was surprised that they had never punched her back. Their old couch was a green, scratchy, and tattered mess, nothing like Dylan's. Padding constantly fell out, and she was always trying to stuff it back in. It was a losing battle, though, as Don's friends often pulled it back out to throw it at each other. They had no crocheted blankets that might have been made by a grandmother or some other old relative. She had no old relatives. She had no relatives at all.

Dylan reached up and touched her cheek, where a tear had fallen. Straightening her shoulders, she attempted to change the subject in her mind. "Where are we going?"

"Everything all right?" It seemed as though he was trying to get back to the sad subject again. She had no interest in going back, though. From now on, going forward was the only way to go.

"Yup." She lifted her chin and forced her grin into a full-blown smile. He kissed her, gazed into her eyes for a few moments, and then let the subject go. He took her hand and led her back up to the bedroom.

There, he helped her out of her clothes, but this time instead of hoping for him to pick her up and toss her back onto the bed, she hoped for a shower. He seemed to realize this and sat on the bed, picking up her toothbrush while she slipped her bra from her arms. As he eyed her body, he held out the toothbrush for her, and she took it, making sure to touch his hand. "What are you trying to say? My breath stinks?" She slammed her hands onto the bones sticking out from her hips.

"Yes. Yes, I am. That's exactly what I'm saying."

She stuck out her tongue at him, then bounced into the bathroom. In the shower, she washed her hair, hoping he had a hair dryer, and knew he probably did if he had all of that makeup downstairs. He had everything else a woman might need. How many women had been here before her?

After her shower and drying herself, she opened the bathroom door. "Hey, do you have a…" She stopped when she noticed him seated on the bed, holding her magic box. "No," she whispered as she ran for him and then snatched it from his hands, almost pushing him backwards onto the bed in the process.

"Whoa. Wait a minute. I didn't hurt it."

As she caressed the box with her hand, then ran one finger over the crack her brother had caused, she was flooded with embarrassment. "I know." She lowered her reddened face and sat next to him on the bed. "I'm sorry. It's just that…" Her throat closed, keeping her words inside, and her jaw quivered as she fought the tears that threatened to come. "It's…"

Dylan stood and went to his dresser. She felt the distance between them growing and put the box down. "I'm sorry, Dylan." She held out her hands as she approached him. With crossed arms, he stood his ground, and she noticed a hair dryer on the dresser behind him. "That for me?" Candy pointed at it.

"Yeah." He picked up the hair dryer.

"Thank you. I was going to ask if you had one."

Without meeting her gaze, he handed it to her. He seemed irritated, and she thought he might change his mind about dinner. "Dylan, that box," she started.

"Don't worry about it." He went back to the bed, away from her.

"It was my mom's. Okay? Please understand. I'm really, I mean, she wasn't the best mom, but it's all I have left," she managed to say before succumbing to her emotions. Still holding the hair dryer in one hand, she covered her face with her other, and was surprised when Dylan came to her. She kept her hand over her face so she wouldn't get tears on his shirt and tried to stop crying, but she was unable to quell the waters. Each time she thought she was under control again, the tears flooded back. She knew if she didn't stop them, her eyes were going to be swollen, and he was going to be embarrassed to be seen with her. Then he might want to stay home, and she didn't want that at all. She never got to go out to dinner. This was a once-in-a-lifetime chance. She had to take it. As she thought about how good the food might taste, she finally managed to stop the tears.

Blowing out a huge toothpaste-scented puff of air, she stood back and peered up at him. "Sorry," was all he said. She got the feeling that was a hard word for him to say, and that he didn't say it very often, and when he did say it, it really meant something. Standing on her tiptoes, she kissed him as his hands rested on her arms, then let go as she pulled away.

She went back into the bathroom and splashed cold water onto her face in an attempt to diminish the swelling. Then she plugged in the hair dryer and dried her hair. It took a long time, though she tried to hurry. But her hair was long, and she had to get it completely dry so she wouldn't be in the cold winter air with wet hair.

Then, the dry air made her hair float from the ends, and she found herself amused at the sight. She fluffed it up and tried to get it to stick out and float as much as possible, then went into the bedroom. "Look…" she started, but he wasn't there.

Disappointed, she went back and lightly wet her hands, then smoothed her hair again. She found some hair spray and lightly sprayed it to keep it from flying away again. Then she found her platform shoes and remembered that she had no socks. Instead of going through his things and getting caught again, she called out for him. "Dylan?" she called from the bedroom doorway.

"Yeah," she heard from the kitchen.

"Can I borrow some socks?"

She heard a sigh. "Yes. Top left drawer."

"Thank you." Candy frowned. She knew she was going to overstay her welcome quickly if she kept asking for things. But it was either ask or get caught taking. Both options seemed to annoy him, and she knew it was going to be a struggle to figure out the lesser of two evils whenever she needed something.

Finally, she descended the stairs into the front foyer and headed for the kitchen. A fleeting thought crossed her mind about wearing makeup, but she quickly dismissed it. When he didn't say anything about it, she knew she would be all right without it. After all, he was the expert in fashion, it seemed. With a sheepish grin, she stood holding her coat, thankfully the newer one. After checking his watch, he picked up his coat and helped her with hers.

He had checked his watch to let her know he was annoyed with how long it took her to get ready. Actually, it hadn't taken her much longer than it had taken him. She wouldn't dare point that out, though. She rationalized it by telling herself he was used to living alone, doing whatever he wanted, whenever he wanted, and not having to share anything. Finding yourself living with a stranger can be very taxing, especially when suddenly they're in your stuff. She knew it must be hard for him. Not that it was any easier for her.

He led her to the back door, and they went outside to a separate garage in the back of the house. Without a word, he unlocked the large white door and pulled it up. He went to the car and held the door for her as she got in. She tried to smile at him as she thanked him, and he forced the same in return. He started the car, pulled it out, got back out to close the garage door, and then got back into the car with a groan. "I've got to get one of those automatic things."

"Automatic what?"

He eyed her incredulously. "Garage door opener. Haven't you ever heard of those?"

"No. I didn't know they made anything like that. Are they expensive?"

"Kind of. You have to have it installed, too. I keep putting it off."

"So, where are we going?"

"I thought we'd go to this place up the road I like."

"What kind of food is it?"

He glanced her way and shrugged. "I don't know. American? Just…food."

"Oh, okay." As he drove, she took in the scenery she hadn't been able to see from the bus. It was a lot like New York with the crowded streets, houses, and buildings close together. But she knew it definitely took more money to live here than in Queens. "Are there boroughs here like in New York?"

"Kind of. In town, in DC, we use 'Northwest,' 'Southwest,' 'Northeast,' 'Southeast.' But then, there are areas like Capitol Hill or Adams Morgan, or other areas that have names, but they're a lot smaller than the areas in New York. It's like different neighborhoods within the city."

"Oh, okay. I see. Are we in DC now?"

"A little north. In Silver Spring."

"Everything runs together like up there, too. You can't tell one city from the next."

"Yeah. It's crowded, that's for sure."

Soon, they were parking at the restaurant, and she watched nicely dressed men and women making their way to and from their cars. She smoothed her hands over her pants. Was she dressed appropriately? But Dylan knew what she needed to wear. She trusted him. She had to. She had nothing else to go on.

As they went in and were seated at a table for two in the dark restaurant, she squinted as she tried to see everything. Paneling on the walls and dimly lit tiffany lamps with red glass covers made it so dark that it was almost impossible to see the other side of the restaurant. When she tried to read her menu, she had to hold it closer to the light to see it. Amused, he snickered quietly at her.

"Well, I can't see. It's so dark in here. Why is it so dark? Something wrong with the lights?"

"Atmosphere, my dear. Atmosphere. It sets the tone."

With a quick shrug, she resumed reading the menu. Meanwhile, he sat like a statue. "You have this menu memorized, I take it?" She spoke while keeping her eyes on the menu.

With a pressed together grin, he nodded slowly. She glanced his way to acknowledge, then looked at her menu again. She hated this atmosphere that kept her from reading the menu. It seemed impractical.

"What should I get?" Finally, she gave up on trying to read it and set it on the table in front of her.

"Get filet mignon. That's what I always get."

"What? Are you sure?" *Filet mignon? It sounds expensive.* She had heard of it before but wasn't sure exactly what it was. Beef? Fish? Chicken?

He took her hand. "Don't worry about it. How do you like your steak?"

She stared for a few moments, trying to figure out what he meant by that. *Chopped up? Sliced? On bread?*

"How do you like it cooked?" he asked, noting her confusion. "Rare? Medium rare? Medium?"

"Um, how do you like it cooked?" She was still in the dark, in more ways than one.

He shook his head in disbelief. She was mortified.

"Well... I'll have whatever you're having." She let go of his hand and slouched into the back of her chair. Then she glanced back and forth and noticed that everybody else was sitting up straight, so she scooted herself back to a straight position again and put her hands in her lap like the others.

As she studied the table, she found a full place setting with more silverware than was possible to use at one time. A bowl sat on her dinner plate, and a tiny plate sat nearby with a strange knife placed over the edge.

When the waiter came, she said nothing as she tried her hardest to appear as though she belonged there. Occasionally, the waiter glanced her way and asked a question, but Dylan always answered for her, for which she was extremely grateful. When the waiter finally left, she let her muscles relax a little and noticed that Dylan was amused. "Whew."

"It couldn't have been that hard. You didn't say a word."

"I didn't want to say something to screw it up." She hoped he would stay in this mood for a while. She needed it.

"You're not going to screw anything up, I promise." He patted her hand. Then, he picked up his cloth napkin and put it in his lap, so she did the same.

Dylan had ordered wine, as Candy had imagined in her vision earlier, and she hoped it was going to taste good. She had never had any kind of alcohol before. The waiter poured a bit into Dylan's glass. Dylan tasted it and said it was fine. Then, the waiter poured wine into their glasses and set the bottle on the table for them.

Candy knew from the expression on his face that something was up. He had to have known that she had never had wine. That smirk told her he was waiting for a chance to make fun of her for some reason. Was wine that bad? Was he waiting for her to drink it first? *That must be it.*

With a quivering hand, she reached for the glass and picked it up by its stem, nearly tipping it over before Dylan grabbed it and steadied it for her. Quickly, she let go and put her hand back in her lap. Her eyes shifted back and forth to make sure no one had seen her improper form in picking up a wine glass, but thankfully, no one had from what she could tell.

Without a word, Dylan picked up his glass and held it in front of him. She picked hers up the same way and held it out exactly as he did.

Dylan thought for a second. "To... your new life."

New life? Yes. New life. This was going to be her new life. She was starting over, learning manners, how to eat in a restaurant, drink wine, wear nice clothes, have money, go shopping.

Beaming, she gently tapped her glass to his like they do on television and nodded. "To new life."

Chapter Ten

The wine was red, dry, and as dark as the room. Dylan had called it Merlot and said it went well with the steak. She didn't like it all that much but drank it anyway, taking small sips here and there to fit in.

The steak was so good, though, she almost moaned with every bite. With amusement, Dylan watched her expressions as she ate.

She couldn't believe people ate like this all the time. Where did their money come from? How did these people get so rich? Would she ever be so rich? Would she ever be comfortable enough with her money to eat in a place like this whenever she wanted?

"So do you think they'll look at the photos soon?" she asked before taking another small sip of her wine.

With a nod and one finger pointed upward, he finished his bite of food, and then answered. "Definitely within the next day or two. Tomorrow's Monday. Kind of busy, so they might not have time. But if I can slip it onto my boss's desk, or maybe casually walk by holding it so she sees it, it will happen soon. I know she'll like the photos. And the way you look…mm-mm."

Hope rose within her, and she couldn't wait to hear what his boss thought of her, and also his photography, which was amazing. Not that she would know, but it certainly seemed amazing to her.

When she became too full to eat any more, she gave the rest to Dylan, who eagerly but gracefully ate it. She watched him, hoping she could learn much from him before he kicked her out. It was going to have to be a lot, and quickly, because she didn't know how much time she had. Tonight, though, she felt she had learned a lot already. He had taught her which silverware to use and when, how to hold a glass of wine, how to cut her steak properly, how to put the napkin in her lap, and how to order. Still, she knew there was so much more.

As they waited for the check, he surprised her. "Are you on the pill?"

That was blunt. "Yes." She thought he might bring this up at some point, but not over dinner. She worried about other people overhearing their conversation, so she lowered her voice. "But I need a new prescription if I'm going to stay on it. I'm almost out."

"Well, call a doctor tomorrow and make an appointment."

"I will need your help. I don't know where any of them are or how to get there. If you're at work and I go, I won't know which bus to take, or which direction. Won't even know where to walk if I do manage to get close enough with the bus. There's no subway?"

"Not yet. They recently began building one. Do you drive?"

"I have my license, but I haven't driven since driver's ed. class back in school. Never needed to."

"We'll figure out something. All right? Don't worry."

Candy's shoulders slumped, relieved. She desperately needed to hear those words from him. Or anyone, for that matter. The only other person to ever say that to her was Rachel. Her joy faded at the thought of her friend.

"What's wrong now?" He leaned more into her line of sight.

"I'm happy, that's all." She hoped he believed her.

"You have issues, Candy."

"What?" She sat up.

"I mean, you weren't brought up right, and you're sad all the time. You gotta get your life together and you'll be okay. I think once you get this job modeling, you'll be able to get back on track to where you should be."

"Like I'm on the wrong road, but trying to get on the right road?"

"Exactly."

Was she on the wrong road? *How do you know?* Certainly, that's how she felt. It's how she had always felt, her whole life. But now, things were changing. Things were going to get better as now she was on a different road.

The next morning, he was gone by the time she awoke. She checked the clock. It was one o'clock. She had never slept so late in her life, unless she was sick. She knew she needed it, though. Dylan's bed was so soft, comfortable, and warm. She took in his musky scent lingering on his pillow.

She sat up and rubbed her face. Last night they had made love only a few times and then went to sleep. She made sure to let him sleep after that, knowing he had to go to work in the morning.

Wearing his sweatpants and t-shirt again, she made her way to the kitchen. She felt awkward in his house, yet strangely comfortable at the same time. This might have been the kind of home she had always wanted, if she had ever allowed herself to dream of such a thing. Not wanting to make a mess, she made herself a bowl of cereal. Once she was finished, she washed her bowl and spoon by hand, even though he had a dishwasher.

She had never seen a dishwasher before arriving at his house. He showed it to her the other morning after breakfast when they were cleaning up. Though she knew the dishwasher automatically washed the dishes, she wanted to make sure she was as little a burden as possible and made it appear as though she hadn't eaten anything.

After taking a shower, she made sure the bathroom was perfectly clean as well and took pride in how well she had covered her tracks. Then, she took her clothes and the clothes from the other bags out and set them aside. First, she threw away their small bags of pot, making sure to cover them with other trash so the smell didn't drift her way. That sickening skunk smell only meant bad things to her. Then she took the clothes to the basement.

On her way down, with her arms full of reeking clothes, she inspected his laboratory. Flat square pans, clotheslines with clothespins, bottles of chemicals, and even more cameras and lenses littered the area. It was in stark contrast to the rest of the house. Since she was afraid of turning on a light and ruining something he may be working on, she let her eyes adjust to the darkness and then felt her way around with her feet, and sliding along the concrete walls with her elbows. Two socks dropped on the way to the little room in the corner that she thought might be the laundry room. *Hehe. Breadcrumb trail back to the stairs, I guess.*

Finally, she found the washer and threw the clothes in. Laundry was one thing she was good at, as it was part of her duties as a groom back at Belmont. As she poured a cup of powdered detergent into the basin, she enjoyed the scent of the soap. Surprisingly, it made her a little homesick.

What was going on at home? What about her brother? Had he been kicked out of the house yet or had he been able to find something to eat? Maybe, if he were lucky enough, he had gotten himself arrested so he would have three square meals and a warm bed at night. It might also give him the opportunity to get clean. She shook her head. She couldn't envision him ever getting clean, as she hardly remembered what he was like before he started using.

More importantly, where was Rachel? How was she? Candy desperately wanted to call Rachel's house again, but she was afraid to upset them. Besides, now it was a long-distance call, and she did not want to place the call without asking Dylan first. As she went back for the two socks that had fallen, she prayed Rachel was all right. She didn't know what else to do.

As she watched television, sitting on the couch, she waited for the washer to finish so she could get the clothes in the dryer and out of the way before Dylan got home. She had no idea what time to expect him home, but if it were a nine-to-five job like all the other city people, he would probably be home around six. Plenty of time.

It was getting dark in late afternoon, which was comical to her, as she had been up only a few hours. But she was bored stiff. She had never sat around so much. She had worked so hard for so many years that she didn't know how to do this – nothing. Watching soap operas was boring, so after throwing the clothes into the dryer, she searched for a book to read. Or something. Anything. She wished she had brought *Pride and Prejudice,* but she had been in too much of a hurry to think about it before she left.

Chewing her lip, she went upstairs to search the other bedrooms in hopes of finding books. At the top of the stairs, instead of going directly into the master bedroom, she walked down a short hallway to find two other bedrooms. One seemed to be a guest room, so she went to the other and found an office. A bookshelf beckoned her from across the room, and with a squeak of happiness, she leapt across the room in only a few steps.

As she ran her fingers across each book, hope began to diminish as she discovered rows and rows of books about photography. Did he own every photography book there was? How ridiculous. Didn't he read fiction? Anything fun?

Then, she was taken off guard when she found a small brown book with Charlie Brown on the front. Handling it as if it were gold, she slid it from the shelf and opened it. As she opened to the first page, then the next, her euphoria grew and grew.

"You only read comics?"

Candy sucked in half of the air in the room as she jumped to her feet and dropped the book. With heated cheeks, she bent over to pick it up and put it back on the shelf. Unfortunately, it fell to the floor again. She picked it up and set it on the shelf, then stood up straight and watched Dylan trying to hold in laughter.

"Jesus, you scared me!" she shouted as she sprung over to him and into his arms.

He moaned ever so slightly as he rubbed her back and squeezed, and then pulled away enough to kiss her.

"Well, I was looking for anything other than books about photography. I was so bored with TV, and well, that's why I'm here. In your office." She hung her head in shame for a second, but he lifted her chin and kissed her again.

"It's fine. I was hoping you would be able to find something to do while stuck here in the house. What did you do all day?"

"Oh, it was so exciting. I slept until one."

"One?"

"One." She nodded once. "Then I did some laundry and watched TV, then came up here. You're home earlier than I thought you'd be. I really had no idea since you left without telling me."

"I wanted you to sleep. You needed sleep."

"I know. It's fine. Thank you." She hugged him tight around his waist as she pressed her cheek into his chest. "What time is it, anyway?"

"Four-thirty."

She knit her eyebrows. "I thought you worked nine to five or something."

"Ha. No, sweet cheeks. I work seven-thirty to four."

"Oh. Did you drive?"

"Yup. Today, I did. Usually I take the bus, but I wanted to make sure I got back at a decent hour. To see you." He took her hand and brought her downstairs again.

"So, any news? Did they say anything?"

He couldn't hide his excitement, and she knew. It was good news. Still he didn't say anything. Tilting her head at him, she waited with her hands on her hips. When she tapped her foot, he winked but still said nothing. She had no choice but to grab his arms and push him. "Come on. Tell me."

"All right. All right. I stopped my boss in the hall and showed her the pictures. Told her I caught you in the city over the weekend, took some shots, thought you would be perfect. And guess what?"

"What?" Candy bent her knees, ready for a jump.

"She wants you to come in tomorrow."

"What?" She jumped. "Really?"

"Yup." He picked up her hand and spun her under his arm. She squealed as she jumped again and reached up to grab his shoulders.

"We have some work to do first, though." He suddenly pulled away then took her hand and led her to the living room. He moved the coffee table and then paused to consider something. Then he moved a chair slightly closer to the wall and stood back to survey his living room. "You need to learn to walk."

"I suppose you're going to teach me to be a model?"

"I'll teach you, all right."

"Good," she shouted as she clapped.

Chapter Eleven

Before the sun was up the next day, Dylan was waking her, but that was all right with her. She was used to getting up before sunrise, for one, and second, this was her big day. She couldn't wait to get started and sprinted into the shower before Dylan was even out of bed.

She tried to be quick so they would both have time to get ready.

"Fastest shower ever," she announced proudly as she bounced from the bathroom. She found Dylan sitting on the bed, leaning against the headboard. He didn't seem pleased. "Right?"

"I guess." Without hesitation, he grabbed some clothes, shot into the bathroom, and shut the door.

"But," she began quietly, but knew it wouldn't do any good.

As she stood outside of the door listening to him brush his teeth, a question burned in her mind. *What do I wear?* She was afraid to bother him, though, especially since he seemed to be in a bad mood. Still, she had to know. She paced back and forth for a few minutes while she tried to decide whether to risk it.

He was in the shower by the time she decided to wait. The clock read six o'clock, she noticed as she put on clothes she already had available. One of Opal's giant bohemian skirts and a blouse to match were going to have to do for now. If he didn't like it, he would tell her to change, and tell her exactly what to wear, or maybe even give her something from downstairs to wear.

She wasn't sure if she should put on some makeup or leave her face a blank canvas for the makeup people at the studio, but she was unable to muster up the courage to ask. She didn't want to bother him.

Finally, she heard the shower stop, and she placed her hand on her heart to calm herself. Why was she nervous? She was unable to figure out if she was more worried about Dylan's attitude or what possibly might be the start of her career as a model.

She waited on the bed in the same position as Dylan had. When he came out with a towel, drying his hair, she mustered up the courage to speak. With a hop from the bed, she stood and smoothed her enormous skirt.

"What do you think? Is this okay?"

He glanced at her after removing the towel from his head, and then went back to drying his hair again. "Fine."

"Should...um." She stopped herself, now afraid to say anything else. She decided to take a chance and leave her face clean for the makeup artists at the studio. That is probably what they wanted, anyway. With her mind made up, she made her way downstairs to get her boots. They did not match her outfit at all, but it was all she had, and she wasn't about to wear the shoes she had worn last night on their date. After donning her boots, she stood in the kitchen, not knowing what to do next.

Finally, he came downstairs. He picked up a cereal box. "You want breakfast?"

"No, thanks," she answered, her voice barely loud enough to be heard. She was hungry but didn't want to upset him by asking for food. She decided at that point that he was not a morning person. That had to be it. And here she was the opposite. She couldn't wait for the day to start.

He put down the box, poured a glass of orange juice, drank it quickly, and then headed her way. Turning sideways, he slid past her and grabbed his coat from the coat rack. She was right behind him, grabbing hers as well. As they walked out the back door, she felt her pocket for her money. If he left her somewhere, at least she had that.

"Can you get the door?" He pointed toward the garage door.

"Um, okay." She went to the large garage door with him. He unlocked it with his key, then motioned for her to lift it. She raised an eyebrow at him.

"Well, I'm doing all the driving. You could at least do this much for me."

Candy fought the urge to let her mouth fall open. After a beat, she grabbed the handle and lifted the door. Fortunately, it was easier than she thought it would be. He went in, started the car, pulled it out, and waited. Candy found a rope and pulled on it, forcing the garage door to close. She turned the latch to lock it again and made her way into the car. *That was weird*, she thought as she slipped inside.

The radio was on with the news, and she hoped to hear something about Rachel. Then again, she was four or five hours away from her hometown, and chances were no one around here knew anything about it. Sure enough, they talked mostly about politics and traffic. Boring. Dylan didn't say a word as he drove slowly down a very straight road with stoplights every hundred feet. Each light seemed to change to red right as he got to it, irritating him even further.

Candy wanted to sink into the seat and found herself sliding down, trying to make herself smaller. She didn't like this at all. How much of his mood swings was she going to have to put up with in order to get this job? Was it worth it? It might be. She decided to tell herself not to take it personally and to hang in there. *Better days are coming.*

Chapter Twelve

Dylan's studio was remarkably like the one in New York, complete with the nasty secretary and tall women walking around in high heels. She felt so small and underdressed. As she glanced up at Dylan, she wondered if he was embarrassed to be with her. Without a word, he led her down a hallway of doors and stopped in front of one open door. Candy couldn't see inside the office, as Dylan was blocking the doorway with his entire body.

"Ms. Evans, this is the girl I told you about, the one I found on the Mall over the weekend." Dylan moved to one side and held out his hand to Candy. She took it, and he pulled her into full view of a woman very much like Ms. Karn in New York. She felt an overwhelming urge to drop Dylan's hand and run. Or cry.

"Oh, my dear, she looks scared to death." Ms. Evans stood up with her arms outstretched. Candy's eyes widened as the difference between the two women hit her.

Dylan put his arm around Candy's shoulders and ushered her into the office to meet Ms. Evans. Candy awkwardly held out her hand for a handshake, but the middle-aged woman in reading glasses placed her hands on either side of Candy's face for a second and then kissed each cheek. Candy wasn't sure what to do, so she stood still but glanced at Dylan. Should she kiss Ms. Evans' cheeks, too? *Is that the way they do things here?*

"Oh, look at you." Ms. Evans stepped back to take in everything about the nervous girl in front of her. "We should get right to work. I'll take care of her, Dylan. Go ahead and get set up in studio B. We'll be in makeup."

Without a word, Dylan disappeared, leaving Candy scared to death despite the woman's friendly manner.

"Um," Candy managed to say, but she was shaking too much to say anything else and stopped for fear of sounding like a child. She certainly felt like one right now.

Ms. Evans gave her a few seconds to finish her thought, but when Candy didn't continue, Ms. Evans took over. "Let's get you into hair and makeup, my dear. Don't worry about a thing. We'll have you fixed up in no time." She spun Candy around and gently pushed her toward the doorway, then led her down the hallway, further into the studio.

When they came to another room, this one full of vanities lit by little, round light bulbs, Ms. Evans stopped and scanned the room. "Nate?"

"Yes?" they heard from deep inside the room.

"He's in here." Ms. Evans led Candy into the room and sat her down on a chair much like the ones Candy had seen on television in hair salons.

Nate approached, wearing tight, low-cut bell bottoms and a paisley shirt. His dirty blond hair was thick and messy. He wore a hint of eyeliner and mascara under his thick, black-rimmed glasses. Candy tried her hardest not to stare.

Ms. Evans inspected Candy's face as though it were a precious vase. The woman's finger drifted over Candy's pronounced cheekbones and jaw line, and when she let go, she nodded. Meanwhile, Nate was already spreading things out on the vanity and a rolling cart full of anything needed to fix hair – a curling iron, hair dryer, hair spray, a jar of something gooey, ribbons, elastic hair ties, and bobby pins.

"Well, I will meet you in the other room, Candy, when Nate's done with you. Be good to her, Nate," Ms. Evans called as she wiggled her fingers and sauntered from the room.

"Hi," Candy managed to say, finally.

"I'm Nate." She took his outstretched hand, but couldn't help staring at his eyeliner-covered eyes again for several seconds. It hit her that she was being rude when he sighed and turned away to grab more stuff from his makeup case.

"Sorry. I've…um…I didn't know men wore eyeliner." Then, she immediately wished to take her words back. Her face turned red, and she lost her breath for a second. When she finally found it again, she sucked in extra air. "Sorry," she repeated.

"It's okay," he answered, still busy with his preparations. Finally, after a few awkward and silent minutes, he turned and let out a big breath as if getting ready to take on an enormous task. First, he pulled back her hair and then went to work, painting her face like a canvas and standing back to survey his work every few minutes. Finally, he turned and checked her face in the mirror as he stood behind her. "What do you think?" Her eyes looked huge, as did her lips. Her eyelashes, although fake, were dark and pronounced on the bottom and thick and full on top. She was surprised that instead of hiding her blue eyes, her eyelashes made them more noticeable. *Just like Twiggy,* she thought as her heart soared. She shook her head and stared in awe of what he could do.

"You're amazing." Candy hoped a compliment might lessen the tension in the air. It was the truth, too. He had performed a miracle.

He waved his hand dismissively. "Oh, it's nothing."

Candy was charmed by his quiet demeanor. He was cute in a boyish sort of way. And just like that, the tension was gone. She wondered if compliments might work on Dylan, too.

"Hair next," he cheered, then pulled the elastic band from her hair and began brushing it. She had never used a curling iron before, but lots of heat and what seemed like a gallon of hair spray later, she now had full, wavy curls that made her look like Bridget Bardot. Candy couldn't be more pleased.

"Wow," she sighed as she bounced a curl in her hand. "Oh, wow."

"I guess that's good?" Nate asked, his whole body beaming with pride.

"Wow," Candy sighed at him through the mirror. He then began packing his things. She didn't know where to go or even if she had permission to leave this room yet.

Nate answered her question before she asked. "All right, you're all set. Go next door to the right."

"Okay. Thanks." Next door was a wardrobe room, full of beautiful clothes one might see on the red carpet before an awards show on television. She wondered if anybody famous had worn any of these clothes, and her stomach turned as she felt out of place. No one like her could ever be on the same level as a movie or television star.

Another man met her in the room, this one looking very much like Nate. "Terry." They shook hands. As she introduced herself, she tried again to hide her nervousness, but these people were so strange. Terry had long blonde hair that was curled much like her hair now, and he wore a long tunic with tight jeans. He also wore eyeliner and mascara.

After Candy tried on several outfits, she and Terry finally decided on a flowing tea length dress, fitted on top, and strapless. Her matching shoes were, of course, four-inch heels. With a nervous glance at Terry, she sat down and strapped them to her feet, then cautiously stood. The words of the store clerk back in Queens replayed in her mind. *Walk normally, but take small steps. Don't walk on your toes.*

Terry made his way to the door, then held out his hand for her, and she carefully walked toward him. She tried not to use his hand as a crutch as they inched further down the hallway, but she couldn't help it. She felt like an old lady. He must have sensed her uneasiness because he didn't say a word.

He led her into a large, dark room with one brightly lit area that had enormous lights and umbrellas. There, she finally saw Dylan. He saw her, faced his camera, and then with huge eyes, turned back to her. She nearly laughed at his double take. He walked over and took Candy's hand from Terry's.

"You did well, Terry," Dylan said as he kept his eyes on Candy.

"Thank you, Dylie." As Terry left the room, he waved his fingers in the air.

Dylan turned Candy around, inspecting her. "You...look...amazing." His words came out almost in sighs.

"Thank you. I can't believe this, Dylan. I didn't know I could look like this."

"You didn't know you were so gorgeous?"

Candy blushed. "Not like that. I mean, I've never done my hair like this, or worn so much makeup, or a dress like this, or even worn heels. I've never had a chance–,"

"Let's go, people!" Another man barged in shouting orders. Dylan hurried Candy into the light-flooded area and stepped back behind some strange equipment.

"That's Phil," Dylan whispered from his spot outside the light. It took her a second to understand his words, and then she nodded.

Without words, Phil pushed and pulled on Candy, shaping her as if she were a rubber toy. He seemed to get annoyed whenever she didn't understand exactly what he was asking for, but he still said nothing. All the while, Dylan was snapping shots of her whenever Phil jumped out of the way for a second. Then he was right back in her face again.

Candy never smiled, knowing she had to portray the sad character again. That seemed to be what they liked. She did her best to make her eyes look saddened despite her excited mood. She was almost shivering with excitement as she hoped that these photos would turn out well and they would love her. They had to. She looked nothing like herself. She was in awe as it hit her that people she knew from back home might see her in a magazine and not know it was her.

After Phil was finished posing her, he left and Ms. Evans came in. Immediately, the atmosphere went from tense to relaxed as her aura lit up even the dark corners of the room. Candy felt everyone in the room let out a collective sigh of relief. Other people had come in to either watch or play with equipment, or so it seemed to Candy. She couldn't tell what they were doing. Dylan was the only one taking pictures, but Candy wondered why it took so many other people.

Then, Candy's stomach growled loudly enough to echo against the white backdrop. Her face turned red under her caked blush and foundation, and Dylan glanced at her and winked. Candy shook her head and rolled her eyes at her stomach, then put her hand on it, hoping it wouldn't make any more noise.

Lately, though, she had eaten more than she had all last month. If she were to maintain her thin and "in" figure, she couldn't continue to eat like that.

"Didn't he feed you before you left this morning?" Ms. Evans shouted, heating Candy's cheeks even more. Candy sighed and covered her face with her hand, but she made sure not to smear her makeup.

Dylan dropped his jaw. "She said she wasn't hungry."

"Of course she said that. She's a lady." Ms. Evans stepped closer to Candy. "I'll get you something when you're done, all right?"

Candy nodded in reply, too mortified to speak. When Ms. Evans stepped away again, she looked at Dylan, who threw up his hands in defeat. But he was smiling. At least his morning mood was gone.

Candy stayed at the studio throughout the day, watching Dylan and other models and trying to pick up as much as possible. Without lessons of any kind, she knew this was the only way she was going to learn anything about the modeling world. The other girls didn't seem to mind being watched and were probably used to it by now. Still, she made sure to stay out of the way.

Occasionally, she gazed out the windowed walls of the studio, down onto what she was told was Connecticut Avenue. It looked a bit like Manhattan, she thought, and it made her homesick. Again, she reminded herself there was nothing left for her in New York. She decided to go back there only after becoming famous and needing to go there for work. Otherwise, it wasn't worth it to go back.

Going forward, she reminded herself. Desperately, she wished to be able to share this with Rachel. There was so much to tell her about her new and promising career, but it wasn't time to think about that now, or she might cry and ruin her makeup. *It might upset Nate*, she thought, then put her hand over her heart as she turned away from the windows.

She stopped to consider her position in this large office. This was the big time, and she was in it. It floored her, and she shook her head as the notion sank in. The difference between two weeks ago and today was so overwhelming that it felt like a dream. She wondered if perhaps she was still asleep on the floor in the subway station at Sixty-First and Lexington.

Dylan rolled over and rubbed Candy's shoulder to wake her. Content and relaxed, she wanted to stay in bed like this forever. She wrapped her arms around him. He kissed her forehead, ran his fingers through her hair, then spoke softly. "Day off today. Want to go shopping? You seem to be in need of a new wardrobe."

"Ha. Well, I guess so." Candy wondered if it would be all right to spend the last of her money.

After dressing, she took her four twenties out of her pocket and counted it again to make sure she still had eighty dollars. Candy chewed her bottom lip.

"I'll loan you some money if you want. You'll be getting paid soon."

"You think?"

"Absolutely. Ms. Evans has taken a shine to you. She would never have offered to pay another girl for sitting around the office watching."

"And learning."

"Yes, that too. You're one lucky girl."

Candy was so excited. This was it. She knew this was her big chance to be in a magazine or catalog soon, and now she was given a whole day to let it sink in and to celebrate. It also seemed as though Dylan was allowing her to stay, as he had spoken of paying him back when she got paid.

With their arms loaded with bags, Dylan and Candy ascended the stairs, then went to their room. *Their room.* Her teeth glistened in her reflection as she slid open the mirrored closet door. "Should I put them here?"

"How about the guest room?"

Candy wondered why she couldn't use the other half of the nearly empty and large double closet, but she didn't push the issue. She decided to get dressed in the other room from now on. No big deal. He even helped her hang up her clothes before scooping her up and tossing her onto the guest bed, tickling her and working his way under her shirt.

They were lying in his bed, having moved over once they destroyed the covers on the guest bed, when the phone rang. Dylan answered.

"Seb. Where you been, man?"

Candy sat up, covering herself with the blanket as Dylan talked to his friend. They were talking about his jail time, but Candy wondered if he knew what had happened to her other friends. And Dylan's. As the minutes passed, they still weren't talking about it. Finally, she couldn't stand the suspense and whispered, "Ask him about Autumn and Opal. And the guys."

Dylan nodded and waved toward her, signaling her to stay quiet. She tried, but it took several more minutes and several taps on Dylan's arm until he finally asked.

"What happened to the others?" he finally asked.

Chapter Thirteen

Candy hung her head in shame as Dylan drove to Sebastian's house. How was she to know that the empty space on the street in DC wasn't their space? That a block away, the VW sat with the entire group inside. They had planned to go back to Dylan and Candy after resting and warming themselves in the van, where they had retreated to when the police showed up. They knew they had to wait for things to die down first. And when they remembered they had left their bags right next to police, they panicked and stayed out of sight for a few hours. They had feared police might find the stash inside Roody's bag and arrest them all.

After things had calmed down, they went back. They had hoped Candy and Dylan were going to be waiting for them, but they never found their blankets, bags, or Dylan and Candy. They had searched for the couple until dark, completely unaware that Dylan and Candy were already on a bus out of the city. The group decided to part ways that night, and Roody, Christian, Opal, and Autumn drove away with the horn blaring.

Candy felt awful knowing that she had their clothes and all of their possessions. She felt even worse when Sebastian had told Dylan that they gave Candy's suitcase to

Hanna, Sebastian's girlfriend, in case they ever found Candy.

She could not feel any lower than she did at this moment, especially since Dylan didn't hold back his disappointment in her. He didn't yell at her, but instead, ignored her and gave her such a glare that it almost scared her. To disappoint him, as well as the other friends who had been so kind to her, was killing her inside. She cried silently all the way to Sebastian's house.

She didn't allowed herself to sniff as her nose ran, but instead tilted her head back so it dripped down the back of her throat. Her fear of facing Sebastian and Hanna made her chest feel as though an elephant were sitting on it. If Sebastian was really such a hot head, she knew she was in for it and wondered if he was going to attack her in some way. She cried, not only from sadness, but from fear as well. She felt as though she were headed right into the lion's den.

By the time they arrived at Sebastian's, Candy's eyes were red and swollen and her face was flushed. She tried to hide it from Dylan, but he saw it, and he didn't seem to care, which hurt her even more.

She knew he would ask her to leave now. He was too old for her. She wasn't mature enough. She was sure he felt that way about her now. The gap between their ages had grown into a giant chasm.

They knocked on the door, with Candy holding all five bags they had gathered from their spot on the grass that day. She stood behind Dylan on the porch, avoiding his eyes, avoiding his anger.

Sebastian opened the door. "Hey," he greeted with his hand outstretched. He took Dylan's hand and tugged him inside. "Who's this?" Sebastian asked as he searched around the pile of bags in Candy's arms. "Oh, Candy. Come on in," he said with a strange displaced happiness.

With her eyes on the floor to her side, she trudged her load across the threshold. Sebastian shot Dylan a severe glare of disappointment and took all five bags from her.

"He made you carry all of this? Dylan? What's the matter with you? Have you no manners at all? I'll tell your mother on you," Sebastian scolded as he set the bags on the floor next to a couch. Candy was still unable to lift her head and face the others, and she was desperately fighting a pain in her chest and a huge lump in her throat. Everything was blurry as her eyes filled with tears again.

"Bathroom?" Candy asked, her voice husky with sadness.

"Here you go." Sebastian pointed to a half bath nearby. Candy quickly jumped inside and closed the door to hide. She grabbed a towel from the ring on the wall and held it against her face, hoping to smother her sobs. She wanted to stay inside that room forever, and maybe if she stayed long enough, Dylan might leave without her.

As she heard Hanna's voice mixing with Dylan's and Sebastian's, they sounded happy, as if none of this had happened. Well, of course they weren't upset. They were able to get their things back, as opposed to Roody and the others. She hoped Opal, at least, had enough money to buy a few things. It was fortunate that none of them had left their identification or money in their bags. They had kept those things in their pockets in case someone walked off with their bags. Kind of like she had done.

After a while, she knew she had to find the courage to face Seb and the others, and to face facts. The first fact was that she had spent the last of her money on clothes, and the second, she was going to be cast out onto the cold streets of DC, or Silver Spring, or wherever she was, without a dime. She wondered if Sebastian might let her hide in the house somewhere. Maybe she could beg him to allow her to stay one night. After that, she had no idea what to do. She had nothing, since everything was at Dylan's. Then she wondered if Dylan would let her back in to get her things.

There was a knock on the door, startling Candy. "Candy?" Hanna's soft voice sounded friendly. *Could she trust this girl?* Candy sucked in a shaky breath of air and blew it out, then checked herself in the mirror. Still a ruddy mess with two swollen eyes. She shook her head, disgusted at the reflection, now even more disappointed with herself. Her jaw quivered and tears fell again. She forgot to be quiet and sniffed as she wiped the tears angrily with the now wet towel.

"Candy? Come on out? Okay?"

She took a breath again, trying to control her voice, and she found a bit of bravery somewhere inside her. "I'll be a minute."

There was no answer, and Candy thought Hanna had gone. But a minute later, she heard Hanna again, this time softer. "Can I come in?"

Candy knit her eyebrows. The girl hadn't said two words to her the other day and now was suddenly pretending to be supportive. Nevertheless, Candy couldn't refuse her request for fear of coming across as a bigger low-life than she already was. She couldn't have that. So she cracked the door.

Hanna opened the door a bit, squeezed herself in, and then closed the door behind her. Candy couldn't bear to face her and kept her eyes on the towel. It had become kind of a security blanket. By now, the tears had stopped again, and while she still sniffed every few seconds, she was regaining more control.

Hanna tried to duck into Candy's view. "He's moody. I know."

Candy raised an eyebrow at her.

"Don't let it get to you."

Candy silently scoffed. "Easier said than done. I've never had anyone treat me this way." Although… that statement was not the truth. This was remarkably similar to how her parents treated her growing up. They ignored her so much of the time that sometimes she doubted her own existence. And when they were mad at her for asking for something to eat or a blanket to keep warm, they shoved her from their room and slammed the door. So to her, this was normal, yet still incredibly hard to take.

"It's not you, hon. It's nothing personal. I'm sure he doesn't mean to be this way. I don't know why he's like that, but he does this with everyone, not just you. Those of us who can stay friends with him don't take it personally. We usually blow it off until he comes out of his mood."

Candy couldn't imagine a tougher job than being Dylan's girlfriend right now. *Was she his girlfriend?* Certainly not anymore, even if she had been for the past few days. It was over. "I don't know what to do. He's going to kick me out. I know it. Everything I have is at his house. Can you help me get my stuff back? I need my clothes and my bag, and hopefully the receipts so I can return a bunch of stuff because I spent the last of my money on clothes today. I have nothing left. I was going to go to work with him tomorrow. But now, I don't know what's going to happen."

"What kind of person do you think I am?" Dylan's angry voice resounded through the door. Candy covered her face with her hands. When she peeked between two fingers, she saw Hanna smiling.

Candy wished desperately to take her words back. Now she had made it worse.

"Candy?" Dylan asked through the door again.

"Come on," Hanna whispered as she reached for the doorknob. Candy reached for Hanna to stop her, but it was too late. The door was open and there was Dylan. He wasn't as angry as he had sounded but he certainly seemed disappointed, now for a different reason, a second reason. Candy sighed. Hanna turned back to Candy for a second, winked, and then walked away to leave the two of them to talk.

Ducking past him, Candy went into the living room, where it was empty. Dylan followed closely.

"Are you going to kick me out?" she asked boldly, faking strength in the hope that it would become reality.

"Of course, not. Where would you go?"

Candy shrugged one shoulder and faced the floor, unable to meet his gaze. "I mean, if you're going to, you need to let me know in advance. I will need to return all those clothes because I don't have any more money. I thought I'd be getting a paycheck soon."

"And you will, Candy. I'm not kicking you out. Sheesh. Where do you get this stuff? I never said that."

"You're angry with me because I made a mistake and screwed up with the parking place and everybody's bags."

"Doesn't mean I'll kick you out. That's ridiculous. Why would you think that if I were upset with you, I would kick you out into the cold without money or clothes? Is that what your parents did to you?"

"My parents did nothing but get high. I pretty much had no parents. And a lousy brother who also got high. So, forgive me for not knowing what it's like to actually have a family." Now, hot and angry tears fell as her jaw quivered and she sought to stay in control. It was like trying to hold back the entire Potomac River.

With a relenting sigh, Dylan wrapped his arms around her. Taking deep breaths, she tried her hardest to stop the tears and reminded herself they were doing absolutely no good to anyone. They served no purpose. She also reminded herself of his words. He wasn't going to throw her out in the cold with no money or clothes. She didn't have to be afraid. Of that, anyway.

"I already feel bad enough for making that mistake. I feel awful. You really don't need to punish me by getting mad at me, you know." Her words were muffled into his chest.

He didn't say anything for a long while but continued to hold her. She felt slightly more open to telling him how she was feeling, though it was still extremely scary. But she felt her last statement really had to be said. He needed to learn a few things, as well, like not treating her like a child. Then again, if she wouldn't act like one...

"You're right. I know. Everybody makes mistakes. Nobody's perfect."

She nodded into his chest.

"But this was a pretty big one," he said into the top of her head, and then kissed it.

She backed up and glared at him, ready to defend herself again, but he had a slight smirk on his face. She relented by lowering her gaze. "I know."

"Not much we can do about it now other than hope they found some more clothes, I guess. The ones they had were disgusting anyway. They needed a little motivation to buy new ones." He put his arm around her shoulders. She couldn't help but agree with him.

They spent the rest of the evening talking and playing a few games of poker. Candy, of course, knew all about poker since they played it often at the track. While they bet only fake chips, she was the one with the most at the end.

"I can't believe you. I need to take you to Atlantic City!" Dylan joked as they drove home with Candy's suitcase in the back.

"You should. I'd win millions."

When they got home, she decided to lay down ground rules and a schedule for getting ready for work. She devised a plan, and as she paced back and forth in thought, she told him about it. "Okay. It takes me five minutes longer to get ready. Plus, I have to dry my hair. So I'll get in the shower first. If you want, you can brush your teeth while I'm in the shower. And when I get out, I'll get dressed and dry my hair in the other room so you'll have your whole room to yourself. Maybe if I have time, I'll try to figure out how to cook something for breakfast. Or maybe make a bowl of cereal. That's all I know how to do, actually." She paused in place. "So, I'd better not commit to cooking. Then, we'll leave at seven. Right?"

He sat on the bed as he watched her pacing back and forth like the CEO of a big company in a meeting. "You forgot your charts. And your pointer. And your business suit."

It took her a few seconds to understand what he was saying. When she finally got it, she rushed to him and playfully pushed him over. "You've got my pointer right here," she said as she grabbed him between the legs.

With the ground rules laid for their living arrangements and schedule set, they fell into routine. Soon, Candy became immune to his mood swings. Remembering Hanna's words, she reminded herself to not take it personally and to ignore it until it goes away. In other words, she decided to treat him nicely when he was nice, and when he wasn't, she vowed to keep her distance. Maybe that's what he wanted. She wasn't sure. But that was fine, because she sometimes needed her space, too.

As the weather warmed and the trees filled out with green leaves and different-colored flowers, her favorite place for her alone time was the front porch.

She sat on the porch swing, her legs folded under her as she held a cup of tea and watched people coming home from work, waving, going inside their homes; she felt happy. This was the kind of life she had always wanted. Only a few months ago, she had been homeless, cold, alone, rejected. However, now, she had a beautiful home, the perfect job, a not-so-perfect man, but then again, who was perfect? She certainly wasn't, and she knew that she shouldn't expect anyone else to be.

Her career was going well, other than not liking the girls she worked with. Still, she did her best, as the money more than compensated for the stress. She had been in several ads in magazines after spending only a few weeks doing catalog work. That part of the job was fun, as she got to try on new clothes, but the underwear part of it was a bit embarrassing. She felt so thin and bony, and white enough to blind someone. Everyone else assured her that she got the job modeling underwear *because* she was so thin.

She didn't quite understand but accepted the situation. Fortunately, she didn't have to spend too much time modeling underwear because a man who worked for a cigarette company saw her and insisted she become one of their models. She hated the smell of smoke, but it was money, and she couldn't turn that down. Ms. Evans was thrilled that Candy was in demand and marketed her to other companies as well, opening her up for many more opportunities. It was nice to be wanted for a change.

Dylan had mentioned when they first met about how she needed a little help getting herself on the right road, and now here she was. Whether she was going to stay with Dylan forever, get married, have kids… that was still up in the air. At least she had found a lucrative career for herself. And she loved it. She was having the time of her life.

What more could you ask for? It might have been nice if she had a girl friend or two, but the other girls in the office were snobs, and she wanted nothing to do with them. Dylan always rolled his eyes and shook his head whenever they talked about it. He didn't see it. It seemed to Candy that to him, those girls were normal, and she was the odd ball.

Nevertheless, he seemed to accept her the way she was, and she didn't want to change. She certainly didn't want to become a snob like them so she didn't bother trying to befriend them.

She had heard one of the girls overdosed on heroin and was in the hospital – another reason not to get involved with them. She knew they all did drugs. Dylan had said that most of them did some sort of drug. Not only that, they took weight loss pills and laxatives. One girl even swallowed a tapeworm, which also put her in the hospital.

The pressure to stay thin enough to appear sickly was overwhelming. The look they were going for even had a name – "heroin chic." It pained Candy to know that she was once that unhealthy without trying.

Everything had turned around, though, and lately, the dark circles under her eyes had cleared, her skin wasn't so pale, she had more energy, and she was happier than she had ever been. How could this be bad? Interestingly, she found that Nate had been painting her face to make her look sicklier than she really was.

When she saw that she had put on a few pounds, she almost panicked, as she wasn't sure what to do about it. She'd never had to lose weight before. Dylan tried to help by telling her to eat half of what she usually ate. She tried that, but it was so hard to stick to it when she knew there was food readily available. It almost felt as though she wanted to eat as much as possible now while it was still around, because one day the food might not be there. She had to remind herself constantly that there was plenty of food to eat anytime she wanted.

Not only was her stomach full, but her bank account was so full, she didn't know what to do with it all. She started giving Dylan money for the bills, and they worked out ways to split food and other necessities. Whenever they went out to eat, he always paid, but she sometimes gave him money for it once they got home. She found it odd that he never refused it, but she knew it was only fair of her to pay sometimes.

Thinking back on her life before, she realized how miserable and unhappy she had been. Even when Rachel was around, she wasn't completely happy. She was unhealthy, barely making it, worried and stressed all the time about her brother. She couldn't sleep well at night unless she volunteered to sleep at the barn, and even there, it wasn't easy because of all the flies and mosquitoes. At home, she was free from the bugs, but wasn't free from Don and his friends. They always made noise partying downstairs while she tried to sleep, and sometimes one would sneak up to her room, hoping to hook up with her. Thankfully, she was always able to get rid of them, but that's no way to live. The stress was killing her, and she didn't realize how bad it was until she was out of that situation.

Oddly, she felt as though Rachel's kidnapping had saved her life. Was Rachel watching over her right now like a guardian angel? Perhaps that's what it was. Maybe Rachel convinced Ms. Evans to give her the job and help her get started last February. Maybe Rachel made the whole thing happen with the confusion over the parking spot and losing her friends, since that was the chain of events that got her on the right path.

Despite her prosperity, her heart ached as she hoped that wasn't the case. She would much rather Rachel be alive and well. When, three months after arriving in DC, she finally mustered up the courage to call Rachel's house again, she couldn't remember the phone number. When they worked together at Belmont, she had hardly ever had to call her because she saw her so often, so she didn't know Rachel's number all that well to begin with. And now it was completely gone. She called information, knowing Dylan was probably going to be upset to see the ten-cent charge on the phone bill despite knowing she was going to pay him back for it, but Julia's number was unlisted. It only made sense, given she was in the public eye as a trainer.

All of this was happening for a reason, she thought. Since she had forgotten Rachel's number, she took it as a sign that she was leaving her past behind her completely.

"Candy, could you do me a favor and wash this for me?" Dylan handed her a shirt. "I need it ironed, too. With starch. You know how I like it. Thanks."

He went into the bedroom, turned on the small television sitting on his dresser, and collapsed onto the bed. Candy stared at him for a few seconds, then made her way downstairs to the laundry room. He hadn't washed one item of clothing since she arrived a few months ago. Resigning herself to the role of woman of the house, she threw some clothes in the washer with some soap and started the machine.

Dylan had also canceled his cleaning lady, since he had one so readily available right here in the house anytime he needed. *How convenient for him.*

She went back up to the bedroom to wait for the laundry to finish and lay down next to Dylan on top of the covers of their bed. "What's the big story of the day?" She noticed that he was watching the news.

"Shh." He pointed to the television.

Candy suppressed a growl, then stared at the television.

Once a commercial came on, she started to ask him the question again, but he got up and went to the bathroom. When he came out, he asked, "That wash done yet?"

"No."

"I need that by tomorrow, you know."

"Yes, I realize that." As if she could make the washing machine work any faster. She rolled her eyes and sulked as he flopped back onto the bed again with a sigh.

After the news, a show about people who live on a ranch came on. He didn't like that show much, but there wasn't anything else better on, so they watched it. Candy was bored, and the closeness of her man sparked urges in her body. She scooted a bit closer and wiggled her way under his arm. He seemed as though he was going to squirm out from under her, but she began caressing his thighs, something she knew he liked. A lot. He moaned as she touched every bit of skin she could get to under his shorts. He spread his legs and closed his eyes, hypnotized by her touches.

Finally, she got what she wanted from him, but only after thirty minutes of driving him crazy until he could no longer resist. Unfortunately, he was so turned on that he pounced onto her, emptied himself into her, spent a few minutes in a weak attempt at satisfying her, then slid off of her with a groan. She wanted more. So she tried again. He was ready again soon, and she decided to use him this time to get what she needed. She still wasn't satisfied.

Despite her aching need, she fell asleep on his chest as he continued to watch television. It was late, sometime in the middle of the night, when he woke her. "Candy, that shirt. I need that shirt."

"Oh, ok." Candy absent-mindedly crawled out of bed, still naked, and stumbled to the basement to put the clothes in the dryer. Out of breath, she arrived two flights up and back in the bedroom, then crawled under the covers as Dylan snored.

The alarm went off at six. The first thing Dylan asked was about the shirt again. "Did you iron it?"

"No. I was sleeping."

"Gee, thanks. You know I needed it." He shook his head, disgusted with her, then got up and stomped into the bathroom.

Candy rolled her eyes and went to the basement again to iron his precious shirt. She turned on the iron to heat it up while she went through the clothes in the dryer. She folded what she could and hung up other things, then set the shirt Dylan needed on the ironing board. She gathered her spray bottles, one with water, one with starch, and began working on the shirt, trying to make it as perfect as possible for him. Maybe he would be happy if it were perfect.

The iron drifted over the back of the shirt, making steam rise as the wrinkles magically disappeared. But then she saw it. A white spot. Bleach. Somehow, bleach must have touched it! *Oh, God. Oh, no.* Fortunately, it was on the very bottom of the shirt and would be tucked in. Hopefully, he either wouldn't notice or would not mind because it would be hidden. Her heart pounded as her fear of his reaction grew. Her hands shook, and she almost could not finish ironing the rest of the shirt, but somehow she managed.

"Candy," she heard him calling from upstairs.

"Be right there," she called back. "Please, please, please," she begged no one in particular as she carefully crept up the stairs. He was waiting at the top of the stairs near the bedroom.

"What's the matter?"

Of course he noticed. He can see it on my face. "Nothing." She handed him the shirt, and he knit his eyebrows at her before taking it into the bedroom. She quickly ducked into the guest room where she changed every morning and found some clothes. There would not be time for a shower now, anyway. Her hair had six gallons of hair spray in it from the photo shoot the day before, so it still looked presentable. She slipped into her clothes and opened the door.

"What is this?" Dylan bellowed. He was standing at his bedroom door, holding his shirt and shaking it in her direction.

"I have no idea how it happened, Dylan. It'll be hidden anyway. Just wear it." Despite what she really wanted to do, hide in her room, she walked toward him.

"I can't wear this now. It's got a huge bleach mark on it. How did you let this happen? Why did you use bleach?"

"I didn't use bleach. Maybe it was leftover in the washing machine or something. I have no idea how it happened. Dylan, you can wear the shirt. No one will see the spot."

"I'll know it's there." He stormed into the bedroom again, threw the shirt in the trash, and pulled another shirt from his closet. "All that, and I still don't get to wear the shirt."

"What the hell's so important about that shirt, anyway?" she mumbled to herself, making sure he could not hear. He had some strange idiosyncrasies, many of which she tried to ignore or play along with, but some were downright weird. This was one of them. He had no reason to choose that shirt over any other button down shirt in his closet. It was blue. Plain blue.

Candy went to the closet and pulled out a blue shirt almost the same shade as the ruined shirt. "What about this one? It's close."

"Close is not what I want. Drop it, Candy."

Candy shook her head slightly, then made her way downstairs to the kitchen to get away from him. She knew what would happen next. He would not speak to her for the rest of the morning and would most likely only acknowledge her presence if they had to work together that day. The ride home would be tense and quiet, and once they got home, she would do her best to make him happy again. She would cook his favorite dinner, give him a massage, caress his thighs again, and she would try to be lighthearted and jovial despite his mood. Most of the time, he would give in and have sex with her, and on a good day he'd tolerate her cuddling with him afterward. Then, the next morning, it would start all over again.

"You going to clean this up?" Dylan waved his hand over the counter, full of dirty dishes. They had spent the lazy weekend day in separate parts of the house, Dylan in front of the television while Candy stayed upstairs reading. Those dishes were mostly Dylan's, but she knew he expected her to clean because she was a woman. After all, that was the woman's place – in the kitchen.

"Yes, sir," Candy mumbled as she made her way to the sink. He left with a nod, and went right back to the couch. Candy shook her head, but went to work, cleaning up after him. It wasn't all that bad, considering she had a dishwasher. But these days, she thought people were trying to push for equal rights. Shouldn't that mean an equal workload of chores in the house? Why did she have to do everything? Dylan helped her cook occasionally, but most of the time, after work, he plopped himself in front of the television and watched the news while she cooked.

Today, she had refused to cook, as she wanted a day off, and she had hardly eaten anything while Dylan spent the entire day eating and making a mess. It had to have been how he was raised. His mother must have been the doting mother like in those shows on television, waiting for her husband to come home and having dinner perfect and ready right when he got home. After dinner, the kids had to stay out of his way, letting Daddy unwind after work with a beer as he put his feet up on the ottoman. That seemed to be what Dylan expected out of a woman, as he had probably known nothing else.

Once the dishes were clean, she went to the couch to sit next to him, hoping he might thank her or at least acknowledge her. Nope. He was so engrossed in listening to Walter Cronkite that she wondered if he had even noticed her there next to him. She tried to watch the news with him but was distracted as she wondered why he was so distant.

Maybe as relationships progress, this is what happens. She might brag to friends, if she had any, that they were so comfortable together that they hardly knew the other was around. *Ha.* She knew that was a load of bull. That couldn't be right. She had seen other couples happy to be around each other, touching, holding hands, gazing into each other's eyes, even after they were married. How do they make it last so long?

She decided to test him. She weaved her fingers with his as she held his hand, and he didn't pull away, making her extremely happy. Almost satisfied. Then, she scooted closer to him, lifted his hand, and placed it between her thighs, which had been a comfortable resting spot for him in the past. As she peered up at him, he finally noticed her, then turned back to the television.

"They're going to land on the moon soon. Probably this summer."

"So, we'll win the space race, then, huh?"

"You got it."

Leaning her head on his arm, she gently stroked his forearm, letting her fingers barely touch him, and she watched his hair standing up on end. She lifted her hand slightly and the hair followed her, as if wanting her to come back. She wished he felt the same. Or did he?

"What are you doing?"

"Watching your arm hairs. I think they like me."

Dylan watched also, fascinated for a few seconds, then pulled her onto his lap. He finally saw her. Sure, there was a commercial on now. At least he was paying attention to her. He pulled her face into his for a kiss, and then quickly slipped her shirt over her head. Soon, she was satisfied.

That night, she wanted more from him as they lay in bed and tried to get his attention, but he wanted to sleep. He groaned with his face buried in the pillow as he lay on his side facing away from her. She had reached over his hips to try to persuade him to pay attention to her, but it was to no avail. She kept trying and trying until he finally told her, "I need to sleep, Can."

Without a word, she withdrew her hand and pulled away from him, making sure she was not touching any part of him. After all, it was summer, and he needed lots of space around him or else he would get too hot and complain. There was a ceiling fan and air conditioning, but that didn't seem to make a difference. He always complained if she got too close.

Silent tears dripped from her cheeks into her hair as she wished he felt the same as he had months ago when they first met. She didn't like this comfortable relationship thing. She wanted excitement, romance, passion, spontaneity. Their lives were nothing like that now, and it had been only three months.

Chapter Fourteen

Dylan peeked into her studio. "Candy, Seb and Hanna are coming over tonight. They wanted to try this new restaurant up the road. Sound good?"

"Of course." Candy tried not to move her face, as there was a makeup girl powdering her nose.

Hanna was the only girl who had even the slightest possibility of becoming her friend, but over time, it hadn't happened. Candy wasn't sure about Hanna's personality at times. She seemed to be friendly, but other times, she was rough, loud spoken, and harsh. It was almost as if she and Dylan were related, as they both had wide mood swings. No wonder she understood Dylan.

After work, Candy was in her room inspecting herself in the full-length mirror on the back of the door. This guest room had become her changing room and the place to keep her things, leaving Dylan's room completely masculine. He didn't want anything of hers in his room, which Candy found odd but didn't argue about it. It wasn't that important. Besides, this way, she had her own room, too, with no guy stuff.

She always slept in his bed but then went to her room to get ready for work in the morning. She had even started to use the second bathroom upstairs, letting Dylan use his own. *A little independence is a good thing, though. You don't have to be in each other's stuff all the time. It's good to have your own space.* She had thoroughly convinced herself that this was a better way to share a place with a man. Married couples had it all wrong. This way was much better.

Since her room was in the front of the house, she saw Sebastian pull up with Hanna. They got out of the car and walked up to the door. Candy was there before they had a chance to knock. She yanked the door open to find Sebastian's hand in a fist in midair.

"Ooo," Hanna shrieked. Candy snickered menacingly and then invited them in. Neither of them seemed to appreciate her silliness and walked by her wordlessly.

"Let me see where Dylan is. I'll be right back," Candy told them, then bounced up the stairs. Dylan's door was closed, and she assumed he was dressing. She cracked the door and slipped in.

"Don't do that," Dylan was saying. He was on the phone and turned away quickly when he saw Candy come in. "I gotta go," he mumbled, then hung up on the person on the other end.

Candy raised an eyebrow at the strange behavior. "Um, they're here." Dylan ran his fingers through his hair as he checked in the mirror for a second, then flung the door open and ran downstairs. Candy glanced at the phone, wondering whom he was talking to and why he was acting so strangely. Dylan did some strange things sometimes. He was a private person. Maybe he was having a fight with a family member and didn't want her to hear. Maybe it was a friend or colleague. However, she knew better than to ask. He wouldn't tell her, anyway.

Candy searched for signs of...something, she wasn't sure what, as they ate dinner and talked. As she analyzed every nuance of his words and body language, she found herself thinking about how ridiculous this was. She wasn't enjoying herself because she was more worried about him doing something behind her back. *He couldn't possibly be cheating, could he? No, there's no time. We're together all the time. We live together. He doesn't spend the night anywhere.*

For the next few nights, he kept his distance, even when she tried to make passes at him. He fell asleep facing away from her again, and this time, she couldn't justify his actions. These things he did to push her away had been too frequent. He was pushing her away for real this time, and it wasn't one of his moods. It wasn't in her imagination.

Her heart burned as she wondered if this was all going to be over soon. While she still had more money than she knew what to do with, she knew it was tough to live around here, as it was so expensive. If they broke up, she would probably have to leave – leave the studio for sure, leave Dylan's house for sure, and possibly even leave the city. She needed more time. *Wanted.* She wanted more time.

She was enjoying her time in DC, learning about history and visiting the Smithsonian, the monuments, and Arlington National Cemetery. They had even walked around the inside of the Pentagon once to see how long it might take to get all the way around. They had gotten lost and were laughing hysterically because every hall, every door, every wall looked the same as the one before. It seemed like one big round maze with no ending, no way in and no way out, and it took them several hours to find their way to the correct exit.

Now, she lay in his bed wondering what had happened. Was their relationship as strong as she thought? Or was it all make believe? Did he only use her for sex? Is that all he wanted her for? Because now, in their bed, his bed, it seemed he didn't even want that anymore, and the rest was breaking down quickly.

The next morning as she watched him, she noticed him diverting his gaze, unable to look her in the eyes. He talked to her, but only if he had to, and still never meeting her eyes. Sometimes that happened after he was mad at her for something. But lately, he hadn't been upset with her, which she found strange. She knew. It was over.

Where would she go?

At the office, she confided in one of the girls as they munched on carrot sticks for lunch. "I think he wants to break up with me, but I don't know where to go. I don't know the city all that well yet. I've been here only a few months. Do you know where I could go? Where would be a good place to get my own place?"

"Honey, it's too expensive to get your own place, even on your salary. You need a roommate. Check the papers," the other girl answered as she chewed her carrot like Bugs Bunny, then stood and walked away.

The thought of leaving him hurt more than she could admit, even to herself. The thought of having to dig through the classifieds for apartments made it even more real. She wasn't ready. Not yet, anyway. Maybe he would come around. Maybe he was merely going through a rough patch. Maybe he would go back to the old him. Her lunchtime carrot was sadly unsatisfying, much like her life with Dylan.

Later that afternoon, she and another model were working together for a photo shoot. They pretended to have fun together, but it was all for show. Candy couldn't stand this other girl, and it was apparent the other girl couldn't stand Candy, either. Her name was Stacy. Candy had always had bad luck with people with that name, and this one was proving to be no different.

When the shoot was over, Stacy sneered at Candy and then walked away. She sauntered over to Dylan, touched his arm with her finger and let it slide up to his shoulder. He watched her finger and then watched her walk away. Immediately, he went back to working with his equipment and ignored Candy.

To Candy, his obvious attempts at avoiding her were most likely his way of breaking up with her without telling her. He was probably too afraid to bring it up. Then again, so was she.

Each day, he became more and more distant, until finally she found the nerve to ask him about it over their silent dinner together at home.

"What's going on lately? Why are you so distant? Why won't you touch me?" Candy held her head high, hiding the fear, as it wanted to choke her and keep her from speaking.

He shrugged and then took a bite. "What do you think?"

"I think you want me to leave," she admitted, then took a breath and held it.

"I don't *want* you to leave, Candy." He peered directly into her eyes. She knit her eyebrows at him but didn't say another word. For the first time in almost a week, he had actually looked at her. It was almost scary.

That night, she reached for him, and after several minutes, he finally gave in and gave her what she wanted. He kissed her as they made love, and was passionate, giving her everything she needed. Tears slipped between their cheeks.

"Are you crying?" he asked, stopping his movements. She shook her head, reached for him, and pulled him deeper.

When he was finished, he rolled over onto his back, leaving her exposed and alone now on her side of the bed. Despite his attentiveness minutes ago, she never felt more alone. It was as if he had been making love to someone else.

The next day, they shared a silent drive to work, and then parted ways as he went right to his studio. She watched him walk away without a word, and then she went to the break room. She needed a friend now more than ever. She had to have someone to talk to about this. There was nobody, though, who she truly trusted. The girls here gossiped and backstabbed each other all the time, and five minutes later, they were best friends again. It was a world she didn't understand and refused to join.

An abandoned newspaper sat on the table, so she opened it to the classified section and began her search for an apartment.

Between shoots, she made a few phone calls but had no idea how to get to the apartments she had picked. They were all so far from her current location, and she needed help. Her only friend in town had been Dylan. She had no one else.

Then, she wondered if he might help her find her own place. If they admitted that it wasn't going to work and she agreed to get her own place, they may, like respectable adults, get along well enough to do this. After all, he was twenty-eight. He was almost thirty. That was old, to her, anyway. He was supposed to be mature by now.

Taking some deep breaths, she decided to talk to him about it during his lunch break. She didn't practice words in her mind beforehand because she knew she wouldn't have to. They could discuss this like adults and work together. Maybe they could still be friends. Maybe they could work together. After all, she had known it was not going to last forever. Though, she didn't think it was going to end this soon.

At last it was twelve, when he ate lunch, and she waited in the break room for him. She didn't see him, but she didn't want to put this off. So she decided to search for him and set off down the hallway and into his studio. He wasn't there, either. She searched other rooms – the dressing room, makeup room, other studios; she couldn't find him. In asking around, no one else had seen him, either. She knew he hadn't left. He never had time to leave for lunch.

As she peeked one more time into the makeup room, she thought she heard something. People talking? No. This wasn't talking. This was moaning. It wasn't loud.

It was as if they were trying their hardest to be quiet. Then, she felt something like a dagger slice through her chest as she heard Dylan's familiar voice.

Her heart sank, then beat wildly inside her chest, and she broke out in a cold sweat as she wondered if she should wait for him at the door or confront him later about it. She stood there for several long seconds, wondering what to do. Then, it turned into a minute. Two minutes. What was she going to do? Where would she go on such short notice? Would he still help her find a new place now that he'd already found someone else?

Silent sobs wracked her until Nate came in and saw her. "What's the matter, honey?" He placed his hand on her back. She covered her mouth and tried her hardest not to cry, but the pain was like a knife in her chest. Now that she had caught him with someone else, that knife was twisting inside her.

"I...um...I," she stammered. Within seconds, Dylan rushed from behind a curtain with wide eyes, running toward Candy.

"Cand–"

"Save it. You're disgusting." She spat her words at him, then stormed away. Unfortunately, he followed.

"Candy, wait."

"Why?" She stopped to ask him that question, but then continued toward the exit. Their conversation was loud enough to be heard from every part of the studio now. But she didn't care. "What the hell do you care? You *don't* care about me."

"But wait. We should talk," he pleaded as he followed her down the hall and into the stairwell. She began running down the stairs awkwardly in her heels, but then it dawned on her that she couldn't leave. She had nowhere to go.

"How could you do this to me? If you wanted somebody else, you should have dumped me out on the street. Where am I supposed to go now? Huh? What am I supposed to do?"

"Stay at my place. It's okay. You can sleep in the guest room."

"Oh. And you'll bring your new slut girlfriend over from time to time in the same bed I've been sleeping in for the past three months. Yeah. That makes perfect sense."

"Why not?"

"Are you serious? *Are you serious*? Do you *really* think that's normal?" she screamed. She heard a door slam downstairs.

"Well, I don't know, but it doesn't mean we can't – "

"Forget it. I'm not going to sit back and listen to you with some slut in the other room every night." She scoffed and shook her head. "You are so self-centered. You can't even see that I have feelings. You can't see that what you did was wrong. You can't see that you hurt me. I don't understand you, Dylan. It's like you're a robot. You have no feelings."

"I do, too. I …well, I'm not in love with you anymore."

"So, why did you let it go on this long? Why did you have to let me find out this way? Did you want to hurt me like this?"

"No," he answered, and then faced the ground thoughtfully. "I didn't mean to."

"You're an asshole. A selfish asshole. Where am I supposed to go now?"

"Hell, I don't know," he yelled, now defensive. "I let you stay in my house for three months. I even offered to let you stay there from now on. How is that selfish?"

"You have no idea. You have no idea that there is anyone else in the world. You're the only one in this world. Right? Is there anybody else? Does anybody else have feelings?"

"Candy...," He tried to keep his voice low in order to calm her. He started to touch her arm, but she pulled away. "Listen, Candy. If you want to move out, then move out. That's fine."

"Where am I supposed to go? I checked the paper, but I have no idea where these places are. I could wind up in Southeast or something and wouldn't even know. And I can't even get there to look at it."

"Well, I'll help."

"You will?"

"Yeah. I'll help you find a place."

"Okay." It was silent for a minute as they wondered where to go next. Then she spoke. "I'll sleep in the guest room from now on."

"Well, that goes without...I mean, okay."

Candy closed her eyes, shook her head, and stormed back upstairs. "Asshole," she muttered, then went through the door and slammed it behind her.

Coming down the hallway was the model she had worked with the day before. Candy knew that had to be *her* and glared. The girl smirked at Candy and thrust her nose in the air.

That's when Candy realized she would not be able to continue to work here.

"Models are bitches," Candy stated over dinner that night. Dylan gave her a disagreeing glance, then set his eyes on his plate again. "I can't work there. I can't be mean like them. I don't fit in. I'm going to quit that studio and quit modeling. It's not for me. This… lifestyle that you think is normal is messed up. It's way too stressful."

"Lifestyle?" Dylan asked with a huff. Candy was surprised he had even answered her.

"Apparently, you change girlfriends like you change clothes, and you think that's normal."

"Well, it is. It doesn't always last."

"You said it had been six months. I bet that was a lie."

"No, it wasn't." Dylan pointed at her. "Look. If you want my help looking for a new place to live, I would suggest not pissing me off any further."

Candy slammed her fork onto her plate and stormed up to her room.

As she sat on her bed, the guest bed, she formulated a plan in her mind. Horses were her thing. She missed horses. It was a much less stressful life, too. Life at the track was hard work, but it was rewarding, especially when your horse won. Being in the winner's circle with your horse is the best feeling in the world. Best feeling ever. She wanted that feeling again.

Forget this modeling thing. Who cares? I have money saved up. I can get a job as a groom at Laurel or Pimlico. I could go there. I could do it. But how? How would I get there? The bus? Does the bus go there?

She stormed back down to find Dylan cleaning up his plate after having left Candy's plate on the table. He glanced up at her with anger still burning in his eyes. "Does the bus go to Laurel? Or Baltimore?"

"Of course."

With a nod, she stomped back up the stairs.

The next day, she read the sports section in the Washington Post left on the break room table and found the horse racing section. *Pimlico.* It was the Pimlico meet. She had been to Pimlico once with Julia, and she was familiar with the track and the backside. She still had her Belmont pass. She could convince them to let her in. But what about all her clothes? She'd never be able to carry all of this. But she couldn't leave it behind for the slut. No way. The slut was the same size as Candy. There was no way she was going to let that girl wear her clothes.

Where could she put her clothes? On the way to work, there was a storage unit building. She could keep her things there until she found a place.

Or, she could buy a car.

Quickly, she flipped through the sections and found the classified ads again. There were more cars for sale than she could count. Some were only a few hundred dollars. If she were able to find one close enough, maybe one along the bus route, or maybe one within walking distance, she wouldn't need Dylan. She didn't want to need him.

"What are you looking for?" Nate asked. She was so grateful it was him and not one of the girls that she let out a sigh of relief.

"A car. I need to buy a car. Nate, I'm leaving. I'm going to have to quit because I can't be like those other…girls. And this…thing with Dylan isn't working out. I'm going to go to Baltimore and work at Pimlico so I can be with horses again. Horses are much kinder than people."

Nate thought for a moment. "You're right about that, I guess. How much are you looking to spend on a car?"

"I don't know. Nothing too expensive. I have money, but I don't want to spend it all on a car if I'm going to need living expenses. Maybe a thousand?"

Nate bobbed his head with a thoughtful frown. "I have a car for sale."

Candy's eyes lit up.

By the end of the week, she had packed everything she had into two suitcases, bought Nate's car, and quit her job. She promised to call Ms. Evans with an address for sending her last paycheck and left without saying goodbye to anyone but Ms. Evans and Nate. She hugged him tightly, knowing it was going to be a long time until she got another hug from anyone. He seemed to understand and obliged. He touched her face one more time before she left, waving her keys to her new 1968 Plymouth Valiant.

It was really a good deal, she thought, because he had paid two thousand for it a year ago. She was thrilled that she got a fairly new car for half price, and proud of herself. There was one problem. She barely knew how to drive. All right, two problems. She had no idea how to get to Baltimore.

After picking up a map from a gas station, she found her way to I-95, the same road she had taken into the city back in February. Driving well under the speed limit, angering other drivers, she carefully leaned over the steering wheel and made sure her car was in her lane. Once she made it to Baltimore, she got lost as she tried to get to Park Heights Avenue, Pimlico's location. Several wrong turns later, she finally found it. Proudly, she pulled into the parking lot and turned off her car.

She checked her face in her mirror, making sure she was put together. She had to be at her best because it was time to charm her way into the backside. Once at the security gate, she took out her Belmont badge.

"Hi, um, Dale," she said, noting his nametag. "I'm a groom at Belmont Park, you know, up in New York. I'm supposed to meet my trainer here. She said you would let me in."

"She?"

Oops. "Uh, yeah. Julia McMahon?"

"I don't see her on my list." He checked over his paperwork and flipping through pages of names.

Candy leaned closer as she tried to check out the list, too. "Hmmm," she moaned. Out of the corner of her eyes, she watched his eyes pop open with surprise. Then she moved closer to him and leaned over him, touching her breast to his arm. At first, he pulled his arm away but then decided not to. "Are you sure? She's got a two-year-old. Derby hopeful."

"I heard that, too, but–,"

"Can I go look around? Maybe if you hold my purse for collateral or something. I could go look for her, and if she's not here yet, then I'll come back. I'll get my purse."

"Well, I don't know."

"Come on. You know a girl's not going to leave her purse with a stranger. But I can trust you, right?" She batted her eyelashes.

"Well, yeah, but –,"

"Please? I need to find her. She'll be upset with me if I miss her. She said she'd be here. And if she's here and I can't get to her…,"

"Well, fine. Leave your purse. Come back in an hour, though. Or I'll come looking for you."

"Okay!" She left her empty furry gray purse with him and walked through the gate and onto the backside.

Men widened their eyes when they saw her, and she made sure to do her best strut, swaying her hips with every stride. She heard some whistles and shouts, and she tried her hardest to keep her lips pouty instead of grinning. *Track guys are so desperate. It'll take me all of two minutes to find a job here.*

One man was talking to another, and he had a sexy accent. Sexy accent man stopped mid-sentence and set his eyes firmly on Candy. It was hard not to let the corners of her mouth creep up the way they wanted. "Where are you from?" She scanned him quickly from his head to his boot-clad toes. Her voice was husky and deep, as if she had recently woken up from a roll between the sheets.

"Hungary," he answered, leaning toward her.

"I love that accent," she purred, then walked away.

"Hey," he called. The corners of her mouth raised, but she quickly lowered them again.

"Hey, yourself," she answered over her shoulder.

"Where are you from?" he asked as he caught up to her.

"New York."

"What's a sexy girl like you doing in a place like this?"

"Looking for work. You hiring?"

"You bet I am."

It hadn't even taken two minutes.

Chapter Fifteen

"I'll get you your purse back. Don't you worry, little lady."

"It's Candy. And thanks," she answered dipping her head and batting her eyelashes.

"Demetri." His R sounded like a purr. Candy's eyes widened as his accent charmed her. He wore a black wife-beater tank top highlighting bulging muscles and a small tattoo of a cross on his upper left arm. When he reached out his right hand with his palm facing up, she placed her hand in his. He lifted her ivory hand to his lips and kissed it, prompting a blush.

"So, do you work with horses? You look like you have 'people' who tend to your horses." He let go of her hand.

"Huh? No." Candy waved her other hand in dismissal of his words. "No, I used to be a groom at Belmont Park, but I left town a few months ago. Had a stint as a model, but it wasn't for me. I'd rather be a groom."

"Ha. You're kidding. You'd give up a career in modeling to rub horses? You must be living off Daddy's money."

Candy's mood darkened suddenly. "No. I don't have parents. And when I did, they never had money."

"Well, I'll be. Okay then. Let's go," he said with a wave of his hand as he turned toward his barn. They went inside, and Candy's heart soared when she saw the horses peeking from their stalls to see the new person. Her eyes lit up, and she suppressed a squeak of excitement and the overwhelming urge to run to every horse and touch their velvety noses.

As she walked down the shedrow, taking the time to inspect each horse in a glance, she finally felt in her element. It was such a relief. One horse nickered and bobbed his head toward her, and she went to him, held his halter, and rubbed his nose. She then found herself smoothing his mane and forelock, inspecting him closely.

"That's Fast Dollar," Demetri said softly from behind Candy. With her eyes crinkling with joy, she turned toward him as she still held the halter. "You'll have to wait for a grooming job, though. We're all full on those. Could use some more walkers, though. You all right with walking hots?"

"Of course." Any job here would be sheer heaven.

Within a few minutes, someone handed her a sweaty horse that had recently come from a race, and she fell into place with the others as they walked in circles between barns.

A half hour later, Demetri caught up with her, carrying her purse. The sight of such a bulky, tough man holding a tiny, furry purse with a gold chain for a strap tickled her. He handed it to her while looking both ways to see if anyone had seen him with it.

"Thanks." She hooked the long strap over her head and arm. She wasn't sure if she should ask how he got it back or stay quiet, but the answer was decided for her when Demetri walked away.

As Candy continued to walk the horse, she wondered where she would live. More importantly, where would she stay for the night? The pace at the track slowed throughout the day, people went home, and she chewed her lip as she wondered if she was going to have to sleep in her car. The thought of it wasn't horrible, but she would much rather have a bed and a place to brush her teeth and take a shower.

"Time to go, Candy," Demetri called to her as he approached from his office. "Everybody's leaving. You got a place to stay?"

"No. I could sleep in a stall, though. Keep an eye on the horses."

Demetri sighed. "I would hate to see you by morning. You'd have bug bites all over you. I couldn't do that to you. You can stay at my place. I have an extra room."

Candy tried not to appear as surprised or as worried as she felt. She barely knew the man. As she tried to formulate a way to say no to him, her eyes darted back and forth, searching for the answer.

However, he insisted. "I promise to keep my hands to myself. You'll have your own bathroom and your own bedroom. I promise I'll bring you back in the morning safe and sound."

"Can you help me find my own place? Maybe an apartment around here so I can walk?"

"Honey, you don't want to live in this neighborhood. I can help you find a place, though. I get the paper in the morning. We can look through it then. Come on." He held out his hand for her.

She wasn't sure why she trusted him, a complete stranger. He seemed so kind, despite his ogling earlier. Once he had calmed down a bit, she found him to be friendly and helpful. His employees seemed to like him. He was the head trainer. The boss. She knew he had to be trustworthy to be in charge.

Giving in as she let her shoulders relax, she walked toward him but didn't take his hand. That was going a bit too far. Demetri dropped his hand, winked, then led her to his car. They drove to her car, picked up her things, and put them in his trunk.

He had a nice car, a Cadillac, and she knew he must have been doing well as a trainer. She wondered if he had a huge house, too.

"So, how is it you decided working on the backstretch is better than modeling?"

"The people, mostly. The money was good, but it wasn't worth it to have to deal with people like that. They were so fake, and many of them did drugs. That's not the life I want for myself."

Pressing his lips together, Demetri nodded for a few seconds. "I'm impressed. That's quite a brave decision to give up a high-paying career for a low-paying one."

"Like I said, no amount of money is worth becoming like one of them. I wanted to be as far away as possible."

She couldn't believe how relieved she felt to be away from Dylan now, too. It was as if a huge weight had been lifted from her, and she was able to breathe again. No more mood swings. No more getting the cold shoulder for unknown reasons. No more, though unsuccessfully, doing everything she could to make him happy. No more broken expectations. She hadn't noticed until now how disappointed she had been throughout their short relationship. Thinking back, she could see now that he had kept her happy enough to stay, and not disappointed enough to leave. That was no way to live. *Never again.*

"We're getting close, but I don't have much food in the house. Are you hungry?"

Her eyes widened. This was all so sudden. And strange. He was almost too friendly. She wasn't used to this. Was he trustworthy? He seemed all right. But...

"No pressure. Just thought you might like a bite to eat. There's a place near my house. If you want, we can order the food and take it home. To my house."

"Oh, um, no. Eating there is fine." The less time she was alone in the house with a stranger, the better. She wasn't sure how she had let herself get talked into this. But she kept telling herself he seemed nice. So far, he hadn't given her anything to be worried about. He hadn't made a pass at her, either, which surprised her after his reaction when she first walked up to the barn. Maybe he was saving it for later. She formulated a plan. Once she got to his house, she planned on going right to her guest room, closing the door, locking it, then staying in there until morning. Then she wondered if there would be a guest room.

"Everything all right?" He turned his left signal on. "You're kind of quiet."

"Yeah, I'm fine. Long day, I guess. Started out this morning in DC, leaving my job, and leaving…well, leaving my home."

"Leaving someone behind as well?" he asked as he pulled into the restaurant parking lot, then put the car in park.

Candy drew in a big breath and glanced his way. "Yeah. Left someone behind."

After they were seated at the table, she couldn't help but be reminded that a few months ago she didn't know the first thing about eating at a restaurant. She hadn't known which fork to use first, or even how to pick up a glass of wine. So much had changed. As she put her napkin in her lap, a vision of Dylan as he first showed her how flashed in front of her eyes. But she shoved it aside. Leaving him behind, despite his cold, insensitive personality, was proving to be harder than she thought.

"I get the feeling you're not too happy about leaving this person behind." He closed his menu. Candy was still trying to read hers, but had trouble concentrating as so many things reminded her of Dylan.

Without raising her head, she nodded a slow and thoughtful series of nods for several seconds as she thought. Was she not happy? She certainly should be. She left behind a real jerk, a guy who cheated on her and then expected her to get over it in an instant. The man had no regard for anybody's feelings but his own, not only in that situation, but in many others as well. He always came first, as if he expected it. His feelings and comfort became more important than hers, and she had let it happen.

She had lost herself. Defeated, she let her head droop. "It was for the best."

"Why's that?" He leaned into her line of vision. His big brown eyes searched her blue eyes and seemed so kind, so gentle. Maybe he really cared. Did he? Or was he trying to get her into bed with him? Didn't matter what he said. She wasn't sleeping with him on the first night as she did with Dylan. But he *was* friendly. He was someone to talk to, and she hadn't had that for many months. Not since Rachel.

"He...I don't know how to describe him. He didn't seem to know that anyone else had feelings. It was as if the world revolved around him and he didn't realize what he did was wrong."

"What did he do?"

"Cheated." Candy sipped her water and swallowed that thought. It still hurt.

"He didn't think that was wrong?"

"Well, didn't think it was that bad. See, we worked together. He was a photographer in my studio, and I caught him with another model. But he acted as if I should let it go, like it was no big deal. Then, get this." She leaned forward. He lifted his eyebrows in response. "He actually said to me, 'You can stay in the guest room so she can sleep in my bed.' Can you believe that?"

Demetri laughed heartily as the waiter approached their table. "I think the lady deserves a glass of wine." Demetri held his hand toward Candy. "Which wine would you prefer, madam?"

Candy smirked at his proper words and tone of voice. It didn't match his words or actions from earlier in the day. She was glad he had thrown a shirt over his tank top, or else they would not have allowed him inside. Surprisingly, he looked distinguished now as he waited for her answer. It was charming. "Merlot would be lovely," she answered with her best British accent laced with a hint of Long Island-ese.

"A bottle of Merlot it is," Demetri said with a nod to the waiter, who spun on his heels and walked away. Candy's freshly painted lips curled into a wide smile. She was so glad to have someone who cared. Or at least seemed to care. Demetri continued. "So, he expected you to stay in the other room so he could bring another girl into his bed?"

Candy nodded slowly with a silent chuckle. "Piece of work, he is." She straightened a fork on the table.

"He really didn't see anything wrong with that?"

"Oh, I promise you. You should have seen his face. He was perfectly serious. It was as if he had done it many times before. I wonder how many other girls had been with him and if maybe one or two of them had so little self-respect that they would stay in the other room while he…" She glanced around as she leaned forward and lowered her voice. "You know. While he had sex with another girl in the same house." Demetri was eyeing Candy as if she had two heads. "You don't believe me, do you?"

"Oh, I believe you. I have seen people in movies like that, but never anyone in real life."

"Well, he's real. Unfortunately," Candy said as the waiter arrived with their bottle. They ordered and spent the next hour drinking, laughing, and talking as if they were old friends. She tried not to drink too much, but two glasses were enough to make her dizzy and cause her to act silly. She made jokes about things, which amused him, but she knew they were dumb jokes. Still, she couldn't stop. Everything seemed so funny to her. Though they were trying to be quiet, sometimes they noticed people at other tables scowling their way.

So they decided to leave. Demetri held her hand as she stood on wobbly legs and found her bearings. Then, to make sure, she hooked her arm around his and allowed him to lead her to his car. "Shh," she hushed as they passed by a table with an older couple who were annoyed with her. Demetri chuckled and patted her hand as it rested on his muscular forearm.

Then, as they drove the rest of the way to his home in Owings Mills, she found herself asking, "How old are you?" She almost slapped her hand over her mouth, but resisted. Then again, it was a valid question.

"Thirty-four. You?"

"Guess," she said, playing the same game Dylan had played with her when they first met. Instantly, she wished she hadn't done this, as it only served to bring up memories of him. Happy memories. One of only a few, she reminded herself.

"Um, fifteen."

Was he serious? Candy backhanded his arm, and he rubbed, pretending that it hurt. "No!"

"Okay. Um, fifty-two."

Candy burst into laughter, throwing her head back and clapping her hands. "Yeah. That's it. I'm fifty-two."

"You look pretty damned good for someone old enough to be my mother." He ducked to avoid another swat from Candy. "Come on. You going to tell me? I have to fill out those tax forms, you know, since I'm your employer now."

Candy made an O with her mouth, then stopped and thought for a moment. Again, nineteen sounded way too young. But it's not as if he expected her to get into a relationship with him. He was merely helping her out for the night or maybe until she found her own place. "Nineteen," she answered, feeling that honesty was the best policy, especially in this situation. Besides, if he had any expectations, he certainly wouldn't now, considering their difference in age.

Demetri turned his whole body toward her as they sat at a traffic light. "You're just a baby."

"Well, I'll be twenty in a few weeks. Then I won't sound so young. I won't be a teenager anymore. Yay." She couldn't wait.

They walked up to his doorway while doubling over at their jokes. Demetri managed to carry both suitcases for her and refused to let her carry anything other than her purse. He put one suitcase down, pulled out his keys, and opened the door.

"Ooo," Candy sighed as she walked into an enormous foyer. The sound of her voice echoed off of bare white walls that needed the attention of a decorator. "So open," she almost shouted, and then slapped her hand over her mouth and faced Demetri with big blue eyes.

"Yes, well, I don't have need of much furniture. I'm at the track most of the time, anyway. And this is my second home."

"Second home? You have two?" She raised an eyebrow as she continued to inspect the place. Just inside the front door to the left was a half wall with a planter on top that spanned the entire length of it. It was empty, aside from dried up topsoil. On the other side of the wall was the living room with a bay window covered with dark curtains.

Demetri carried the suitcases into the large room and sat them down with a groan. "Yes. My main house is in Miami, Florida. Do you know where that is?"

"Of course I do. Wow. Why are you up here, then?"

"Just for the Pimlico meet. I rent this house out during the winter while I'm in Florida for the Hialeah meet, and sometimes Gulfstream."

"Wow. Must be doing pretty well to be able to afford two houses." Candy peeked around a corner into the hallway and saw several doors, which she assumed were bedrooms. The one level rancher was very large, she thought.

"It helps to rent them."

"That's neat."

"Yes, let's get you to your room." He picked up both suitcases again and carried them down the hall to a bedroom on the right, right across from a bathroom. "Here's your room, and your bathroom."

Candy peered inside to see a plush bed with lots of pillows. She couldn't wait to jump onto the soft surface and let herself sink into the luxury. So, with a sharp breath, as if getting ready to dive into a pool, she ran and jumped onto the bed, making the pillows leap into the air and almost fall onto the floor. "Ahh."

"Well, I can see you are tired. I will leave you now and let you rest. You've had a long day."

Candy sat up. "Yeah, it has been a long day. Thank you so much for letting me stay here, Demetri. I'd be sleeping in my car right now if it weren't for you."

After a nod, Demetri left, closing the door behind him.

Candy found her summer pajamas, a tank top and pajama shorts, and changed. It was only eight, but she was exhausted and quickly fell asleep.

It was still dark when she heard a soft knock on her door. It almost didn't wake her, as she wasn't sure she had actually heard it. But then she heard, "Candy?"

With a disgruntled moan, wanting to stay in bed, she sat up. "Yeah," she answered as she rubbed her face and pulled her hair together over one shoulder.

"Time to get up. I'd like to leave in an hour. Is that enough time?"

"Oh, yes. Of course. Thank you," she answered, more awake now. She reminded herself that she loved mornings, though it is hard to convince yourself of such things when you're half asleep. With newfound energy, she got up, grabbed her things, and headed for the bathroom across the hall.

It was modern and clean, and the shower felt good on her head, which ached from too much wine the night before. Leaning against the shower wall, she rested her head and let the hot water pound on her shoulders. The water pressure was awesome, allowing her to wash her hair in no time, and it massaged her muscles, threatening to put her back to sleep. Finally, she was ready to come out, and she found the house to be dark. *Demetri must be in his room.* She headed for the kitchen.

She wanted to be a good guest and stay out of the way, not make a mess, but then again, she thought Demetri might like it if she made breakfast. In the past, breakfast was not cooked; it was poured into a bowl. However, Dylan had taught her how to prepare foods like eggs and bacon, or even pancakes. She hoped to surprise Demetri with a delicious breakfast, and as quietly as a mouse, she searched Demetri's kitchen.

She was placing a pan onto a gas burner when she heard something behind her. She jumped, sucked in a whole room full of air, and dropped the pan on the floor. The noise was deafening in the empty house, and she slapped her hands over her ears to avoid it. Then she snapped around to face him.

"Demetri!" she gasped with her hand now over her heart. "Jesus, you scared me."

With a patient look in his eye, he came into the kitchen and picked up the pan. "You don't need to make anything for breakfast. I usually eat at the track."

"Oh. Okay. I wanted to surprise you. Well…surprise," she joked, then took the pan from him and put it back into the cabinet.

"It was nice of you. Thank you." He smelled of after-shave and a fresh shower, exactly like Dylan in the mornings. The memory burned in her chest, souring her expression.

"Are you okay? If you really want, you can make breakfast."

Candy stopped him with her hand on his arm. "No. No. I was, well, my head hurts. Do you have any aspirin?"

"Yes, ma'am." Within a few seconds, he had filled a glass of water for her and had given her two aspirin. Surprised, she kept her eyes on him as she took the medicine, and put down her glass. What would Dylan have done in this situation? He would have asked for breakfast and never would have troubled himself to find aspirin for her. There's no way he'd fill a glass of water for her, either. Already, she began to feel spoiled, something she had never felt before. It made her feel a bit guilty.

"I guess I'm ready, then."

As they were walking out the door, she remembered about her things. "Should I bring my stuff? In case I find a place to stay today?"

"Oh, I'm sure you won't find anything available immediately. Just leave it here. In the off chance we find something, we can always come back and get it."

She thought it might be a bit of a pain, considering they had driven for almost thirty minutes last night from the track to his house. But she trusted him and followed him to his car.

When they got to the track, they fell into routine, with Candy spending the whole morning walking horses. It was boring, and her feet and legs were tired, but still, it was all part of the life she loved at the track. Anything was better than dealing with snobby and prissy young women. And Dylan.

She shook her head as she considered how selfish he had been. It surprised her that she didn't see it until she had separated herself from him. It was now obvious.

Demetri was so sweet and sensitive. She knew he was too old for her, but he was a good man. He took care of her, something hardly anybody had ever done for her. Normally, she was the one taking care of other people. Candy wondered if Demetri thought of her as a daughter. Certainly, a father wouldn't take a daughter out for a night of drinking wine. On second thought, her father might have, had she been old enough at the time.

During the break between workouts and races, she sat down at a table inside the barn and rested her head in her hands. Strangely, there on the table was a Washington Post – the very same paper from back at the studio. It seemed that life was already so far away, but it had only been a day, and maybe only forty miles.

Demetri passed by the door, so she called him. "Demetri!"

He peeked in. "Yes?"

"Can you help me look for apartments or something? I don't know where any of these places are."

"Oh. Yes, um, I'll be back in a few minutes." He held up one finger, then two, then hurried away.

She circled a few places that seemed promising. Once that was done, she read the rest of the paper, searching for news from home. There was nothing about Rachel, and no mention of Julia or her stable in the sports section. It seemed they only wrote about local horse racing. Then she noticed that the Pimlico meet was going to be

over soon. Was Demetri going to Miami? Or close by to
Laurel?

"Hey." The greeting came from a short-haired girl
as she sat down at the table with Candy. She leaned back in
her chair and wiped her forehead with her arm. Then, she
fanned herself with her hand. "Sherri," she said, holding
out her hand.

"Candy." They shook hands. Sherri's hands were
soaking wet and smeared with dirt, and Candy wiped her
hand on her jeans once they let go.

"New here, huh?" Sherri asked her.

"Yeah."

"You going to be riding? Or you walking the
horses?"

"I was a groom at Belmont for a few years. I'm
waiting for a grooming job."

"You don't ride, then?"

"My friend was trying to show me how to pony
horses to the track and stuff. But we didn't get very far on
that before I had to leave."

"Why'd you have to leave?"

Candy didn't like the girl's nosy interest in her, and
her questions were starting to sound like an inquisition, as
if she expected Candy to be some sort of underground
criminal or something. *Hmmm, criminal…*

"I um, see, I was with this guy, and he taught me
how to um, rob banks. We were like a team. You know?
My job was to go in and seduce the teller, get him away
from the little buzzer thing they push if the bank is being
robbed, you know? And then my guy's job was to go in and
snatch the money when the teller wasn't looking. But,

sadly, this guy um, he got shot. Yeah, he was shot in the bank because the teller, he had a gun. But I got away. I ran out, and um, I dyed my hair and all that. No one knew it was me. Or so I thought. One night I saw the police coming, and I knew they were there for me. You know? So I left. I just ran. I ran completely out of New York City. Through the tunnel and everything. Wound up in Jersey somewhere. Then, I took a bus here. And…here I am." Candy finished proudly with her arms wide open.

Sherri's eyes grew wide at first, but then about halfway through Candy's story, her mouth curled higher and higher. She then lowered her gaze and did her best to keep from laughing. When Candy's story was over, Sherri shook her head and held up her hand for a high five. Candy slapped her hand and leaned back in her chair like Sherri.

"What about you?" Candy asked.

Sherri stared at Candy for a second. Then, she told her story. "I started in California, you know, digging for silver, 'cause all the gold's gone. And well, the silver's gone now, too. So I decided to try my hand at train robberies. I found myself a horse tied to a post outside the saloon, and being the expert horsewoman I am, I hopped aboard my new mare and rode her away into the sunset. We stopped and listened, and we heard a train. So I kicked her into a full out run across this field, and we caught up with the train. We ran next to it for a minute, and um…oh, um…I couldn't leave my horse. So we found this flatbed car. It had nothing on it. I told my trusty steed to jump up onto the car, and then told her to stay. I went through all these cars until I got to the banking car. I punched the guard, knocking him out. Then I rushed inside, took the money, and ran back to my horse. I hopped on, and we ran all the way to Baltimore. And...here we are."

"Is that so?" Candy put her hand on her stomach as she laughed.

"Yeah. And I still have her, too. She's the track's best lead pony."

After the laughter died down, they sat in silence for a few seconds, proud of their own creativity. Then the mood shifted. Candy shrugged. "Well, that's better than the real reason, I guess. I think I'll stick with that story. It's much happier."

"Yeah. I could say the same."

They nodded silently in agreement, and then changed the subject. Candy pointed to the paper. "Maybe you could help me find a place in town?"

"Well, you could look for a place, but the meet's over in a week. Wouldn't do much good. Are you planning on staying here or going with Demetri to Miami? We'll be going to Hialeah. That's where that girl jock got to ride last February. Did you hear?"

"Oh, did she actually go through with it?"

"Yeah. She didn't win, but another girl won a race last month."

"There's more than one girl jockey?"

"Got a few already. I'm planning on going for it myself. Maybe when I get down there."

"Really? That's... Wow. That's awesome. I wish... Um, never mind." Candy opened the paper, trying to change the subject again.

"You want to be a jockey?"

"I don't know. I don't think it's for me. But my friend, she would have..." Candy sighed as she shook her head. "She would have..." But then she had to cover her face as she thought about Rachel again. Rachel would have been ecstatic to find out that the race had happened. Other races with girl jockeys had to be canceled because every trainer had pulled their horses out of the race in protest.

"That's why you left?"

Candy nodded, scanning the paper now, distracting herself, hoping Sherri had figured it out on her own so she wouldn't have to say it. She wasn't sure exactly what Sherri thought, but whatever it was, it was better than the truth.

"You have family up there?"

Candy shrugged as her throat constricted. Briefly, she wondered what had happened to her brother. Hopefully, he was in jail.

"So this girl was your only family."

Don wasn't much of a brother. Candy reluctantly nodded and held her breath, hoping to hold in her emotions as well.

"You might as well go with us, then. I mean, it's hot for the next couple months, but then, once it's winter, you'll really appreciate it. You might never want to come back."

"Would there be a place to stay down there?"

"Yeah. Track apartments or there are rooms for rent off track. You'll be able to find a place pretty easy."

Candy glanced back and forth for Demetri again, but he hadn't come back yet. She wondered if there was enough steady work there. What about a place to live?

Friends? She met Sherri's eyes again, wondering if the two of them would ever be close friends. It was worth a shot. She nodded. "If he'll have me, I'll go."

Sherri's face lit up as she nodded in approval of Candy's decision.

Sherri had to go back to work ponying horses, as afternoon races had begun. Demetri finally came back, but he was in a hurry again and had to go to the paddock for his horse. He promised Candy he would be back later. Candy stayed and sat around waiting for a horse to walk.

An hour later, a small ecstatic group of people walked with a horse to the barn. Demetri was with them, and Candy stood to greet them. Excitement bubbling inside her, she congratulated the owners and Demetri on their win.

"Want me to walk him?" Candy offered, hoping for something to do.

"Nah, Scotty's got it. Scotty," he called. A small man jogged from the barn and took the horse. Demetri put his hand on Candy's back. "Let's go get some lunch. You must be hungry. You didn't eat breakfast."

Candy was taken aback but managed to reply. "Yeah. I am kinda hungry."

"It's on me. Let's go." He took her hand and led her to the track kitchen. Candy slipped her hand out of his after a few steps.

"How many more races do you have today?" she asked as they sat down with their food.

"Only two. Slow day today. They don't run until later. Sorry I couldn't meet with you earlier about the apartment. We should have brought the paper with us.

Maybe there's one in here somewhere." He searched the room for a stray leftover paper on an empty table.

"Well, Sherri said the meet is almost over, and you will be going to Miami."

Demetri stopped his search. "Do you want to go with us?"

"Well, I might as well. I have nowhere else to go." Candy's words stung her heart, reminding her of her lack.

"Then come with us."

"Sherri said there were track apartments."

Demetri nodded. "Yes. Or you rent a room. Whatever you want."

"So is it all right if I stay with you until then?" Candy asked with a soft voice, almost scared.

"Of course. Of course. You stay with me. I will take care of you."

A weight lifted from her shoulders.

That night, Demetri took her home after going out to dinner again. Candy joked about how often she had eaten out in the past, and how much she had eaten out lately. It was almost as if she were living somebody else's life. This couldn't be her life. Demetri, flattered, seemed to enjoy taking care of her, maybe spoiling her a bit. Candy certainly didn't mind.

Candy wondered what his expectations were and why he was taking her out so often. He also seemed to be favoring her around the barn, not making her work as hard as some of the others. At first, she thought it might be because she was new. But now, she wondered if he thought of her as an escort, or date, so he wouldn't have to eat alone. If so, did he realize what he was doing?

After a few more days of the same routine, she began to wonder about his intentions. He never made passes at her, but everything else he did made her wonder if he thought of her as a girlfriend. He treated her like a girlfriend but never kissed her. He held her hand sometimes when bringing her home or leading her into the restaurant. Sometimes he placed his hand on her back or around her waist. It was all very confusing. She wondered if Europeans did this normally. *How exotic,* she thought.

The night before they left, he had packed his clothes, Candy had packed hers, and they sat in the living room watching television.

"I need a drink. You up for a drink?" Demetri asked, standing.

"No, thanks." She didn't like alcohol all that much, and wondered why people even bothered to drink it. All it did was give her a headache. Maybe another European custom.

"Suit yourself," he answered, then went to the kitchen. He came back after a few minutes with a short glass of something yellowish. Sipping it little by little, it was gone by the time the next show was on, and he got up to get another drink. Another half hour later, he had finished that drink, and Candy sensed he was getting drunk.

He started yelling at the people on the television. "He's behind the shed," he yelled, laughing. "No, no, not that one." Candy laughed like he did to be polite, but she didn't think it was all that funny.

Finally, Candy decided to go to bed. "It's late, Demetri. Thanks for dinner again. I'm going to hit the hay. Okay?"

"Sure, Can. Sure. Go ahead. Have a good sleep. Dream of me." He tipped his glass toward her.

That was odd. She almost couldn't sleep wondering if Demetri, being drunk, might somehow lose his self-control and come in after her. She got up and locked the door. However, the television was on all night, and she didn't think he had left the living room.

The next morning, he was still in his chair, with an empty glass on the table next to him. The test pattern on his color television filled the screen, and she wondered if she should wake him.

Well, they were planning to leave for Florida today. She softly made her way to the living room, worried about waking him for some reason. He had been nothing but nice to her, so caring and protective. She knew she had no reason to be nervous. He wasn't Dylan. Besides, he had to get up. They had to leave today.

"Demetri," she whispered as she touched his arm. He grunted. She tried again. "Demetri." Again, she repeated his name, and her touches became rougher and rougher as she attempted to wake him. Finally, his eyes opened.

"Can...dy." His voice was rough with exhaustion. He sat up and took a breath, then blew it out. Candy backed away from the stench of old liquor.

"Time to get up, Demetri. Today's the big day."

"You are right, my dear. Thank you for waking me. I might have slept all day. Where would I be without you?"

"Asleep in your chair?"

"True. True." He stood, wobbled, and Candy held out her hand steady him. He took her hand, then caught his bearings and let go. "Thank you." Then he picked up his glass and brought it to the kitchen as he stretched his back. Meanwhile, Candy made her way back to her room to get ready.

"You okay to drive?" Candy asked as they walked to his car. Her car was still in the lot at the track, and she wondered how to get it all the way to Florida. She wasn't all that comfortable with driving.

"Of course. I'm not drunk. Never was. I can hold my liquor."

"Oh, okay." Despite her response, Candy was not convinced. He *was* drunk last night. But she wasn't about to point that out.

When they got to the track, they found the crew already lined up, passing their things to the trailers to be packed in. He had only ten horses at this track, with many more waiting for him in Florida. But for those ten horses, a lot had to be moved along with them. They had feed, tack boxes, hay, and toys. Two large trailers were packed to the brim with five horses in each, along with their belongings.

"I guess you will be following us, Candy?" Demetri asked as he put his hand on her back. She passed a bag of feed to the next person and then spoke.

"Yeah," she answered, out of breath. The bags were at least forty pounds each and she wasn't used to this.

"I'll ride with you, then."

"You're not taking your car?"

"No, I leave it here. I'll be back up every once in a while, and I leave it here so I have a car when I fly up."

"Oh. Okay."

Finally, they were packed and ready to go, and Candy, now in her car, caught up to the caravan as they were getting ready to leave the backside. Demetri hopped in on the passenger side.

"Um, I'm not really a good driver. This is my first car. Do you want to drive?"

"Oh. Okay. Sure." He got out and they switched places.

"Oh man, what a relief." She settled into the passenger side. "You'd probably be scared to death the way I drive."

"How bad can it be?"

"Have you ever seen 'I Love Lucy' where Lucy learns to drive?"

"Yes, I have seen that. You are that bad?"

"Worse."

"How did you make it all the way from DC, then? Your car seems fine to me."

"Luck."

They honked and cheered as the caravan finally pulled out of the Pimlico backstretch and headed for the interstate and Florida.

Occasionally, they stopped and walked the horses at rest areas. Since they had the horses, they couldn't stop for lunch or dinner, so they ate vending machine food from the rest areas. That night, they made it as far as Georgia before stopping.

"Do we sleep in the car?" Candy asked.

"We can get a hotel if you want. Some will sleep in the trailer, in the trucks, some in cars. We can meet up with the others in the morning, though. How does that sound?"

"Oh. Okay." Candy, again, felt strange, not knowing what to expect from him.

"We'll get two beds. Don't worry."

Candy stiffened. "Okay." *Same room?*

Demetri talked with the others and arranged a meeting time for morning, and then he and Candy drove off in search of a hotel. They found a Holiday Inn nearby and pulled up to the front door. Demetri told Candy to wait in the car since the front desk might want to make sure they were married before allowing them to sleep in the same room.

Candy wasn't too sure about this.

Soon, they were able to go to their room, and they brought in their things. Candy's eyes darted nervously.

"Which bed do you want?" Demetri asked.

"Um, I don't know. This one?" she replied, sitting on the bed closest to the front door.

"Sounds good to me." He plopped his suitcase onto the bed and opened it. Candy watched him pick up some shorts and head for the bathroom. He came out again wearing his shorts. So Candy did the same, taking her pajamas into the bathroom to change. By the time she came out, her arms wrapped around herself, hiding, he was already in bed and watching television.

"It's in color," he noted as he pointed toward the television. "This is a nice place."

"Yeah," Candy replied as she crawled under the covers on the side farthest from Demetri.

"You cool enough? I can turn down the air if you want."

"Oh, no, I'm fine. Thanks."

Demetri nodded, then continued to stare at her for several seconds. Candy shifted nervously, wishing she could hide under the sheets. Trying to be polite, she smirked at him but still tried to find a way to avoid his gaze. She tried to lift her sheet to hide, but felt funny about it and let it fall again. Finally, he spoke again. "You seem nervous."

She sucked in a quick breath as her eyes shot open. Then she caught herself and tried not to seem surprised. It was too late for that now. "I'm okay." She didn't know what else to say.

"We're all very close, my employees and I. Everybody's like family. I want you to feel comfortable. Would you like me to get another room?"

"Oh, no, Demetri. I understand. I don't want you to have to pay for another room on my account."

"As long as you're comfortable. That's all that matters."

Candy couldn't help but tilt her head at him. "You are so nice to me. I don't know what to make of it. No one has ever been this nice to me." *Except Rachel.*

Demetri sat up a bit, leaning on his arm and facing her. "What do you mean?"

"Never had much of a family. I had some good friends, and my friend, you know, the one I told you about, Rachel? She gave me things, or tried to, but most of the time I refused because I didn't want to admit that I needed anything. But the truth was, I did. I guess I was too proud. Or something. Plus, as I said, I'm not used to anyone being so nice. And thoughtful. No one's ever treated me as good as you treat me, Demetri," she managed to say before her throat constricted and cut off her words. Then she covered her face to hide from him, but knew it was impossible.

Demetri shook his head, then sat up, tossed aside his covers, and went to Candy's bed. He sat on the side and put his hand on Candy's shoulder as it bounced with her sobs. "Come here." He offered his chest and she accepted. He wrapped his huge arms around her and stroked her long hair as she cried while trying desperately to control herself.

"I'm sorry." She wiped her face with her sheets.

"It's okay, Candy. I had a rough childhood, too. I know what you're feeling."

She sat up to meet his eyes. "You did? Wh-what do you...I mean, how? What happened?"

Demetri slid his hands down her arms to her hands, and held them as he took in a breath. His thumb tenderly swiped over her knuckles as he thought for a few seconds. She worried she had overstepped her boundaries. Before she was able to apologize, he found his words.

"We were very poor. We lived outside of Budapest. In Hungary, of course."

Candy nodded.

"My father was a hard man and worked hard. He came home from work exhausted every day. He was trying his best to provide for us. And my mother did what she could to make extra money. She made things with needles. What do you call it? Knitting?" Candy nodded again. "And she went into the city to sell her things to tourists. But if she didn't make enough that day, my father got mad at her. He hit her. And me. Then, when I turned ten, he made me find work as well. That's when I found horse racing. I did what I could and gave all my money to my father so he could pay the bills, but it was never enough. Nothing was ever enough for that man. He always wanted more. He said it was for us, but it wasn't. It was so he could buy vodka. You know I drink, but I will never drink vodka. It ruined my family."

"Your dad beat you?"

"Yes, but in the end, I believe all of that made me a stronger person."

"Adversity makes you stronger. I know I'm only nineteen, almost twenty, but like you, I believe what I went through has made me a stronger person. I know exactly what you mean."

"We have a lot in common," Demetri said softly as he glanced at her lips for a brief second.

Candy nodded, and she wanted more than anything to be closer to him. Before she knew it, he was leaning in toward her. For a second, she panicked and wanted to push him away. Despite her practical side telling her it was too soon and that he was her boss, she found herself wanting this. His kiss melted her and her shoulders dropped as she gave in to the feeling. *Just a kiss couldn't hurt*, she told herself. He was so soft and gentle with her that she never wanted to stop. Her head spun, and she almost felt dizzy.

Several minutes later, as they were becoming more and more excited, he stopped suddenly and pulled away, leaving them both breathless. They peered into each other's eyes as they communicated without speaking. They wanted more. They didn't want to stop.

Demetri reached up and ran the backs of his fingers down her soft cheek, then pushed his fingers into her hair. She couldn't help but close her eyes.

"It's too soon," he whispered.

"What do you mean?" She opened her eyes again.

"I mean, Candy, I would love nothing more than to get under those covers and make love to you, but it wouldn't be right. I don't want to rush. I feel we should get to know each other better."

She dropped her gaze for a second as she considered his words. She agreed with him. *After all, look at what happened with Dylan.* She found herself nodding as she met his eyes again. "You're right. It's better not to rush into things."

As a defeated air swept over him, Demetri let his hand slide from her face to her shoulder, then down her arm to her hand. He stood, still holding her hand, then kissed it, and finally let go. He went to his bed and crawled under the covers.

He was such a gentleman, wanting to wait like this, that she couldn't help but respect him even more for that. As he had stood from her bed, she noticed the evidence of his body wanting hers, but his mind and his maturity made him strong enough to overcome that urge and stop. Any guy her age would never have said that. This was something to be admired, she thought. Other men could learn a thing or two from him.

"You haven't told me much about your parents, other than that they were inattentive," he asked after pulling the covers over himself.

Candy shrugged quickly, and then spoke. "They did drugs. Your dad drank, and my parents were into drugs. Heroin. It was really big in New York City when they were younger, then they just never stopped. They had always done it, and I don't remember a time when they were not high. Then my brother started using, too, but I refused. I didn't want to be like them. Sometimes I wondered if I was adopted or something, because I was so different. In school, I learned that not all parents did drugs. In fact, none of my friends' parents did drugs. So I spent time at their houses instead of mine. That's where I got my meals. I got free lunch in school, and then I went to my friends' houses at night. Sometimes I would spend the night, but I don't think my parents even knew. Or cared. So I decided I wasn't going to be like them. I was going to be like my friends. They were much happier, and that seemed to be a better life."

"That's admirable, Candy. You're a strong young woman, and I respect your courage to live up to a higher standard."

Candy nodded and considered his words. It was something to be proud of, and she was quite pleased with herself for not following that awful path her parents and brother did.

"Did they…hit you?"

"No. At least I had that. They just didn't pay attention to me. But it wasn't all bad. There were a few minutes here and there when my mother played with me when I was very young. We had some games that I played by myself most of the time. I was both people in the game, you know? And my mom watched me, and sometimes played with me for a few minutes. Then my dad always came and took her away from me."

"She tried. Maybe she was like my mother. Afraid of your dad."

Candy thought for a moment. "Maybe. I never thought of it that way. Maybe he intimidated her. I don't think he ever hit her, though."

"Did they fight a lot? Yelling?"

"Yeah."

"Maybe it was behind closed doors, and you didn't see it. That's how it started with my parents. I didn't know it was happening until he started in on me."

"How old were you when he started beating you?"

"Five. Six, maybe."

Candy shook her head and sighed, feeling sorry for him. "Sounds like you had a much harder childhood than me."

"It was hard, yes. But you suffered from mental abuse while I suffered from physical."

"Definitely. That's what it was." Candy reached up and swiped away a stray tear.

"I don't want to go to bed thinking about miserable things, though. Let's change the subject."

Candy took in a shaky breath left over from crying. "Okay. How? What will we talk about?"

"Horses."

"They saved my life." Candy's face lit with joy.

"Mine, too." They continued to talk until they were both too exhausted to continue, then finally fell asleep.

Chapter Sixteen

"Which horse do you like best?" Demetri asked with a grin.

"Um, I don't know. They're all so beautiful." She then walked down the shedrow spending a few seconds with each horse, rubbing their ears, feeding them mints, patting their necks. It didn't take her long to pick one. She found a beautiful black colt with a white blaze down his nose.

"He seems very well mannered. I can see it in his eyes that he's smart and aware. It's like he understands us."

"That's Shadow Dancer. He has Northern Dancer's sire in his bloodline, Nearctic."

"Wow." She stroked his neck as if touching gold. "He's like royalty, then."

"Yep. Pretty good runner, I think. He's three but was a little late maturing. Never made it to the Triple Crown races but he's improving."

Candy nodded as she peered into the horse's right eye again. "He tells me he wants to run," Candy announced confidently.

"Well, he's telling me he wants you for a groom. What do you think? Would you like that?"

Candy squeaked in excitement and jumped into Demetri's arms. "Oh yes. Thank you."

As Candy brought the black colt to a grassy area to graze, Sherri approached and then stood with her hands on her hips.

"Hey," Candy greeted.

"Hey." Sherri's voice was rough with anger and Candy's heart skipped a beat. Sherri moved closer to Candy and stood right in front of her face. Her eyes burned into Candy's.

"What's wrong?"

"Listen, Miss Perfect, I'm just gonna warn you one time, and one time only. Don't get involved with that man." One finger waved in the air as she spoke.

"Who?"

"You know. Demetri."

"What? Why?"

"He'll just wind up hurting you."

"Well, firstly, we aren't really an item right now. But I'll keep that in mind." Candy turned away.

Sherri followed Candy as she began walking again. "I'm speaking from experience, here, Candice. Not me, but my friend."

"Just because it didn't work with her doesn't mean it wouldn't work with us. We have so much in common. We were both brought up in bad families, and we got away. We both plan on being better people than our parents."

"He's not much better than his parents. But if you think he'll actually change…" Sherri shook her head.

"…then, go right ahead." Sherri dismissively waved her hand.

"Change? He's so sweet."

"Yeah. Now he is." Sherri turned and strode away quickly, so quickly that Candy didn't get a chance to ask her any more questions. *What did she mean by that? Would he change later?* Despite Sherri's warning, Candy wholeheartedly believed that because they had the same sort of upbringing, and a mutual love for horses, they could make it work. He might change with her help. Maybe he had already changed. He had a warm side to him, loving, caring, and protective. Candy would make sure he stayed that way.

The lights were dim in the restaurant, evoking the romantic atmosphere Dylan had mentioned a few months ago. It looked strangely like that restaurant they had been in, too. With the red Tiffany lamps, wood paneled walls, and dark carpeting, it seemed that this was the quintessential modern restaurant décor nowadays. Demetri helped Candy push her chair in, then sat down. She loved how thoughtful he was.

"It seems like everybody already has a place to go tonight. You can stay with me again, if you want," he said after placing his napkin on his lap.

Candy remembered to do the same as Sherri's words from earlier replayed in her mind. "Well, only one night. I don't want to be a burden. I'd like to get my own place."

"Whatever you think is best."

Once their food arrived at their table, it was quiet and Candy felt the urge to fill that silence with conversation. "So, I had an interesting conversation with someone today." Candy cut her chicken properly with her fork and knife, just the way Dylan had taught her.

"Yeah?"

"Yeah. This person, someone who shall remain nameless, warned me about you." Candy grinned and pointed her fork his way. Candy felt a change in the atmosphere and she regretted her joke. The air was heavier, the joy gone from Demetri's face. "Don't worry. I'm a big girl. I make my own decisions."

Demetri sat still and without a word as he stared at Candy, while it was obvious his mind was elsewhere. Candy let him think.

"Where'd you go?" she asked when he landed back in the present again.

"Oh, nowhere. You talked to Sherri, didn't you?" he asked, and then casually took a bite of his chicken. Candy knit her eyebrows slightly.

"Yeah."

Demetri nodded for a few seconds. "Had a bad experience with her friend, that's why. We used to fight like cats and dogs. Never did get along."

"When was this?"

"I guess it ended about, oh, a year ago." He shrugged.

"Ended badly, I take it?"

"That's putting it mildly."

He didn't seem to want to go into details about it, and Candy did not push the issue, as she did not want to pry.

"Shadow seems to like me." Candy changed the subject, hoping to lessen the tension, and knew that any time Demetri talked about his horses, he was happy.

"I can't wait to see him race. He's got the speed, but we just have to figure out if he wants to use it."

"Would be such a shame if he didn't. It would all go to waste, you know?"

"Yes, definitely. His owner is fine with me taking my time training him up for his first race, but at the same time, he keeps asking when Shadow will be ready."

"What do you think? How much longer will it take?"

Demetri took in a long breath and held it for a few seconds, then blew it out. "I think by this fall he will be ready."

"Groovy."

"Groovy?"

"Groovy."

"No one uses that word anymore, little red. You sound like a hippy."

Candy sort of liked his new nickname for her. "Little red," he had called her. That was cute. She was far from little, but she was smaller than his large frame. He wasn't overweight, but big, like a football player. She wondered what sort of nickname she could come up with for him.

After dinner, he took her to his rancher and showed her around. It wasn't a big house, but it had three bedrooms and a garage. In the middle was the kitchen and living room, with the garage on one side and the bedrooms on the other. It was strangely like the house in Maryland; only the outside and roof were different. This one had a Spanish tile roof and stucco siding, while the house in Maryland had plain black shingles and aluminum siding.

"The insides of both your homes look remarkably similar," Candy pointed out as she inspected the place from her spot.

Demetri nodded and winked. "You noticed, huh? I used the same blueprints, but changed the outside."

"Oh wow."

"Saved some money that way."

"Oh, I see. Good idea."

"Want the same room?" he asked as he headed down the hallway toward her room.

"Sure."

They put her things in her room and then went to the living room to rest.

"Long day." Demetri sighed and lowered into his plush couch.

Candy sat on the opposite end of the couch, then took off her shoes and curled her legs under her. The furniture here was much more comfortable than in the Maryland house. She knew he must spend more time in Florida than in Maryland. "Feels good to sit down," she said as she massaged her back with her hand.

"Your back hurt?"

"A little. All that lifting yesterday, and driving, sitting in the car, and then having to lift all that weight again, I'm not used to it."

"You need some muscle. I've got some weight equipment in the garage if you ever want to use it."

"Are you serious?"

"Yeah, sure. Why not?"

"Well, I don't know. I guess that would help, huh?"

"Sure would. Here. Come here, let me get that for you," he said, waving her toward him.

"Huh?" She was hesitant but moved closer to him.

"Turn around," he said as he touched her shoulder.

"Oh, okay." She wasn't sure about this, but when Demetri began rubbing her shoulders, then her back, and down to her lower back, she couldn't help but grab a pillow, lean forward, and let him work his magic. His hands were strong, and he knew exactly which muscles were hurting her. She moaned with relief as he worked out kinks in her lower back with his thumbs.

After a long while, she sat up and then turned to thank him. She smiled first and then gave him a quick kiss on the cheek.

"You're so sweet."

"You're the one who's sweet, like candy," he purred, then scooted closer and took her into his arms. She let it go that she had heard that line a million times, and wrapped her arms around his strong shoulders as she leaned in to kiss him. Their tongues danced and their hands wandered. His kiss melted her and made her feel warm all over. He slid his hands up her sides and under her shirt, and then slipped it over her head. Within seconds, her bra was unhooked and off as well. His kisses felt good not only on her lips, but on the rest of her body, too. She sighed as goose bumps decorated her skin.

She lifted his shirt and ran her fingers through his thick chest hair and down to his waist. She wondered if his large build also meant he was big everywhere, but she didn't wait long to find out, as she found her way into his khaki pants. He moaned as she touched him, and she wasn't disappointed. In just a few moments, the rest of their clothes were tossed onto the floor, and she was moving sensuously over his lap.

Only six hours later, the alarm went off in Demetri's room and was answered with two low groans, one from each of them.

"I'm getting too old for this." Demetri's voice was so low that he didn't sound like himself.

"Thirty-four is not old." Candy stretched her arms over her head.

"When is your birthday, anyway?" he asked as he ran his hands over her prone body. She closed her eyes, enjoying his touch for nearly a minute before she could answer.

"July fifteenth."

"We'll have to celebrate, then," he said before planting kisses on her neck. He lifted himself over her and she reached for him, opened herself, and pulled him in.

At work, they smiled at each other, giving knowing glances from time to time. They tried to be discreet, but by the end of the day, she found herself under his arm and wrapped around his chest. Then Candy caught sight of Sherri walking by and shaking her head.

Just before Sherri was about to leave that evening, Candy caught up to her and stopped her with one hand on her arm. "Hey, Sherri."

Sherri peered down at Candy's hand, and Candy let go. "Hey."

"I um, it looked like, well, we couldn't help it. I think it's going to get serious with him, Sherri. But don't be mad. I think it will work with us."

"I'm not mad. I just didn't want to see you get hurt, that's all."

"I'll be careful."

Sherri looked at the ground and pursed her lips, then walked away with her head lowered.

Candy knit her eyebrows as Demetri walked up to her and put his hands on her shoulders. He squeezed, making Candy moan involuntarily. "You keep moaning like that and we won't make it all the way home," he whispered into her ear.

"You are so sexy." She eyed his body up and down.

They skipped dinner and went straight to his house. They made it as far as the living room, and then the kitchen, where he had tossed her onto the counter first. Then they were back in his bed again, where they stayed for the night.

Again, she found that her current man was better than the last. Each one seemed to get better and better. Or was it her? Improving her skills between the sheets? With Dylan, she had finally found the ultimate satisfaction, or so she thought. However, Demetri knew ways to excite her that Dylan never knew, and that Candy hadn't even heard of before. Demetri was experienced, and she had never been happier.

The idea of finding her own place vanished once they realized they were never going to separate themselves. They were stuck together, always touching, always gazing at each other with intense desire, and everyone at the track knew it.

Sherri kept her distance from Candy. Candy knew the two of them couldn't be friends. And other girl friends? There were not many to choose from, and those who were there didn't seem to like her. There was a girl named "Jo," who exercised horses in the mornings, and another girl nicknamed "Bubbles," but Candy had no idea what her real name was. They didn't spend much time with Candy, and for the longest time, she couldn't figure out why.

It took about a month of Candy trying to get close to them, starting conversations, trying to be friendly, joining in while they stood around the barn talking, before Candy decided to give up. The girls would glance at Candy but never include her. It was obvious they didn't want her around. She wondered if they were jealous. Maybe they wanted Demetri. Maybe they were upset with her because she had been given one of his favorite horses to groom. She really didn't have to work her way up the ladder like the others. She had spent only a week walking horses before she was given a horse to groom.

It drove her crazy, though, because it was as though she was back at the modeling agency again with the stuck-up girls. Only now, she felt they saw her as the stuck-up one. But she wasn't, and it was frustrating that they thought that way about her.

So she tried befriending the guys and had better luck. They were much friendlier and loved to laugh at things and have a good time while working. That's what she loved. She considered herself one of the guys.

Chapter Seventeen

"Shadow, my buddy," Candy called softly as she entered his stall. It was his first race day, and she hoped he was going to win. His works had been excellent, and he had been worked hard. He was in top shape and ready to run, and he seemed to know that today was a big day for him. He whinnied loudly to greet her, and she kissed his nose and fed him a mint. "You're my best buddy, aren't you?"

"I'm your best buddy." Demetri's soft voice came from just outside the stall.

"Yes, you are." Candy moved over to give him a kiss. "He's ready to race today. He told me."

"He did, did he?"

"Uh huh." After an affirmative nod, Candy took out her hoof pick and began cleaning his feet.

"He's going to go for a jog this morning with Sherri. She'll be by soon to pick him up."

"Okay. I'll have him ready."

Demetri tapped the wooden wall of the stall twice, then left. Candy quickly brushed her horse down, making sure he was beautiful for his morning work. Today, all eyes were on him, and he had to be perfect. *Good looking horses get the money*, Demetri always said. Bettors bet on the healthiest and most aware horses. They had to be on their toes, but not too much. They had to be clean and shiny, with their muscles visible under their coats. Their hooves had to be perfect. No cracks. She polished his hooves, then wrapped his legs, and was finishing up when Sherri came to the stall.

"Ready?" Sherri asked.

"Yeah." Candy stood up straight and ran the crook of her elbow down her face. Sherri came in, and Candy helped her tack up the horse and then gave her a leg up. Candy led Shadow out of the stall and toward the gap in the rail that led to the track. There was a constant flow of horses in and out of the gap, and sometimes a line as people and horses waited for their time slot. Candy walked Shadow in circles as they waited for seven o'clock.

"So how are things with Demetri?" Sherri asked bluntly.

Candy was surprised the girl had actually spoken to her and widened her eyes at Sherri. "Fine. Things are great. We're very happy."

"Mm," Sherri answered, diverting her gaze.

It was quiet for a minute while Candy struggled to decide if she should ask the question that had been bugging her for so long. Then it slipped out before she was ready and before she could figure out the best way to word it. "Why don't you guys like me?"

"What?"

Candy sighed as she lowered her gaze to the ground. "Never mind."

"No. Wait a minute. Are you really asking that question? You really care?"

Candy gave her an incredulous glare. "You guys hate me, and I don't know why. Is it because I'm with Demetri?"

"You don't get it."

"No. I don't. That's why I'm asking."

"You're just not one of us. That's all."

The guard then allowed them to walk to the track, and Sherri left Candy standing by the fence.

Here she was again on the outside. Would she ever find girls for friends? Or would she be doomed to the boys' club for the rest of her life? Not that it was all that bad. The guys were a lot of fun. However, a girlfriend would be fun, too. Then again, maybe not these girls. They were not like her at all. Candy felt like such a girl around them, and so feminine. They were masculine with short hair and deep voices. And they even walked like guys with that little bounce guys all do. She didn't understand them. She definitely wasn't one of them. That was the truth. She had to accept it.

Once Shadow had worked and was washed and put back in his stall, all they had to do was wait for the fifth race. Demetri was busy as usual in the afternoons, and he had the stable running like a well-oiled machine. Everyone knew their jobs and did them to the best of their abilities, mostly because they wanted to. They loved their jobs, though they did not pay well. Candy understood that aspect of the business all too well. Still, this was much more rewarding to her than modeling.

It was most rewarding when your horse won, and she couldn't help but have high hopes for Shadow Dancer as she led him to the paddock for his first race. Butterflies tickled her stomach, as she was nervous and excited for him at the same time. She knew his jockey probably was not. This jockey rode in almost every race and very often rode for Demetri. He was a veteran rider, and Candy knew this was routine for him.

She held Shadow still as Demetri saddled up his horse and the jockey stood back watching. Candy couldn't help the smile permanently imprinted on her face. Demetri didn't seem happy, but she knew he was probably thinking about race strategy. So she tried to stay out of the way and not talk. Her only way of communicating was to smile at everyone, and those who passed by greeted her with their own smiles.

"Riders up," called the paddock judge.

Their jockey marched over, and Candy couldn't help but smile at him, too. He returned her expression and nodded just before grabbing the horse's mane and holding his leg out for Demetri to boost him up.

"You're gonna win today, buddy," Candy softly told her horse as she led him around the walking ring. She inspected him one more time just to make sure he was perfect, and he was. She knew she had done a good job with him and felt proud to be part of his team.

Demetri had withdrawn, though, and was quiet as he walked next to the horse. Candy wondered if he was nervous or upset about something, and she kept her distance. They walked silently around the circle, through the tunnel, and onto the track, where Candy handed Shadow over to the pony girl. Without a word, Demetri hopped into the stands and went to his box, while Candy made her way closer to the winner's circle. Just in case.

She couldn't see the race very well, as it had started in the backstretch. But as she listened for Shadow's name, she grew more and more excited as the race progressed. Shadow was running well and swallowing up ground quickly as the pack of horses shot around the far turn and into the homestretch. Shadow was gaining on the leader and was only a few lengths behind. Candy jumped up and down, screaming for him. "Come on, buddy!"

When he finally passed the leader, she threw both arms into the air and jumped high enough for a slam dunk. It took everything in her power to stand still while he galloped out and came back. Having gone as far onto the track as she was allowed, she stood impatiently, hopping from time to time as she awaited his arrival. Finally, the outrider brought Shadow to her, and she clipped the lead line onto his bridle.

"You did it." She patted his sweaty neck, displacing spittles of foam from his coat. He was breathing hard, his eyes were huge with excitement, and she knew he wanted to run even more. "You gotta save some for your next race, big guy." Then she held up her hand toward the jockey. He slapped it and they cheered together. "Good job."

Demetri was there soon and was finally happy. She was glad to see a smile on his face and knew that he was probably nervous before. That was all over now. She glanced at him after their picture was taken and wanted to jump into his arms for a big kiss, but she knew she had to restrain herself in front of the fans.

They went back to the barn and the hotwalker took Shadow to walk him. Candy went to get the brushes, soap, and water ready for him. Demetri came over to her and took a deep breath.

"Hey," she shouted when she saw him, and ran to him. She flung her arms around his shoulders and kissed his cheek. "He did it. We won."

Demetri smiled politely and nodded, but he didn't say a word. He tried to pull away, but she wouldn't let go. So he relented and put his arms around her again.

"What's wrong?" she said softly into his ear, keeping her words private.

"Nothing. It's nothing."

"I love you." Candy kissed him gently.

He smiled, kissed her, and then answered. "You promise?"

"Of course." Candy made sure to catch his eyes.

He nodded and then replied, "I love you, too."

She squeezed him, letting her head rest on his shoulder. He let out a breath of air and gently rubbed her back.

"We'll celebrate big tonight," Candy said just before he pulled away and left. Now he seemed happy, and she was relieved. Whatever the problem was, she had negated it.

Back at home for the evening, they ate in, Candy making dinner as Demetri watched television. For a moment, it felt eerily like the situation with Dylan. However, Demetri never got on her case about keeping the house clean or making dinner. If she didn't feel like making dinner, they went out. It took all the pressure off, making it more fun for her to cook whenever she wanted.

After eating, they sat on the couch together with his arm around her. She ran her fingers through the chest hair sticking out of his tank top. "You're my furry teddy bear."

He kissed the top of her head then ran his fingers through her long ginger hair. "So, uh," he started, then stopped.

Candy waited patiently, but when he didn't continue, she gazed up at him.

"Never mind." He stopped himself from saying more.

"You can tell me anything, Demetri." She feathered her fingers up his thigh, hoping to relax him.

"You're only in love with me, right?" he asked. Candy felt his hand shake a little.

She sat up and opened her mouth, but wasn't sure exactly what to say. Finally, she managed to find words. "Of course, Demetri. Of course. Why would you even think…oh, my gosh, Demetri. I'm only in love with you. I promise."

Demetri nodded as he let out a breath of air. "I love you, too."

"I don't know what I did to make you think that, though. Tell me, and I won't do it again. I'm so sorry."

"Oh, it's nothing. It was just in the paddock today, you seemed to be flirting–,"

Candy stopped him with her hand on his chest. "Oh no. I was just so happy that I couldn't wipe the smile from my face. I was so excited for Shadow. I knew he was going to win, and I couldn't wait to get to the winner's circle. I wasn't flirting with anyone. Oh, my goodness, Demetri. It was so exciting." She bounced up and down next to him.

"It was."

"I can't wait until he races again. When is he running again?"

"Couple weeks, I think. I'll have to look over the books when I get back to work tomorrow. We'll get him in an allowance race. Make some more money."

"Groovy." He always laughed when she said that word. Then she let her head fall onto his chest again.

That night after making love, Candy thought it was time to sleep, but Demetri had other ideas. "Hey, Can."

"Yeah?"

"Hey, um, will you let me, um, you know. Do that thing? You know. Just to make it up to me."

Oh, oh. That meant doing the thing she hated most. So, she stalled. "Thing? What thing?"

"You know. Back door thing."

"Well, I guess. Just to make it up to you."

"Man, I love you, Can. You're the best." He leapt from the bed and grabbed a condom and KY Jelly.

As usual, she hated it and was unable to even pretend to enjoy it, but she did it for him. She went to sleep sore, while he slept behind her, sated and relaxed.

Certainly, she knew that he had to be more insecure than she had originally thought. It must have been because of his parents. Like him, she felt insecure at times and had to tell herself she was being silly. Sometimes she went a bit too far with it, though, such as with Dylan.

She had found herself doing things for Dylan to make him happy so he wouldn't leave her. Sometimes she did things for him for the tiny bit of attention he gave her afterward. When he didn't notice things she did for him at all, it made her try all that much harder. However, all that did was get her stuck in a routine of giving him everything he wanted while denying herself. She hadn't realized this until she was out of that relationship.

Now, here she was with a man much like herself – insecure. She knew she should try harder to make him feel better about himself and to make doubly sure he knew how dedicated she was to him. So far, he was the best thing that had ever happened to her. He had been so kind and supportive. Never a cross word to her. Never bossy. It was the opposite of Dylan and was quite refreshing.

Long ago, she had moved her things into his room, and he had been excited to share his room with her. This is what she thought might be normal for a relationship of two people living together. As she lay in the bed with Demetri's arm around her, she listened to his breathing as she inspected the room. There was an even mixture of her things and his things. Her magic box sat on top of a tall dresser that he had cleaned out for her to use.

"What's in it?" he had asked.

"Nothing."

"Oh. I thought it might be a dead relative or something. People keep ashes, you know."

"Ha. No. This was my mom's. Only thing I have left of her."

That was the end of that conversation. She was glad he hadn't asked too much about it. She really didn't want to talk about it.

Tonight, as she lay there staring at it, she wondered if she was ever going to find the nerve to open it, or to keep anything inside. *Not yet.*

Two weeks later, Shadow was racing again. Candy tried to appear less excited this time. She made sure not to so much as catch sight of another man this time. No one in the male species made it into her line of sight, except Demetri. Occasionally, she winked at him, blew him kisses, and always smiled at him, and only him. He seemed to appreciate the difference and seemed much happier this time. She also managed to squeeze in a quick "I love you" before he left her for the stands.

She handed the horse over to the pony girl and made her way toward the winner's circle again. From there, she peered up into the stands to find Demetri standing tall with his binoculars pointed toward the starting gate. The announcer came over the loudspeaker and announced that the horses were in and ready to go. Candy held her breath.

With a distant ring, the gates opened in the backstretch again, and the announcer reported that Shadow Dancer was taking the lead. Candy clapped her hands and paced nervously as the horses continued around the track. Finally, she saw him. Shadow was running his heart out, was still in the lead, and began pulling away. She cheered, jumping and screaming as he swept under the wire in first place.

Again, she met up with the horse, walked him for a few minutes to cool him, and then took him to the winner's circle for his photo. She stood proudly at his head, with Demetri on the other side of her. After the photo, Candy faced Demetri. "We did it again."

Demetri patted Candy's back, and they walked back to the barn together with the proud owners.

"Two wins in a row. I can't believe it," Candy said as she stood holding her plastic cup of champagne.

"Of course. I never had a doubt." Demetri cheered and then raised his glass. Everyone held his or hers up as well.

One of the owners filled everyone's plastic cups again with champagne. Candy didn't like it and kept pouring hers into Demetri's cup, and Demetri gladly accepted it. By the time the party was over, he was drunk.

"He's gonna win next time, too," Demetri shouted over the small crowd. It was the tenth time he had shouted that tonight, and by now, no one reacted to it anymore. "You hear me?" He tugged on one of the other grooms from the barn. The groom shrugged him off and walked away.

Sherri and Jo stood by, their faces scrunched with concern. Candy had seen Demetri drunk plenty of times. She could handle him. It wasn't that bad. He was only a little obnoxious. She had to get him in bed, that's all.

"We should go," Candy suggested.

"No, way, Can. It's party time," he bellowed in return and walked away.

Sherri nonchalantly walked behind Candy, and as she passed her, Sherri leaned into Candy. "Meet us in the office." Candy watched Sherri walking away, and wondered why she had said such a thing. But Demetri was stumbling around, leaning on people, cachinnating, and Candy saw her chance to break away. They slid away and into the office.

"What's up?" Candy saw Jo sitting at Demetri's desk and Sherri standing nearby.

"Can you handle him when he's drunk like that? 'Cause we'll take care of him if you want."

"No, thank you." Candy crossed her arms. He was her boyfriend. Her responsibility. Not another girl's.

"We're not trying to hit on him. Lord, no. We're just trying to help. But if you got it…" Sherri held up one hand and ducked her head.

"I got it." Candy walked away, anxious to check on Demetri. A few steps from the door, she turned back to see Sherri and Jo standing together in the office doorway. Candy narrowed her eyes at them for a second but then turned away again.

Demetri didn't want to go, but everybody else did and wound up leaving one by one. Finally, the last two at the barn left, and she was able to convince him to go home. It was easy to snag the keys from his pocket, as his reaction time was extremely slow. He was very drunk this time, and she knew it was partially her fault for dumping her drinks into his all night.

"Where's my keysh?" he asked as they approached the car. He stumbled. She walked.

"I'll drive." She opened the door and got into the driver's side. Demetri stepped next to the door, blocking her from closing it.

"Uh, no. You're Lucy, remember? You can't drive."

"I know how to get to the house. I'll be okay. Better than you driving drunk. You could kill someone."

"Ha. I always drive like thish. I can handle it, Can. I know what I'm doing. I can tell."

"I'm not moving." She crossed her arms in front of her, making sure to hide the keys from him.

"Move it!" He grabbed her arm and pulled her from the car. She screamed as she fell onto the gravel parking lot, and a rock cut open her hand. She picked up her hand and watched blood drip down her palm.

"I have to...Oh no. I have to go clean...Oh no," she stammered, then scrambled to her feet and ran back to the barn.

"Get back here with my keysh!" But Candy had run off for some first aid supplies.

By the time he caught up to her, she had rinsed off her hand and wrapped a bandage around it. Blood seeped through, making her wonder if she needed stitches.

"Let me see," he said gently. She peeked up at him, and he seemed calmer now, more rational, and she wondered if he realized that he had caused this. She held up her palm. "Is it deep?"

"Yeah."

"I know a doc. He can fix you up in a jiffy."

"Really? At the hospital?"

"No, his houshe," Demetri answered, snickering, as if it were funny. "He's got an office in his houshe."

"Can we go there?"

"Sure, Can. Let's go."

When they got back to the car, she stopped before getting in this time. "Only if you let me drive. I never get to. You said I could drive," she added, hoping he believed her.

"All right, all right, ginger bear. You drive."

"You have to tell me where the doctor is, though."

"Gotcha." Finally, he got into the passenger side of the car.

As he guided her through several wrong turns, Candy drove patiently, hoping they made it to this doctor's house before dark. It was going to be much harder to drive in the dark, especially driving with one hand. During their excursion, he only gave directions and didn't talk about anything else, but that was fine with her. She didn't feel much like talking.

Finally, they pulled up to the doctor's house and parked in front. "Think it's all right to come in unannounced?" She turned off the motor.

"Oh yeah. Come on." He opened the door and stepped out with a stumble. Candy also stepped out of the car and closed the door. She made her way around to his side and shut his door as well, as he had walked away without closing it. "Oops," he muttered as he noticed, then snickered.

They stood on the front porch with Candy holding her hand up, trying to keep it above her heart to prevent it from bleeding too much. The palm of her hand was entirely red now, and blood had smeared onto the open areas of her palm. She bit back tears.

"You're going to just say you fell, okay?" Demetri said. Candy blinked as she turned toward him, and just then, the door opened.

"Demetri, my friend." A black-haired man with a thick accent greeted them. They kissed each other's cheeks, and the doctor invited them inside.

"And who is this lovely young lady?"

"Uh, this is Candy. Candy, this is Doctor Slavin. Old friend of mine."

"Oh, yeah. We go way back. What seems to be the trouble? I see blood."

Candy stood, open mouthed and as still as a statue as she stared into the doctor's eyes.

"Yeah, she uh, fell on the parking lot at the track. Wanted to know if you'd look at it and see if she needs stitches."

"Oh, gladly." The doctor led a flabbergasted Candy and a jovial Demetri further into the house. They went into a room with a table and some medical equipment. Dr. Slavin had Candy sit on the table, and he put a piece of plastic over her pants to keep the blood from dripping onto them. Then he unwrapped her hand. Candy closed her eyes and turned her head after glancing at the cut. She couldn't tell what was what through all the blood.

As he examined it, she flinched and grunted in pain a few times but tried to be strong and brave. He finally made a decision. "Yeah. I'm going to sew this up. Sorry, Candy. Looks like you cut yourself up pretty good."

She glared at Demetri, who stood with a sheepish grin but didn't say anything.

Candy whimpered and cried as the doctor cleaned the wound area and numbed her hand with a few shots. She wasn't sure if she was more upset about the painful shots of Novocain, or that Demetri had done this to her and was hiding it. While the drug was taking effect, the doctor brought out his curved needle and black thread. She couldn't believe he was going to sew her hand back together. She'd never had stitches before.

"You've got one long one here, about an inch long, and we'll just put that back together and you should be all set."

Candy still didn't say a word, but she turned her head away as he stitched up her hand carefully. He cleaned it one more time and then wrapped it with bandages.

"Come back in a week, and I'll take them out. Or you can if you want. You just cut them and pull them out. No big deal."

"I can do that," Demetri offered.

"Yeah, he's done it before," the doctor answered. It made Candy wonder how many times he had done it, and why. Had he hurt other girls before?

Was this what Sherri meant when she said I would get hurt?

Candy hyperventilated and passed out before she realized what was happening. She woke up again lying flat on the table. She saw Demetri above her, and the fear returned.

"No," she whimpered. "No, please."

"No, what?" Demetri asked with a misplaced grin. "Come on, Can. Let's get you home. I'll take good care of you. I'll draw up a bath for you, I'll rub your shoulders. I'll take good care of you, Can."

"Keep that hand dry, though."

"Got it."

Shaking, but powerless to do anything but go with him, she sat up. She swayed a bit, and they caught her. Dr. Slavin and Demetri made small talk while she regained her bearings. Once she was ready, she stood up. Demetri took her arm and led her to the front door.

"You going to be okay to drive?" Dr. Slavin called to Candy as they walked down the front walkway.

"Yeah." Candy did not turn to face him.

"Sure you don't want him to drive?"

"She says I'm too drunk. She's right. She's absolutely right. I shouldn't be driving."

"Okay. You two have fun. Take good care of your girl, Demetri."

"You got it," he replied, then opened his door and fell into the seat. Candy went around to her side and got behind the wheel.

As tears slipped down her face, she drove home, wondering how to leave him. *Now what?* Now she was even further from home. She had nowhere to go. Her money was still in the bank, but she might have a hard time getting to it, as she had never taken it out of her account before leaving Maryland.

"You crying?" Demetri asked softly as they pulled up to his house. He reached over to touch a stray tear, but she pulled away.

"No," she bellowed, then got out of the car and stormed inside. She threw the keys onto the kitchen counter and went to her old bedroom to hide. She heard him come inside the house and close the door.

"Can? Come on, Can. I'm sorry. It was an accident, Can."

Don used to call me that.

"I'm sorry, Can. I will take care of you. Okay? I'll make it up to you. Just give me a chance," he said through her door. "Can I come in? Please?"

She wasn't sure what to do but began breathing quickly again. In order to avoid passing out, she leaned over. This hurt her hand, so she sat up again. There was no comfortable position, no answer, no way out.

"Can? Please?"

There was no getting rid of him, at least not for now. "Fine!"

He came into the room, his apologetic eyes meeting her angry eyes. "Please, Candy. My sweet Candy," he purred, his voice just loud enough to be heard over the blood swirling in her head. He touched her arm so softly and gently that it instantly took some of her anger from her. When he touched her again, the anger faded even more. He let his hand drift down her bare arm to her injured hand, and then picked it up. As she continued to sit on the bed, he stood before her, leaned over, and kissed the back of her hand.

Then he sat down next to her and gently touched her chin, bringing her face toward his. "I love you," he whispered, then kissed her softly the way she liked and the way it melted her every time. Finally, she relented and kissed him despite the taste of champagne in his mouth. *It's not that bad*, she thought. *It's kind of sweet, actually.*

That night, she didn't have to move a muscle. He tasted every inch of her body, sending her into a whirlwind of ecstasy and desire. Everything she needed, he gave her. An hour later, she found herself sated, happy, relaxed, and in love, as he held her in his arms and cuddled behind her.

"What happened?" Sherri asked, alarmed as she saw Candy's hand.

"I fell in the parking lot."

Sherri glared at her.

"What?"

"Did he do that?" Sherri asked bluntly, and loudly, too. Candy shushed her and looked around.

"No," Candy whispered.

Sherri waited for more, but Candy wasn't giving. "Candy, tell me the truth. What happened? If he hurt you –"

"No, Sherri. It wasn't like that. It was an accident, that's all."

"What kind of accident?"

"The kind where I fell and landed on a pointy rock in the parking lot. Like I said."

"You'd tell me if he ever hurt you?"

"Of course."

"I hope you're telling me the truth. I'd love nothing more than to put his ass in jail."

"Why?"

"He hurt my friend, that's why. She had to move away because of him."

"What did he do?"

"Beat the shit out of her, that's what he did."

"Demetri? He's so gentle."

"Not when he's drunk."

That, she knew was true. When that realization hit her, Sherri saw it all over Candy's face.

Sherri nodded. "I knew it. He did it. He probably pushed you down, didn't he?"

"No. Okay? He was drunk, and he wanted to drive. He pulled on my arm to get me out of the driver's seat, but I pulled back. I lost my balance and fell out of the car. It wasn't entirely his fault, Sherri."

She stood staring intently into Candy's eyes for several long seconds. "If he touches you again, I'll kill him," Sherri muttered under her breath and then walked away. Her words made Candy's knees quake.

Demetri walked up just then and saw the fear in her eyes. "Hey, sugar." He kissed the top of her head and wrapped his arms around her. He rubbed her back as she rested her head against his chest. Her favorite spot in the whole world was right here, like this. "You okay?"

"Better now."

Chapter Eighteen

"I know when I drink I get too rough. So from now on, I will try not to drink so much. All right? I'll listen if you say I need to stop next time. Will you help me?"

"Of course."

"I don't think I'm an alcoholic because I don't have to drink all the time. It's just when we have parties or celebrations. But I will be more careful, all right? I know I shouldn't drink so much. It's gotten me into trouble before."

"What kind of trouble?" Her heart beat hard against her chest, and she hoped he couldn't tell.

"Well, I mean, you know. Accidents happen. I really didn't mean to pull on you that hard, Can. I just don't know my own strength when I'm drunk. So, things happen."

"Like what?"

Demetri released a resigned sigh. "Well, with my last girlfriend, the one Sherri mentioned, I accidently bumped into her and her head hit the wall. Of course, everybody thought I hit her. Then she lied and said I hit her, but I didn't. It was an accident. I just couldn't see straight because I was so drunk. But if I can keep from getting drunk, I won't be so clumsy."

"Okay." It made sense to her, since things only happened when he was drunk. And then the girl had lied to everyone. No wonder Sherri hated him so much. Besides, as he said, if he stayed sober, nothing would happen. "Maybe we should throw out the rum in the kitchen?"

"Well, I think it should be all right to drink. Just not too much. And if you say stop, I'll stop. I promise. No exceptions."

"Promise?"

"Promise." He held out his pinkie, and she hooked hers around it.

Demetri avoided alcohol all together for a few weeks. The weather was cooling, the humidity was finally releasing them from its heaviness, and it seemed all of Miami had breathed a collective sigh of relief. Candy was also relieved that Demetri was not drinking.

So far, they hadn't been to any parties or winner's celebrations, though he had won plenty of races. When they finally decided to go to a party, Candy dreaded every moment leading up to it.

"How do I look?" Candy stood in front of the mirror admiring her Cat Woman costume.

"Damn, woman!" His exuberance prompted a blush from Candy. "I don't know about this. You might have every tom cat on the block following you around tonight."

"Well, I'll make sure they know who I'm with, Batman."

"That's right." He took his place next to her and inspected his own costume. He wrapped his arm around her waist and kissed the side of her neck.

"I can't believe it's late October and it's still warm. Back home, we'd be in coats already." Candy sat down in the car and Demetri closed the door, then got in his side.

"That's why we're here, my dear." From the driver's seat, he couldn't take his eyes off her tight black body suit. He shook his head, and she lightly tapped his arm.

"Come on, super hero. Let's go to the party."

Finally, he took a deep breath, calmed himself, and started the car. They drove just a few miles away to the home of another trainer who lived near Hialeah. They parked as close as they were able, but the street was lined with cars. "Everybody's here already."

"We're just fashionably late. We'll make a big entrance."

They heard loud voices inside and in the back yard and decided to walk into the house without knocking. As they walked in and closed the door, their host came out of nowhere and greeted them.

"Demetri. Candy. You guys look amazing. Hey, everyone, check this out!" Grant shouted into the crowd.

Candy smiled nervously, as did Demetri, while the others stared at them with wide eyes. Candy noticed every man's eyes on her and instantly felt self-conscious. She wanted to wrap herself in a huge coat and hide. Apparently, Demetri noticed as well.

"They're all looking at you, sexy mama," he said softly into her ear.

"Can I hide behind your big muscular chest and cape?" she asked with a small voice. She wrapped her arms around his waist and slid herself under his cape to hide.

"Don't be nervous, my dear. But if anyone touches you, you let me know. I'll take care of 'em."

Candy nodded, a bit apprehensive about spending the evening avoiding leering looks from other men. She thought it would be a fun costume, as it matched Demetri's, and while she knew it was sort of sexy, she didn't think she would get this much attention.

"Want a drink?" Demetri's eyes lit with joy as he pulled away. She shook her head without a word. She didn't want him to drink either, but she remembered their talk a month or so ago about when to stop. He promised to stop whenever she said to. She hoped and prayed he would live up to his word.

While Demetri was getting a drink, Candy made her way to a group of people. Sherri and Jo stood with a group of other women, and when Candy approached, they inspected her up and down. She thought women would be safe to be around. Apparently not. Candy tried to blow it off. "Oh, come on. It can't be that bad, is it?"

"Whew," Jo said and then diverted her eyes. Sherri was stunned but didn't say a word.

Candy tried to keep her reply low. "Maybe I need a cape to wrap around myself." Sherri and Jo nodded silently.

Finally able to work her way into the conversation, she started to feel more comfortable. Demetri came by and handed her a cup of water, but then left her again to find other friends.

As the night wore on, Demetri was becoming louder and louder, and Candy got some urging glares from other people as if they wanted her to control him. Controlling him was impossible, but she figured she might be able to seduce him and get him to leave.

"Hey, baby," Candy purred as she wrapped herself around him again.

"My hot girlfriend. Boys, this is Can, I mean, Cat Woman. My hot girlfriend. She's hot."

"I see that," one of the other men said, ogling Candy.

"But she's mine." Demetri pushed the other man away.

"Okay, okay." The man put up his hands, then walked away.

"Can we go home? I'm so tired." Candy touched her cold fingers to her heated cheeks.

"We're just getting started, Can. You want to leave now? It's just now starting to get fun." The smell of the liquor on his breath made her stomach turn, and she wished desperately he would never drink again. She knew that would never happen.

"Remember a couple months ago when, you know, I hurt my hand?"

"Yeah?"

"You promised me you would stop drinking whenever I said it was time to stop. And well, I think it's time to stop. You're getting too drunk."

"I am not," he insisted, pulling away from her.

"You are, honey. You promised me. Please? Please stop? I don't want anyone to get hurt. Namely me."

"I would never hurt you, Can Can. I love you."

"You said accidents happen when you drink too much. Remember?"

Demetri relented. "I guess."

"I think we should get some sleep anyway. Five o'clock comes awful early when you've been partying the night before. I'll let you strip this tight leather pantsuit from my body, if you want."

"Oh, man," he growled, then wrapped his arm around her waist again. "First let me say goodbye to everyone."

"Goodbyes, then we go home and give in to our animalistic needs," she moaned directly into his ear, making him shiver with excitement.

"Hey, guys! I'm going now," Demetri shouted over the crowd. Candy faked a smile as everyone stared at him with puzzled expressions. She then saw relief build in their eyes.

Candy waved as she directed Demetri to the front door. "Can I drive again?"

"Naw. I can drive. I'm not drunk." He took out his keys. She didn't want to argue, didn't want to upset him, so she hoped he was sober enough to drive.

They drove home slowly and carefully, with Demetri peering intently over the steering wheel. "Gotta be extra careful." She knew he was trying to make sure he didn't appear drunk and get pulled over. Meanwhile, she had a death grip on the door handle inside the car and clenched her jaw. Finally, they made it home, safe and sound. Candy pried her hand from the door and let her shoulders drop.

She helped him through the front door and began untying his cape. As she pulled it from his back, he walked into the kitchen.

"I'm hungry." He began grabbing things from the cabinet. Potato chips, peanut butter, crackers… "Are you hungry?" Then he started toward the liquor cabinet.

"Hungry for you," she purred softly, hoping he wouldn't reach for the bottle of rum. But he did. She put her hand on it, and moved closer to him. "I want you," she tried again, this time in her sexiest and huskiest voice.

"One more?"

"You don't need it, baby. I love you just the way you are." She reached for his chest and ran her fingers over the hard plastic costume. Then, she let her fingers drift down, but he stopped her and pushed her out of the way, making a clear path to the glasses.

Without a word, he poured himself a drink, then leaned back on the counter and reached out for her. She stood her ground. He waved his hands for her to come to him, but she refused and stood still. "Come on, Can."

"You want that drink more than you want me?" she asked with her bottom lip in a pout as she peered through her eyelashes.

"Ha. You're kidding, right? This drink makes me a better lover, my dear. You will be quite pleased tonight."

Candy had her doubts.

Demetri took a long sip of his drink, and then held out his hands again for her. Still, she refused, this time turning her back and heading for the kitchen table.

He rushed toward her, grabbing her from behind, and picked her up by her waist. She screamed as he carried her to the living room and threw her onto the couch. "You like it rough, don't you?"

"No!" She tried to roll herself off the couch, but he pounced on top of her, pinning her. "Get off me!"

"You just said you wanted me. Now you don't? Make up your damned mind, woman." Still, he did not move.

"You're drunk, Demetri. I don't want you drunk. I want you sober." Candy struggled again, but he had wrapped his hands around her wrists.

"Well, you're going to have to wait, because that ain't happening any time soon, my love." His sour breath filled her nostrils and burned. She turned her head.

It was silent for a few seconds as she grimaced. The expected alcohol-laced kiss never came. Instead, he released her and sat on the couch at her feet. Stunned, she lay still for a few seconds and then got up. Before she could walk away, he grabbed her again and pulled her onto his lap. "Do me like this, baby." He unzipped her costume.

At this point, she was afraid to argue with him, but she certainly wasn't in the mood anymore. Then again, she also knew he might get angry with her if she didn't try. So she let him slip off her costume and touch her. He groaned as she stood before him in her underwear and then slipped down her panties.

"You want me?"

No, she thought, but tried to fake it. She helped him get his costume off and pretended to want him. He was silent as she slipped onto his lap.

"What's the matter, Can?"

"Nothing. Keep going." She pushed her hips into him again and again, wishing it were over.

"I can tell. Something's wrong. What is it?"

"Nothing, okay? Just...let's just –,"

Before she could finish her thought, he shoved her from his lap and she fell onto the coffee table, hitting her back against the edge, then slid onto the floor. The pain nearly took her breath away. He stood up, shook his costume from his ankles and walked away, leaving his costume in a pile near the couch.

"Hey!" She rubbed her back. She could picture a purple bruise in the shape of a line forming on her back already. "Why'd you do that?"

"You're obviously keeping something from me. I'm not going to make love to a woman who's lying to me."

She got up, resisting the urge to rub her back again, and ran to him. "Come here. I'm not, Demetri. Let's make love. Come on."

Then, surprising her again, he picked her up. Purely on instinct, she wrapped her legs around him. Then he slammed her against the wall, and shoved himself into her with such force that she yelped. It took her a few seconds to gather the scope of what was happening. She had been thrown into the wall and had hit the back of her head. She reached up to touch a painful spot, hoping there wasn't a bump.

"You like pain?"

"No," she cried, the fear rising to a head.

"I do." His voice didn't sound like his. It was lower, more evil than she had ever heard it, and it scared her to death. But she could do nothing but wait. The torturous minutes went by slowly.

Finally, he finished and let go of her, watching as she slid down the wall onto the floor. He laughed at her and walked away. After a second, she felt the pain in the back of her head again, and she reached up to touch it, hoping there wasn't a bump, but there was.

"You son of a –" With sudden fury, she ran toward him with the intent of pushing him. But he stopped her, grabbing her arms with his strong hands, and pinned her against the wall again. She was breathing hard, her fair-skinned face mottled with anger.

"Son of a what?" he growled as he grew closer to her face.

She couldn't speak. It was too much. She was too scared. The only option was to cry and close her eyes to escape.

As her cries turned to sobs, she felt him let go, then wrap his arms around her, holding her, trying to comfort her.

She was never more confused in her life.

He gently wisped his fingers over her bare back, massaged her head, and then began kissing her. The more he kissed her, the more he touched her this way, the more she melted in his arms. She needed this touch, needed him to hold her and love her. She wrapped her arms around the man who had saved her from the evil. He caressed her until she couldn't resist, and then she let him carry her to the bedroom and lay her on the bed like a china doll. Then, as he did everything she liked, she forgot all about the fear.

She thought only about his hands, his lips, his body enveloping hers.

Chapter Nineteen

The next morning, Demetri woke with a groan. Candy sighed and then got up to get him some water and aspirin. Strangely, this felt like old times. Back home in New York, she often took care of her brother, who seemed to always have a hangover. He spent mornings begging and begging until she gave in and got him the water and aspirin he needed, and sometimes a cold washcloth. Every time, she asked him, "Why do you do this to yourself?" He always answered, "It's fun." Candy would shake her head. Sure didn't seem fun to her.

As she handed Demetri his water, he sat up, and she felt with certainty that this was going to be the pattern for the rest of her life. This was all she knew how to do – take care of people with hangovers.

"Might as well be a nurse," she mumbled, getting up again.

"What's that?"

"Nothing, dear," she answered with distinct sarcasm. While in the shower, she wondered if that was what her life's goal should be. Maybe that's what fate had in store for her – going to college, becoming a nurse, and spending the rest of her life taking care of other people for a living. But she didn't want that.

Was there a choice? Do you choose your own fate? Does God choose it for you? Does God even care? Is there a God? Or was everything just random? So many questions rattled in her brain that it almost hurt her head to consider them. She shrugged them all away and washed them down the drain with her shampoo.

She came out of the bathroom to find Demetri fast asleep again in his bed. She pushed on his arm to wake him. "Demetri?" After saying his name, something hit her.

He often called her "Little Red" or "Ginger Bear" or something similar. There was "Can Can," too, but she hated that one. It reminded her of her brother. She wondered why she didn't have a nickname for him. There was "baby," but everybody uses that one. She really only called him by his full name. Not even half of his name. "Dem" didn't sound right. Nothing sounded right except "Demetri." It was strange.

"Hey," she tried again. He opened his eyes and grabbed her arm, scaring her. She gasped and tried to jump back, but he had a firm hold of her arm.

"Help me up," he groaned, making sure to keep her arm in his grip. Candy whimpered from the pain, but helped pull him up to a seated position. Finally, he let go.

She inspected her arm to find red marks where his fingers had dug into it. "You don't know your own strength, Demetri." She checked her arm once again.

"Huh?" She showed him the marks. "Oh. Sorry, Can." Then he stood up, wobbled just a bit, and made his way to the bathroom.

Candy went to the kitchen to make coffee for them and waited at the kitchen table for him to finish getting ready. As she waited, she reached up and touched the back of her head where he had slammed her into the wall the night before. Sure, it was the heat of passion. He was drunk and didn't know his own strength. Before that, it was a bit of a struggle to keep him from drinking too much, and then he had one more drink when he came home, though she told him not to.

Well, she was just going to have to stop him earlier next time.

"You okay?" Sherri asked. Candy knew why Sherri was so concerned with her well-being. She was digging for more evidence to put Demetri in jail. She couldn't give it to her.

"Yeah, I'm fine." She picked up her bucket.

"He was drunk last night." Sherri set her hands on her hips.

"Yeah, but I was able to control it. He didn't get that bad."

"He's holding his head. Seems he has quite a hangover this morning."

She peered outside to find him walking by with a washcloth on his head.

"Yeah. I guess. But he wasn't violent or anything." Candy set her eyes on the bucket again.

Sherri appeared to be trying to inspect Candy's bare arms for bruises, but she wouldn't let Sherri get close enough. She kept moving, and finally, Sherri gave up and left. Once she was gone, Candy checked her arm. A faint green bruise was on her upper arm, probably from this morning. He didn't do it on purpose. He wasn't trying to hurt her. He wasn't beating her. It was an accident. Nevertheless, with Sherri around digging for evidence, she knew she had to hide it somehow. So she borrowed a sweater from someone and wore it for the rest of the day, though the temperature was in the mid-seventies.

"You cold?" people asked.

She lied every time. "Yeah."

By the time Thanksgiving came around, she found herself hiding more and more bruises. None of them were on purpose. None were from fights. He never got all that mad at her. Whenever he was drunk, he didn't know his own strength, that's all. Things happened, but they were all accidents. He wasn't like the normal or average wife-beater type, whatever that was. He didn't mean it.

Candy felt as though she was living well with Demetri, who never asked for rent money. She bought food for the house, but he took her out to eat at least three times a week. It was because she was working hard at the track, and he didn't want her to come home exhausted and still have to cook dinner. She loved that she had opportunities to rest after work. It was much easier to sit at a table and have someone bring your food right to you.

She leaned over to give him a kiss as they sat together and held hands at their favorite restaurant. They gazed into each other's eyes and were happy – happy and in love. With a glimmer in her eyes, she asked, "What do you want for Christmas?"

Demetri's face lit up. "Hmm," he started with his hand on his chin. "I could use a new saddle."

"How much are saddles? You want a western, right?" She sipped her water.

"Yeah. Um, but that might be too much. Couple hundred, probably. Let me see." He stopped to think again. As he thought, she wondered if she had the money for it here in Florida. Her modeling money was still in Maryland. She had called the bank to ask how she could get it, and she learned that all she had to do was have it wired down and put into her bank account here in Miami. Demetri didn't keep track of her money. He didn't seem to care how much or how little she had. She didn't get paid much for grooming Shadow Dancer, but it was enough for food and a little extra for clothes or other things each month.

"I know. A fifty-year-old bottle of scotch." He pumped his fist in the air in front of him.

"Oh, yeah, I'll be able to afford that. No problem." Candy rolled her eyes. "I think the saddle would be cheaper."

"Yeah, probably right about that. I'll have to think. I don't really need anything, Ginger Bear. I just want to spend the day with you."

Candy smiled warmly and tilted her head. "You're so sweet."

"What do you want?" He took a sip of his wine.

Candy thought for a few minutes but couldn't come up with anything. "I don't know. I don't need anything, either. I have everything I need right here."

Demetri touched the tip of her nose with his finger. "You ain't getting out of it that easy, baby. You gotta come up with something."

"I'll think. But really, considering a year ago, when my only gift was a sweater from my friend, and I only had a cold house to go home to every night, I can't imagine wanting anything else. I have so much more than I've ever had in my whole life."

Demetri nodded. "You're right. I feel the same. Considering my past, too, I could say the same. I'm very grateful for you and everything I have. Two houses, cars, horses, and the most beautiful girlfriend the world has ever known."

"Oh, you're good. You're good," she said, pointing at him.

"Come on, Can, have some wine. I love it when you wind down a little."

"You saying I'm uptight?"

"No, no. I just love it when we have fun and joke about everything. Anything and everything. Last time you were tipsy was over the summer sometime. We had such a good time."

"I'll have a bit more wine just to loosen up. How's that? I don't want to wake up with a hangover in the morning, though."

"We'll drink lots of water before bed. That's how you avoid a hangover."

"Really?"

Demetri sipped his wine again. "I should know."

Candy agreed.

After one glass, she felt tipsy and played it up to seem as though she was more drunk than she really was. He was fooled, as she had started making dumb jokes she had learned as a kid and made sure to giggle at everything everybody did.

Finally, they left the restaurant and drove home.

"So where are we going to put the Christmas tree?" Candy asked as they walked through their front door.

"Usually, the front window there."

"Looks like the perfect spot. Do you buy a real tree? Or do you have a fake one?"

"Ha. Real? You're kidding, right? Only palm trees around here."

Candy loved the thought of a palm tree in their living room. It would be hilarious. "Oh my. We ought to try that, too. That would be the talk of the town."

Demetri agreed, then immediately wrapped his arms around her and dove under her shirt. With clothes strewn on the floor, they made love on the couch, then in the kitchen, and finally in their bed.

Demetri groaned as he stood up just after their last time. He stretched his back and then headed for the bathroom.

Candy relaxed with her arms behind her head and her eyes closed, as she relished feeling like an overcooked spaghetti noodle. Demetri came back out and walked between her dresser and the bed, heading for her side. She grinned up at him.

He stopped. Turning his head, he noticed her box, still sitting on the top of the dresser, and still the only item there. She had kept it free of dust over the past several months but still had not opened it.

"You should use this as a jewelry box," He picked it up and Candy jumped up, snatching it out of his hands before he could open it.

"Damn, girl. What's the big deal? I'm not going to hurt it."

Candy tried her best to catch her breath. "Sorry. I know. Sorry. It's just...you know..."

"Your mom's. Yes. But it doesn't mean you can't use it. I'm sure she would have wanted you to use it for something."

"But..." *I'm afraid to look inside* sounded like such a ridiculous reason, and she was unable to come up with another one. "Um, I just don't want to."

"Why not?"

She sat the box back on the dresser. As she stood in front of him, she hoped for the subject to be over, but he didn't stop. "Candy," he started. Usually he used her full name only when he was annoyed with her. Her stomach turned sick. "You're being ridiculous."

"I know, Demetri. I know. I'm sorry. I guess I just need time to heal. I don't know."

Narrowing his eyes, he turned again toward it, then, without warning, he lifted the lid. Candy screamed "No!" and slammed it closed again. His thumb was still inside.

"Ow!" he bellowed as he dropped it and then glared at her with pure anger and hatred in his eyes.

"Demetri, it was an accident. I'm sorry. Accidents happen to me all the time." She inched backwards.

"So you're getting me back?"

"No, I mean, accidents happen. Right? You've just been…lucky." She moved away a little more but he followed.

"Bullshit!" He pushed her shoulders, sending her backwards and into the nightstand. With a gaping mouth, she tried to take in air but couldn't. She grasped at her chest, hoping to find a way to breathe again. Carefully, she lifted herself onto her knees and knelt on the floor on all fours, her long hair cascading around her arms, hiding her face. She wanted to cry, but she wanted to breathe even more.

Finally, she was able to breathe again, and she gasped for air as she sat up. Demetri was gone. He was in the bathroom running cold water over his thumb. He came back in to find her kneeling on the floor, shaking, but trying her hardest to keep her eyes on his.

"You knocked the wind out of me," she finally said, swallowing her fear with a gulp.

"Sorry," he said simply, then crawled into bed. "You coming?"

She was surprised, but what other options were there? Yell? Fight physically? There was no way to win against this man. So she crawled into bed. He rolled over to face her, and she tried to meet his eyes, though she didn't want to. Finally, she was able to face him.

"I forgive you, Can. I know it was an accident." Then he stroked her arm gently, tenderly. "Are you okay?"

"I guess." Then she couldn't help the tears. Instantly, sobs overtook her whole body and she hid her face with the covers. He held her and ran his fingers up and down her back, but her back hurt, so she wiggled and writhed until she finally had the nerve to tell him. "Please, that hurts. Stop. Please."

Instead, he ran his fingers through her hair, and touched her everywhere but her back. "I'm sorry, Can," he whispered, and then kissed her forehead. She continued to cry, filled with confusion and fear, but soon she felt better as he put his protective arms around her and pulled her in tightly, just the way she needed.

He was more careful with her now, making sure not to get angry. He did his best to control himself, especially after a few drinks. While it was extremely difficult for Candy to keep him from drinking too much at times, it was possible. She kept ahead of him, thinking of ways to trick him into leaving a party or putting his glass down.

Until he figured out what she was doing.

Chapter Twenty

After a New Year's Eve party, Demetri was smashed and hardly able to walk. Candy contemplated whether to leave him there or to get him home. As she sat on a couch in thought, Sherri was there, again, in her business. Candy very nearly told her to go away but tried to be polite.

"Candy, we know what's going on."

"What are you talking about?" Candy kept her eyes on Demetri.

Sherri touched Candy's arm and she flinched. Candy frowned as she stared down at her arm and remembered what was beneath her sweater. Demetri had been upset with her for accidentally burning his dinner, and he had singed her arm with the hot frying pan.

"What happened here?"

"Look. Why are you always asking me about him? You're always looking for something. If you keep looking, you're going to find it whether it's there or not. Any time I hurt myself, you think it was him. And it wasn't."

"Then what happened?"

"I burned myself. On the stove."

"You putting medicine on it?"

"Of course. What do you care, anyway? What's with the fascination with him hurting me?"

"I don't want to see you get hurt."

"You say that, but you hate me. You never talk to me unless you have to."

Sherri shrugged. "You wouldn't understand. I don't hate you. I like you. A lot. I just, you know, hate when he hurts you."

Candy stared at Sherri for a few moments before it finally hit her. Sherri had a crush on her? Candy's face lit with surprise. Now she got it and knew why Sherri hadn't wanted to say it. Candy's body chilled from the inside. Suddenly Candy knew why she wasn't one of them.

She didn't want to be.

"Oh."

"Yeah. See what I mean? You're not one of us." Sherri lowered her gaze.

"I-I see now." Candy swallowed noisily.

"I'm gonna quit, though. I'm not gonna be around next week."

"What? Why?"

"I just, I've had enough. No one will give me a chance to race, anyway. Bubbles and I have a place down in Key West now. We're going to move there and become beach bums. Maybe run a fishing shop or something.

"Oh. That's… nice, Sherri. Cool." Candy blinked.

Sherri nodded a few times, glanced Candy's way, then stood and walked away. As she was leaving the house, Sherri stole one more glimpse of Candy and then walked outside.

"Oh my goodness," Candy said with her hand over her mouth. "What the hell?"

"What the hell, what?" Demetri asked loudly. He shoved a drink into her hand.

"Thanks." She had no idea she had replied, as her mind was still on Sherri.

"What the hell what, Can Can?"

"I'm just surprised. Sherri's um…did she…?"

"Yeah. She quit. Last day is Friday. Bubbles, too." He took a swig from his lowball glass, then his ice clicked as he lowered it.

"Jo's staying?"

"Jo got the short end of the stick, I guess. Sherri and Bubbles decided to run off together." He shuddered and his whole body shook. "Ugh," he said and then giggled like a child for a few seconds. He burped loudly, then laughed at that, too. Candy rolled her eyes.

She glanced at Jo. Jo was talking but not smiling, and her young face sagged as if it were fifty years older. "She's upset. I want to go talk to her," Candy said, then tried to walk away, but Demetri stopped her by grabbing her arm. Candy eyed his hand angrily as it gripped her. "What are you doing?"

"I thought we'd go home."

"I'd like to talk to Jo first. Then we can go." Candy ripped her arm from his grip and tried to walk away again. Demetri ran up behind her and picked her up, cradling her in his arms. "Put me down!" Demetri laughed as he ran to the front door with her in his arms. Everybody stopped and stared, jaws dropped, drinks in hand.

"No!" she screamed as she gripped the door frame. At this point, it wasn't just because she wanted to talk to Jo. She wanted control. Of herself.

He brought her back in, away from the door frame, and she expected to be put down. As she searched his face, she found what she feared most. He was angry now and probably embarrassed. She was certainly embarrassed. Next, instead of letting her go, he barreled through the open door. Candy wasn't ready, and her head slammed into the door frame, knocking her out.

People inside screamed as they chased after Demetri, who was still headed for his car. Candy's head flopped backwards, but Demetri didn't notice or care. Someone ran up and cradled her head. They were yelling at Demetri when she came around.

"No, you're not. She's going to the hospital," a man was yelling.

"She's coming with me," Demetri bellowed.

"Candy!" a woman screamed and tried to rip Candy's body from Demetri's arms.

"What the hell are you doing? Get off of her!" Demetri pulled Candy away from the woman. But then three men came from behind him. Two grabbed his arms while one grabbed Candy. Now she was free and seated on the grass while two men dragged Demetri back into the house.

Candy was so dizzy that she couldn't see straight, and she had no idea what was going on. Everybody was in her face, asking if she was all right, but she couldn't answer. Then, a sudden wave of sickness came over her, and she leaned to her side and vomited in the grass.

"She didn't drink," someone said.

"Hurry. Get her to the hospital." Before Candy knew what was happening, she was in the back seat of someone's car and speeding down the road. She didn't even know who was driving. She was so tired that she couldn't stay awake.

She woke up again in an emergency room with doctors and nurses scurrying around her. "Honey?" she heard. She focused her eyes and saw a nurse. "Can you hear me?"

She tried to nod but was not sure if her head had actually moved.

"Lay back, honey."

Candy let her body relax and fell asleep again.

The next time she woke, she heard Demetri's voice in the distance. She struggled to sit up, as no one was there to tell her not to. Finally, she was upright, but still dizzy and swaying a bit. Demetri's angry voice grew louder and louder as he grew closer to her room, and she became more and more frightened. She began crying loudly and sobbing. "Please, no, get him away from me," she screamed as he came into the room, followed by a doctor and nurse.

"Candy. Wh-what are you saying? Candy?" Demetri asked, his voice now softening.

"You slammed my head against the door."

"I didn't mean to. It was an accident."

Candy bent over her knees, hid her face, and cried. Still dizzy, she lost her balance and almost fell off the bed, but Demetri caught her. The doctor helped get her back into the middle of the bed.

"Is that what happened, miss?" the doctor asked.

She reached up for the side of her head and then brought her hand back down to see if it was bleeding. It thankfully was not. Then she spoke. "He ran out the door while carrying me, and my head hit the door."

"So it wasn't on purpose?"

"Well…I guess not."

Demetri stood next to her, holding her hand, and Candy gazed up at him. His face was wet with tears, and his eyes drooped. "It was an accident, Can," he whispered.

The doctor believed their story and sent them home with instructions for Demetri to keep an eye on her, but to let her sleep it off. She had a mild concussion and was given some pain medicine to help get her through the next week.

Demetri took time off work while Candy stayed in bed, sleeping and taking the pain medicine for her horrible headaches. Demetri was by her side with ice packs and wet towels. He even crushed ice for her to eat. He brought her anything she wanted to drink and let her watch any show she wanted on television. For nearly a week, he took better care of her than he ever had.

Finally, she was ready to go back to work, and they returned to the barn to find everything running smoothly. No one mentioned the incident. No one asked her how her head was. No one.

She hadn't had a chance to say goodbye to Sherri and Bubbles, which saddened her even more. And just when she had discovered Sherri's reasoning, too. She hadn't had a chance to talk about it with her, though no one talked about that sort of thing. Ever. In fact, just a few years ago, Sherri might have been locked in a mental institution for even suggesting such a thing. Candy's heart burned with sadness as she wondered how hard Sherri's life was going to be and had already been. There was nothing anyone could do about it now, but still, she wished she'd had a chance to say goodbye.

Several weeks later, with no incidents, she finally began to relax and trust Demetri again. He had even stopped drinking, knowing these things always happened when he drank.

But it didn't last long, and he blamed her for keeping him from the drink. He knew that she had been tricking him into leaving parties early. So he blamed her for having cravings and for drinking too much. He blamed her by saying that the more she fought his drinking, the more he wanted to drink. Much to Candy's disappointment, he started drinking almost every night.

One night, after losing a tough race, he came home angry. She was in the kitchen but slithered quickly to her old bedroom to hide. Unfortunately, he saw her and followed. She had locked the door, but he kicked it open, shattering the door frame. Candy screamed as he came for her with his hands outstretched like Frankenstein. She ducked under his arms, taking advantage of his slow reaction time, and ran back into the hallway.

"Demetri, please," she begged as she backed herself down the hallway. Demetri came out of the bedroom with intense anger burning in his eyes. It scared her so badly that she felt a huge lump in her throat, already threatening to choke the life out of her. As she tried her hardest to breathe, he caught up to her and pushed her into the wall of the hallway.

A large framed picture tilted above her, and the glass front hit the top of her head, shattering into a million pieces as she fell to her knees. She screamed as she saw blood and glass everywhere. Tiny shards of glass littered her hair, and as she touched her head, she found glass in her scalp as well. She pulled her hand back and saw blood on her fingertips. As she shook violently with fear, almost expecting him to hit her again, she lifted her head to find him gone.

Candy stood on shaky legs and finally found the nerve to look outside for his car. She made her way down the hallway as she held onto the wall for support. Then, she pulled back the curtain over the front window. His car was gone. She cried desperately with relief, but for just a few seconds. Quickly, while she had time, she got a broom and a vacuum and cleaned up the glass. She also used the end of the vacuum hose to suck the glass from her head and hair as she faced the bathroom mirror. She was only able to look at her hair and the hose of the vacuum, not at her eyes.

When she was done and there was no evidence of his tantrum left in the house, she headed for the shower. She had little cuts all over the top of her head, which she hoped to be able to hide in a hat.

She wore a ski cap for a few days, thanking God it wasn't too hot yet. Nevertheless, she did get some puzzled looks, as it was March and in the seventies. She kept telling people she had a slow metabolism and was cold.

While at work, she thought she was safe and decided to talk to him about his temper.

"Why'd you do that to me?"

"Do what?" he asked as he flipped through his condition book as if nothing were wrong.

"You made that picture fall on my head. I had glass in my hair and on my head."

"It was an accident, Ca–,"

"How many accidents have to happen before you realize that this isn't normal? There have been too many accidents, Demetri. It's not safe for me to live with you. I need to –"

"What?" he screamed, making her jump back with fear. Again, that familiar feeling returned of the air being stuck in her chest and not being able to breathe. It was as if the air in her lungs was afraid of him, too. When he stood and towered over her, her knees almost buckled beneath her. He grabbed her shirt in his fist, and she whimpered. "You need to what, Can?"

"Leave," she managed to say, somehow. Instantly, she was sorry she said it because he balled up his fist and struck her across her cheekbone, sending her flying backwards into the wall. She fell with her hair over her face and could not see him, could not tell what was coming at her next. As she cried out in fear, he picked her back up and forced her to sit in the chair next to his desk.

She was whimpering from the pain and fear with every breath.

"Shut up," he bellowed and then bent down into the hair covering her face. "If you leave, I'll find you. We

belong together, Candy, and you know it. You can't leave."
He pointed at her, his finger almost touching her. "I will
bring you back home and you'll be sorry you left."

She was too afraid to cry, too afraid to face him, too
afraid to look away. She was too afraid to close her eyes for
fear he might hit her again, so she sat shaking on his chair,
unable to say a word in reply.

"You'll thank me for this, later, young lady," he
murmured with his face only a few inches from hers. "Have
to treat you like a child, I guess." Finally, she closed her
eyes and turned her head as he huffed and went back to his
desk chair.

The bruise on her cheek was too obvious, and she
couldn't hide it, but surprisingly no one said a word about
it. So she left it open for all to see, like a prize from a
boxing match. She noticed a few heads turned toward her,
some stares, but still, no one mentioned it. It made her
almost miss the days when Sherri bothered her about her
injuries. At least she knew someone cared back then.

That night when they made it home, she tried to run
and hide from him, but he grabbed her arm and stopped
her.

"No, no," she whispered through fear-induced tears
as she closed her eyes and anticipated another blow to the
head.

"My ginger bear," Demetri whispered as he
loosened his grip and then wrapped his arms around her.
Still, she shook with fear despite his attempts at calming
her. Then she wondered if he might get mad at her for

being afraid. So she tried her hardest not to shake and not to appear scared. It was next to impossible, but she finally managed to relax in his arms. She hoped he wouldn't hurt her again, and hoped for him to take care of her so tenderly, as he always did whenever he hurt her.

He pulled her face into his chest, and when her cheek touched him, she flinched and pulled her head away from him. "Shhh," he whispered, then helped her turn her head and put her other cheek on his chest. He lovingly caressed her hair, her back, and held her for several torturous minutes.

Two weeks later, her face had cleared up. Demetri had also managed to keep his temper under control and did his best not to drink. But Candy knew it wasn't over. It was far from over.

Chapter Twenty-One

"Things have been going well, my little Ginger Bear, haven't they?" Demetri asked over dinner one evening at their usual restaurant.

"Things have been going well. Yes," Candy answered obediently, then sipped her wine. Things had been going well, but she knew it was not going to last. It never did. He was always good and they were happy for a few weeks, but then all hell would break loose and she would get hurt. The hard part was trying to predict when he was going to explode. She knew, at the very least, that she was never going to be able to disagree with anything he ever said. She became a "yes man" for him at work, where he asked her questions and she regurgitated things she had heard him say. Of course, he ate it up.

It pained Candy to disagree about things yet have to say she agreed with him. Despite this, on the inside, she tried her hardest not to give up. She refused to give in and lose herself, lose her opinion, lose her mind. She always kept her own opinions to herself, but she still *had* her own opinions, because she knew one day she was going to leave him. She knew this was never going to last. *She* was never going to last. She would die one day if she stayed long enough.

The hardest part of all of this would be leaving and hiding for the rest of her life. After his threat to her, telling her she would be sorry if she ever left, she knew he would come after her, no matter where she went. She knew she could never run, never escape, no matter where she went. It was a life she didn't want. Yet she didn't want her current life, either. So she stayed as she tried day after day to decide what to do.

Pretending she was attracted to him was becoming harder and harder, as well, but she had to maintain her façade or else make him mad. She did her best to pretend to enjoy having sex with him. Sometimes she had to pretend she was with someone else. She closed her eyes and tried her hardest to imagine a movie star or past boyfriend, even Dylan. Demetri made her say his name sometimes, and she managed to force herself to say it, but she refused to believe it. She was determined to stay strong and hide her true feelings from him.

Candy lay next to him in his bed, in his favorite position, Demetri spooning behind her. He told her that it should make her feel secure to lie with him like this. Instead, she felt trapped. She finally managed to fall asleep, but woke up with a sudden start with him yelling at her. She was hardly able to comprehend what he was saying for several seconds as she stared at him with knit eyebrows.

"...you. How dare you say that about me? Do you really think that way? Do you hate me? What's the matter with you? Don't you appreciate all that I've done for you?"

He was sitting up, peering down on her as she lay there trying to wake up and figure out what was going on.

"Demetri, what –,"

"Shut up," he yelled as he slapped her.

"What's going on? What happened?" She reached up and held her cheek, feeling its painful heat under her hand.

"Were you talking in your sleep?"

"I don't know. I guess." Candy sat up, still holding her cheek. "What did I say?"

"You said you hated me. You said, 'You hit me and I hate you'."

Candy's eyes widened. She had no idea she talked in her sleep. That is what she really felt, but she knew better than to say something like that to him. It would set him off. And it surely did.

"You said we were supposed to be together, Can. You said we were meant to be. Have you changed your mind?" he asked, his voice raised in desperation. It surprised her that he didn't hit her. His eyes were pleading, concerned, scared, maybe of losing her. *How could this be?* "I love you, Ginger Bear," he finished softly. Candy thought she saw a tear in his eye.

"I…um…I do love you. I guess…well…I guess I just wish you wouldn't get mad at me. For things."

"I'm trying, right? I haven't lately. I have been controlling my drinking and my temper and everything. I've been trying really hard, Can."

"You're right, Demetri. You're right." This time, in saying those words, she honestly believed what she said. He had been trying. He had been good, and she hadn't appreciated it, hadn't noticed it, and hadn't praised him for it. "I'm so sorry. You're right. I love that you try so hard for me."

Demetri nodded and set his eyes on the bed. She had never seen him so sad. Is this how he was going to be if she left him? She knew she could never bring herself to do that to him. He loved her. He had tried so hard to be good for her. Maybe one day he would change and not do this anymore. She moved closer to him, though part of her worried he might suddenly become angry, and touched his face. She slid her thumb over his cheek, wiping a tear. Then, she gently kissed him.

"I feel awful that I haven't thanked you for trying so hard for me. I see that now. I'm so sorry, Demetri," Candy whispered into his ear, and then kissed his cheek. He took a breath, then turned and kissed her. He lay down on his back, and pulled Candy until she was straddling him, and they made love for the first time in months. Candy hadn't been that happy in so long. She had almost forgotten what it was like to be with the good Demetri.

Over time, she felt even more comfortable with him. It had been two months since his last temper tantrum, and she started to believe he was going to be able to stay in control forever. As she became more comfortable, she found herself feeling freer to do what she liked to do.

She loved to go shopping because it felt good to be able to buy the things they needed. Even grocery shopping was a fun activity for her, and she found herself wanting to stop by the store almost every day to pick up something fresh. She didn't have much time off from work, but occasionally she went shopping for clothes and even for little things they might need at home. She bought a new rug for the foyer, a new painting to replace the one he broke, some new pillows, towels, and an electric can opener to help her feel as though she were a modern housewife.

She went shopping so often, though, that Demetri started to worry.

"I know. I guess I'm just too happy to be able to buy things like this for us. I'm so excited to finally have money and be comfortable."

"Just try to watch it, that's all. Don't overdo it because you might find yourself without money for something you really need one day."

"Okay. I'll be more careful."

He gave her an approving nod and went back to his meal. He wasn't eating his salad, though.

"Don't you like it?" Candy nodded toward his salad.

"Not really. It has those green watery things. What are they called?"

"Cucumbers."

"Yeah. I hate those."

"Oh, I thought you said you liked them. So here, I've been putting them in the salad all this time, thinking you liked them," she said in her most jovial voice, hoping it would lighten his mood.

"It's not funny. You're so busy worrying about which towel to buy for the bathroom that you couldn't listen to me long enough to hear me when I say I don't like those things. Maybe if you listened more, and spent less –"

"Okay. I'm sorry." This was the sort of thing that set him off, and she tried her hardest to put out the fire before it got to be too much and burned her.

"You're going to put me in the poor house one of these days. See? This is why we aren't married. We'd have to put our money together, and I'd be broke. You'd spend every living cent I had."

"You're right."

"Damned right, I'm right." Then he threw down his fork and stood up. Without a word, he went to the bedroom and slammed the door.

She knew he was trying his hardest to control himself and had separated himself from her to protect her. He did it for her, and she knew it with certainty. That's how much he cared about her. He cared enough to try this hard to keep from getting mad enough to hit her.

She cleaned the kitchen after dinner while trying to decide what to do. Should she go to the bedroom and apologize again? Or seduce him? Or tell him how much she appreciated his concern? Finally, once the last crumb was cleaned up from the counter, she had decided to go to the door and speak to him without opening it. That way, at least she had a barrier between them in case he did lose his temper.

"Demetri, you all right?" she asked softly through the doorjamb.

"Fine."

He was still mad. However, this situation wasn't that bad. How could he be this mad at her? She didn't spend his money. All she did was forget that he didn't like cucumbers. "I love you," she tried. He didn't answer. "Can

I come in?" she asked, then wished she hadn't said that. She didn't want to go in. She had wanted to keep her distance, just in case.

"Fine," he barked again.

With her eyes closed with dread, she turned the knob and opened the door. She found him seated on the bed. The television wasn't on, he wasn't reading, he was only sitting. Perhaps waiting for her? So she went to him and put her hand on his shoulder. "Miss me?" Her teeth shone as she hoped to cheer him up.

"You do hate me, Can. I can tell. You aren't thinking of me at all. You're just like that last boyfriend of yours. What's the word? Narcissistic? You only think of yourself."

"What? I mean, it was an honest mistake. I just forgot. That's all. I'll remember next time. I promise."

"No, I see what's going on here. You may not realize it, but you're trying to do your best to make me mad. You're doing all these things to get on my nerves. You're testing me. Well, I'm tired of being tested." His voice continued to rise with every word, each one louder than the previous. "Are you trying to make me mad again so I'll hit you and you can call the police on me? Huh? Is that what you're trying to do? You're trying to put me in jail?"

At this point, Candy wanted to run, as she knew she wouldn't be able to get a word in edgewise. Even if she did, he wouldn't listen. So she stood still, hoping he would be able to calm himself.

Instead, he stood up, and she knew. *Here it comes*, she thought. "No," she whispered.

"No, what? No? What the hell do you mean by that? You think I'm going to hit you again? Huh? Is that what you think of me? You think so little of me?" He continued his rant as he towered over her, and she stood like a statue with her eyes closed, waiting for the pain.

After a minute, she couldn't control her sobbing and began crying and desperately wishing he would stop yelling and hit her, but he kept going. "You're so skinny. No wonder you bruise so easily. Maybe if you wouldn't put cucumbers in the salad, you'd be healthier." The insults continued, as it seemed several months' worth of pent-up anger was spilling out all at the same time.

Finally, she covered her face with her hands and turned away. "Stop," she protested, though it was barely loud enough to be heard.

"Stop? Stop what?"

"Yelling," she said just as quietly.

"Would you rather I hit you? Is that what you want? I knew it. You're just waiting for me to hit you so you can have an excuse to leave. Well, you're not leaving."

He moved behind her and pushed her onto the bed. Her long hair fanned outward as she fell face first, catching herself with her hands. She stayed in that position, afraid to move, afraid to make him madder. Then, she heard him leave the room with a slam of the door. Stunned, she twisted around and stared at the door.

"Thank you, God," she whispered as she began crying with relief. Just in case he came back, she stayed on the bed. She buried her face in her pillow and cried with desperate sobs.

But only seconds later, Demetri came back in, now wielding a screwdriver. He pointed it at her, and she looked at him incredulously as she wondered what he was going to do with it.

"You'll never leave me, Candy. You'll see."

He spun around and began unscrewing the screws on the doorknob. Within seconds, he had turned the doorknob around so that the lock was on the outside. Then he stepped out and closed the door while holding her eyes with his. He locked the door.

She sat there staring at the door for a long time as she wondered what had just happened, fighting the denial in her mind. He locked her in her bedroom? Their bedroom? Wouldn't he have to come in at some point? How long was she supposed to stay in here? Finally, she went to the door and tried to open it, but it was locked. "Demetri," she screamed. "Let me out!"

She heard faint laughter from the living room.

"What is this?"

He never answered. She heard him leave the house, then go to the garage. He shuffled around in the garage for a while, and then she saw him just outside the bedroom window. He had a bucket and a hammer. He began nailing nails into the window and frame. The whole house shook and at first Candy feared the glass in the windows would break, but it never did, much to her chagrin. It would have given her a way to escape.

She decided to watch television once he was done, but softly so he couldn't hear. It distracted her and kept her occupied until dark. She wondered if he might come into the room then, but he never did. She was grateful for the bathroom, at least, but she was hungry and wished she had something to eat. She wondered if he had fallen asleep on the couch. She then searched for something to pick the lock with, but there was nothing that fit. Her stomach growled.

She reminded herself that she had always been this hungry in the past. This was normal for her growing up. She knew she would last until morning. She also knew he had to let her out then because she had to go to work. Shadow Dancer was racing again tomorrow. So she crawled into bed and finally fell asleep.

The next morning, she got up, but the door was still closed. She tried the knob, but found it still locked. So she took a shower, knowing Demetri had to come into the room for his clothes and a shower as well. But then she felt the water pressure drop, and she knew that he was taking a shower in the other bathroom.

What about clothes? She knew that he had to come in for clothes, but he never did. Thirty minutes after his shower, she heard the front door open, then close. Then she held her face as she heard his car drive away.

She stood at the door with wide eyes and her jaw dropped. This was unreal. No food? What about Shadow? His race? As she sat on the bed, she wondered if she should call the police. If she did, Demetri would finally get in trouble. But this is what he was waiting for. It seemed he was daring her to call police. Her punishment for doing that, she knew, would be far worse than being locked in the bedroom. She had to resist. She turned on the television again, hoping to distract herself from the hunger and boredom.

While locked in her jail cell, her cage, she seriously considered leaving him. However, she knew he would hunt her down. Somehow, he would find her, and she knew it. At that point, he would be so mad that he might even hurt her badly enough to kill her. She didn't want that pain. Although the end result wouldn't be so bad. At least it would be the end of her misery.

She went to her magic box and wiped off what little dust had settled there since she had last dusted. Seated on the bed, she held it and traced the crack from her brother's temper tantrum last year. If she left, she was going to have to take her box. Then she and her box would go somewhere safe, away from Demetri, and start over.

She imagined herself changing her name and moving to a hippy commune or maybe one of those Mormon camps in Utah. She desperately wanted to hide and start over. There was no way she'd ever be with another man as long as she lived. It seemed as though she was only meant to be unhappy in relationships. She always chose the wrong men, or they chose her, and she let them choose her. Next time someone appeared to be interested, she was going to resist, no matter what, because she knew what was going to happen. They'd turn into an abusive monster, whether it was mental torture or physical. This was it. This was her life now – doomed to be alone forever, or doomed to be abused forever.

She decided that being alone was better than being in pain.

Finally, Demetri came home. She fought the urge to run to the door and beg for forgiveness for whatever it was she had done. She couldn't even remember what it was now, as she was so hungry she couldn't think straight. So she sat up, leaning against the headboard of the bed with her eyes half closed, her face gaunt with hunger, as she watched television.

Suddenly, the door opened with a bang as it hit the wall behind it. Candy jumped, and then when she saw him, she slithered to the other side of the bed and onto the floor to hide. She huddled in a tiny ball in the corner of the room between her nightstand and the wall near the window, waiting to be struck.

It was silent. She wondered if she looked up, would he hit her?

"Candy," he said softly, and then sat on the bed. "What are you doing?"

For a few seconds, she wondered what he wanted to hear. Back and forth, her mind tossed itself around as she wondered what to say that might appease him. Her mind was in a whirlwind. Her stomach growled loudly in rebellion, and she quickly covered her belly with her arms, hoping to hide any more sounds.

"Go get something to eat," he said, then stood and walked to the television, turning it off. "No more TV, either."

She was too tired to argue, and crawled to the kitchen, too afraid and too weak to walk. Demetri laughed at her from the living room as she made herself a sandwich with trembling hands. As she spread the peanut butter, he threatened that if she ever called the police on him, or threatened him in any way, he would lock her in the room again. She nodded silently and bit into her sandwich.

Over time, she learned her new and stricter boundaries. If she tried to overstep them, he made sure she was punished. He had locked her in the room a few more times, but had taken the television away to keep her from watching anything. If he caught her trying to watch a show, even while he was watching, he always ran after her, pushed her down onto the floor in the bedroom, or into her dresser, and then locked the door. He had pushed her into the dresser so many times that she gave up trying to straighten the mess he made on top of it. Eventually, she took her box and a few other things that had accumulated there and put them all in a flat cardboard box under the bed.

She wasn't allowed to leave the house without him unless it was to go to the track, and in that case, most of the time, he went with her anyway. Fortunately, sometimes, he drank too much the night before, and she drove herself to work after he had told her to go ahead without him. Those were the times she cherished the most. Still, he always asked people what time she came in. If she arrived even a few minutes too late, he punished her later, assuming she had gone shopping. *At six in the morning.*

Before he came in one morning, she called her bank in Maryland. Quickly, before anyone came into the office, she gave the teller her information and asked that her money be sent to her account here. She had to figure a way out. Summer was coming, and she wouldn't be able to hide the bruises for much longer. It was getting too hot to wear long sleeves. It was a miserable existence, and she wanted out. If only she knew how.

Chapter Twenty-Two

"Can't wait to see who wins the Kentucky Derby," one of the grooms said as he raked the dirt floor.

"Really? I can't believe I have missed all the prep races. I don't even know who's running. I've, um, I've been so busy," Candy answered. Demetri hadn't allowed her to watch the races because she had begged to watch them. He said it was to teach her not to beg and to grow up and act like an adult.

"Yeah. Should be good. I used to work for the trainer of the favorite, you know."

"Really? Which trainer is that?"

"Julia McMahon, up at Belmont. I was a groom for her five, maybe six years ago. Or was it seven?"

Candy's heart jumped. To hear Julia's name again nearly knocked her over. And Julia was going to be in the Derby? Finally, she found words. "You're kidding. I used to work for her, too."

"No!"

"Yes!"

"We weren't there at the same time, were we?" he asked, knowing his memory was shot from the drugs in his past.

"No," she giggled. "No, we weren't." Then, she sighed as she considered how excited Julia must feel, and she desperately wished she were able to call her somehow. But not only did she not remember Julia's number, she was too scared to call.

"Race is tomorrow," he said as he continued sweeping.

"Tomorrow," Candy mused. She *had* to find a way to watch the race. Would Demetri let her if she begged him and told him her former boss was the trainer of that horse? Probably not. Maybe she could hide from him and watch at someone else's house. But then, when she went home, she would really get it. She had to decide which was worse – missing the race or getting beat and locked in the room. Quickly, she knew she was more afraid to get hit again than she was excited about the race. So she hoped to hear the results the next morning at the track. If she were going to miss the race, at least people at the track would be talking about it the next day.

Before Demetri awoke the next morning, she got herself to the track. She avoided his hangover-induced anger by getting to work early and making sure everything was in order before he got there. Maybe, if he were happy enough with her, he might let her watch the big race today.

With her horses groomed and ready, their riders already taking them to the track, she decided to go to the kitchen for coffee. While she waited in line, she overheard two men talking about the Kentucky Derby.

"Finally got a good horse that might have a shot at the Triple, and they screw it up by putting a girl up on him."

"Yeah. I can't believe it. Even if she knew how to ride, the other jocks will ruin it for her. I guarantee you someone's going to whip her behind," the second man said, making everyone at his table laugh. "I would." There was more laughter.

The first man continued. "Damned broads. That horse must be extremely good to be able to overcome having a female trainer. *And* rider."

Candy's heart was pounding out of her chest now as she wondered if the girl jockey was Rachel. Did she live after all? She had to ask, so she got out of line and slipped over to the two men, who stared at her with one eyebrow raised and wide eyes. But she didn't care. She had to know. "Excuse me. I couldn't help overhearing about the female jockey. Is that jockey the trainer's daughter?"

"Yeah. Why?"

"Oh, my GOD!" Candy covered her face with her hands as tears started to fall. Everyone in the entire track kitchen was staring at her, but she still didn't care. "Oh, my God. I have to see that race."

"Well, it's on CBS. Just watch it."

"Um," she searched around but didn't see him. "Demetri won't let me."

"What? I've never heard such a ridiculous thing."

She shook her head, then repeated. "I have to see that race. Rachel was my best friend when I lived up there, and I thought she was dead. But she's alive. And she's a jockey now. I can't believe it." As the entire cafeteria stared in disbelief, she scanned the place for someone, anyone, who might allow her to hide and watch the race at their house. It was definitely worth the beating now.

"Jo," she shouted, and then sprinted to Jo's table. Jo and the few girls she was sitting with made room for her to sit with them. Candy plopped into the only empty seat, her eyes wide with excitement and wet with tears. "Jo, please. I have to watch that race. He won't let me. He'll be mad at me, but I have to watch it. I thought she was dead." Candy said more softly this time.

Jo nodded and put her hand on Candy's. It was such a relief that Candy giggled and cried at the same time.

"Oh, my God, she's alive. She's alive," she repeated many times as her voice shook with excitement and joy. But now she felt horrible for not checking on Rachel. *How long had she been gone? How did they find her? Did she escape?* A million questions rattled around her brain.

Candy and Jo planned to meet while Demetri was in the stands watching his horses race or perhaps watching the simulcast of the Derby inside the grandstand. It was the perfect opportunity to sneak away and go to Jo's house for the television coverage of the Derby.

All morning, her heart beat strongly as she anticipated watching Rachel on television. She knew that they probably were going to interview her, considering the circumstances. Female trainer, female jockey… it was probably the biggest story in horse racing since the Seabiscuit days.

Candy made sure not to let anybody know where she was going so Demetri wouldn't find out. He knew where Jo lived, and knowing him, he would come get her and beat the crap out of both of them.

Finally, Demetri was in the stands for his races, and it was time. Taking a deep breath, she sneaked around a corner, hoping no one saw her, and jogged over to their designated meeting spot, two barns away.

"Jo," she called in a loud whisper.

Jo snickered as she appeared from a stall. "What's the big secret?"

"Oh, I guess I was trying to be quiet so..." She peeked around, worried he might come after her. "Can we get out of here? Like now?"

"Sure." Jo began packing up her things. It couldn't happen quickly enough for Candy, and she hid in a stall and petted a horse to keep herself calm while she waited. Finally, Jo was ready and peeked in. "Let's go."

"He's not there, is he?"

"Of course not."

"Could you look, please?"

Jo rolled her eyes and sighed, and Candy felt awful for making her do this, but it had to be done. She had to make sure. Jo glanced back and forth and didn't see him. "Nope. He's not here."

"Okay." Candy glanced around for herself to make doubly sure, and then followed Jo to her car.

"I can't believe this," Candy kept saying.

"How exactly did you think your friend was dead?" Jo started the car.

"She was kidnapped. She had disappeared, and no one could find her. I couldn't bring myself to go back to the track knowing she wasn't there. I had no family or friends other than her. And since she was gone, I had to leave."

"Well, I guess she got away."

"Yeah. I wonder how. I wish I could remember her phone number."

"Didn't Manny work for her mother a while back?"

"Yeah, but he wouldn't have her home phone number. Besides, even if he had it at one point, he would never remember her number. He can't remember his own name sometimes."

"That's the truth." Finally, they arrived at her house. Jo offered Candy a drink and some lunch. They ate and talked while they waited for the coverage of the race to start. Candy was shivering with fear inside, knowing Demetri might find out she was missing and come after her. She wondered if she would even live through the night. Regardless, it was all worth it to see Rachel ride. It was Rachel's dream come true.

At two, the coverage finally started, and Jo and Candy sat on the couch with their eyes glued to the television.

"Today, history will be made, whether or not Chivalry wins the Derby, because today, we have a very interesting set of circumstances. We not only have a female trainer poised to win, we have a female jockey. Considering there are only ten licensed female jockeys in the country, it is unprecedented to see a female in such a big race. She has been riding for her mother as an exercise rider since the tender age of fourteen, and now she is nineteen and has acquired her apprentice license in New York. For them to allow such a young rider in the Derby is news enough, but for it to be a girl, well, that's just unheard of. The Churchill Downs stewards maintain that she is quite capable, and some even say she's a better rider than some of the men. They expressed that they have faith that she will be able to ride Chivalry today in the Derby, and ride him well."

"Show Rachel," Candy yelled, and just after that, the camera showed Rachel seated next to a young man with crutches. "Rachel!" Candy screamed as she jumped up toward the television. Candy desperately wished she could jump inside the television and hug her friend. She was unable to hold back her tears any longer, but she stayed quiet by covering her mouth so she could hear Rachel's voice. Her free hand quivered as it reached out toward the television, but she kept her distance so she did not block the screen.

Rachel was wearing the navy blue silks of Hanover Farms, the stable that had employed Julia for many years and had given her a chance at being the first female trainer at Belmont. And now, the stable had given Julia's daughter the chance at being the first female jockey at Belmont.

"Firstly, congratulations, Rachel, on securing this ride."

"Thanks, Tim," she answered. Candy whimpered as she heard her friend's voice for the first time in a year and a half.

"You're making history today, whether you win or not. How does that make you feel?"

"It's a dream come true for me to be able to ride in any race, let alone the Derby. As for making history, I didn't really come into this planning to be the first female to ride in the Derby. I just want to win the race for my mom and for the Hanovers."

"Erick, you must be proud of your wife."

"Wife? She's married already?" Candy whined, but then she shut herself up again so she wouldn't miss anything.

"Yes, I am. I knew this day would come sooner or later. She's an excellent rider, and so good with the horses, especially Chivalry. I've always maintained that she should have been the one riding him all along."

"Why didn't she?"

"Her mother was being cautious. This last year, it's been rough for females getting into racing, and she wanted to protect her daughter. It's understandable. But we all knew she would get the chance sooner or later."

"I guess it took a broken leg for this to happen. Was it worth it?"

Rachel and Erick gazed into each other's eyes. "Definitely. I'd do it all over again," he answered.

"Aww," Candy sighed with her hands clasped in front of her chest. "He is so cute."

"Shh," Jo scolded.

Finally, Candy sat back down on the couch, and they watched the entire show leading up to the big race. By the time post time came around, Candy was a nervous wreck as she hoped Demetri hadn't discovered her missing yet. At the same time, she couldn't wait to see Rachel ride. Jo rolled her eyes at Candy as she paced around the couch, back and forth to and from the kitchen, to the front door, everywhere.

"You're going to wear a path in the floor," Jo joked as she watched Candy walk from place to place, but Candy was too excited. She couldn't stop.

They had interviewed other jockeys and trainers in the race, and Candy and Jo were not surprised to find that every one of them was upset about Rachel being there. No one, of course, was going to admit potential plans to hurt her, but Candy knew it was possible. She had heard about violence against the "jockettes" and had even seen it at her own track. Candy's stomach turned sour as she hoped Rachel would be all right. It might kill Candy to see Rachel get hurt now, especially after recently learning she was alive.

Candy had hoped the reporters would discuss the kidnapping, but they never did. Candy vowed somehow to get back in touch with Rachel no matter what. This time, she had to try everything. Every avenue. Even asking Manny if he remembered the phone number, and that would be the longest shot of all.

Finally, post time arrived and Candy watched Rachel getting a leg up from her husband. Rachel seemed stern and focused, but she knew her friend well and saw that hint of fear in her eyes. Candy couldn't help but cover her face with her hands again and peek between her fingers. "Hold on, girl," she told her friend. During the post parade, Rachel waved to the crowd when her horse was announced. The close-up of Rachel on her horse sent Candy's heart soaring again with pride. She couldn't believe it. Rachel was going to do this. She was going to realize her dream, and Candy felt privileged to watch it, though it might get her killed later tonight.

Finally, the horses were in the gate. The last shot Candy saw before the break was of the jockey next to Rachel eying her with sinister eyes. She was able to see them even through several layers of goggles, each one to be pulled down as it gets dirty during the race. Rachel seemed as though she didn't notice the man, though, and kept herself focused on the race ahead.

"They're off in the Kentucky Derby!" The announcer started his call. Candy jumped to her feet, as did Jo, and they silently urged on Rachel and Chivalry. They watched as horses surrounded Rachel, and they knew she was going to have a tough time getting out. The jockeys were going to do anything and everything within their power to keep her locked in a box, ruining her chance at winning. Not only were they against her winning because she was a girl, but they wanted to upset the favorite as well. They each wanted to go down in history as the one to ruin Chivalry's chances.

Candy watched as Chivalry shook his head angrily. "She's trying to back him out." Jo grunted in agreement. Unfortunately, the other horses and riders continued to slow with Chivalry and were able to keep him boxed in for most of the race.

Finally, as they rounded the far turn, the last turn before the home stretch, the horse next to Chivalry tired and was unable to keep up with the pack. It seemed as though Rachel might be able to take the opening that horse had left behind, but another horse came up on her inside and blocked her path. Candy and Jo yelled "Ugh!" at the same time as they clenched their fists.

Just after that horse passed her, the rider glanced back at Rachel and Chivalry and then yanked his reins to the right, bumping another horse hard and nearly causing a spill right in front of Chivalry. Both horses thankfully righted themselves, but that bump opened up the rail. Chivalry jumped into the open space and took off like a bullet.

In an instant, the cheers from the crowd grew to a sound so loud that it distorted the television speakers. But that sound could barely be heard over Candy and Jo. They jumped up and down as Chivalry pulled away from the rest of the field and won by eleven lengths.

Candy was crying so hard that she couldn't see, and she wiped her eyes so she could watch her friend's reaction. Rachel appeared not to react at all, and Candy knew that she was probably overwhelmed. Then, as Rachel slowed Chivalry, she saw Billy, Rachel's brother, ride up to them while pumping his fist in the air. Before grabbing Chivalry's bridle, he lifted Rachel's arm in victory, prompting even louder cheers.

In the stands, Julia and Erick, Rachel's husband, were jumping up and down as well, and when they finally stopped jumping, Candy saw tears in their eyes. Then, when the camera switched to Chivalry for a close up again, Candy got closer to the television to see Rachel's face. She was smiling, but stunned, as if the emotion were too much to take. But when Rachel leaned over and wrapped her arms around her horse's neck, Candy knew it was finally taking hold. They had won the Kentucky Derby, every horse person's dream.

Candy was surprised to see tears in Jo's eyes as well. "Oh, stop," Jo said with a wave of her hand. Candy wondered how many other thousands of people, especially women, were crying with joy for Julia and Rachel. It was a win for females everywhere in a time when "women's lib" was on everyone's mind.

When a reporter interviewed Rachel, asking her thoughts on the race, Candy listened closely. She was impressed with Rachel's quick thinking and strategy.

"Very good, Rachel. Congratulations on your first Kentucky Derby. Hopefully not your last," the reporter said as he shook her hand.

"Thank you," Rachel said, gripping his hand tightly with what Candy was sure was her strongest handshake, as she always did with men.

But then, Rachel spoke again. "And Tim?"

"Yes?"

"I need to thank two men who saved my life a little over a year ago. I've had no way of finding them, so I hope they're watching today.

Candy held her breath and listened closely.

Rachel continued, "Two garbage pickup men from Harlem saved my life one night in the middle of the night. I was kidnapped, but I had escaped by jumping out of a second story window. I was knocked unconscious when I fell, but those men saw me, wrapped me in a coat, and took me to the hospital. I can't go into many details about it, but since they never gave their names when they brought me to the hospital, I was never given the chance to thank them for saving me. So, to the two brave men who saved my life that night…Thank you."

Soon after the broadcast ended, Candy found the nerve to go back to the track. Demetri wasn't there, thankfully, and Candy wondered what had happened and where he was. But she was grateful for the break. Then she saw Manny.

"Manny," she shouted as she bounced up to him.

"Did you see?" he cried with his arms outstretched toward her.

"Yeah," Candy answered and then clenched her jaw to keep from crying again. She held his arms and jumped.

"Oh, man. I am so excited. Now I wish I wouldn't have left. What it would be like to work there now…Oh…"

"Manny, I need to call them. I need to talk to Rachel."

"Why?"

"To congratulate her, of course." She hoped she was a decent liar. While it was partly true, she needed to call Rachel for something entirely different. "Do you know how I can get in touch with them?"

"Call Churchill Downs, I suppose. I'm sure the number's gotta be around here somewhere."

"Oh. In Demetri's office?"

"Of course."

After scanning the area for Demetri and finding it safe, she ducked inside his office and flipped through his books. One book was a list of tracks in the United States, and she ripped it from the shelf. With one peek in back of her to check for Demetri, she grabbed a piece of paper and wrote down the number to Churchill Downs, then put the book back on the shelf the way she found it.

Candy knew Rachel and her family were probably celebrating, so she tried her best to wait until later to call. But dare she try to call from home? Never. Demetri let her use the phone? Impossible. And where was he, anyway? Did he know where she had been all afternoon? Then she heard him yelling from behind her.

"Can Can? Where's my ho?" he asked, laughing at himself. Candy closed her eyes with dread. He was drunk again. She searched for a place to hide, but it was to no avail. "There you are. I've been looking for you."

Fortunately, he had spent Derby time in the clubhouse drinking at the bar with his friends and wasn't aware that she had been gone. She let out a huge sigh of relief, knowing that at least she had that. Of course, he was going to treat her miserably at home, but at least he wasn't going to hurt her. Physically.

Anxious to move on with the inevitable, she took him home and was glad when he finally passed out later that night. He had ripped off her clothes and had his way with her, but was unable to finish, as he was so drunk. He blamed her, of course, telling her that she was too ugly, too skinny, that her hip bones were hurting him. Inside, she told him *Good*, but she never said a word aloud.

It was after ten when she finally found the nerve to sneak out of the room and make the phone call. She knew there was a slim chance she would find anyone left in the Churchill Downs office. Most likely, the only people there were security, as the entire Hanover staff had to be at some hotel ballroom or something. Still, she had to try.

The phone rang seven or eight times, and she lifted the phone away from her ear to hang it up when she heard someone pick up.

"Churchill."

"Hi. Um, this is Candy O'Neil. I'm looking for Rachel Bennett," she said softly, as to not wake Demetri.

"Are you press?"

"No, sir. I'm a friend of hers. There's been an emergency, and I need to speak to her right away."

"Who is this?"

"Like I said, Candy O'Neil. Can you please help me find her? I need to get in touch with her. Please, sir. It's life or death. Please."

It was silent for several seconds, and Candy cringed as she felt the phone bill increasing with every one of the seconds he so carelessly wasted. Demetri was going to be teed.

"Please," she whispered. She wasn't sure he heard it but didn't care, honestly. She was praying internally for his help, as well as begging aloud. "Please?" she said more loudly this time. "I need her, and it has to be soon. Please… Mister, I could die, okay?" Candy covered her mouth to smother a sob.

"Just a moment, please," he said, then the line clicked and it was dead silent. Her jaw dropped and so did her heart as she wondered if he had hung up on her or if she was on hold. She continued her silent pleas for mercy as she hoped she was still connected.

She glanced down the hall to find the door to the bedroom still closed, and she simultaneously prayed for him to stay asleep and for the man at Churchill to come back to the phone. Her blood pressure rose steadily as Demetri could discover her missing at any time now, and every second racking up the phone bill was that much closer to death.

"Hello?" Candy heard a faint female voice. *Is that really her?*

"Rachel?" Candy tried to keep her voice down and project her voice through the phone lines at the same time. She cupped her hand over the receiver.

"Yes?"

"Rach. It's me. It's Candy."

"Candy?"

"I saw you on television, Rach. I saw you. You're alive." Candy broke down in tears, sobbing into the phone, and in hearing this, Rachel followed suit.

"Candy, where are you? Where did you go? What happened?"

"I left, Rach. I was stupid, but I couldn't stay there anymore. I couldn't face it without you. I thought you were…well…you know. I thought you were gone. I'm in Miami."

"Miami? What on earth possessed you to go there?"

"Long story, Rach. But I need to get out of here. I'm…sort of…in trouble." Candy's voice lowered. "I need help."

"What happened?"

"Well, this guy, he's my boyfriend, he's um…well…"

"Does he hit you?" Rachel shouted into the phone.

"Um…"

"Candy, drive away. Leave him. Get on a plane. Do you need money? Cause –"

"I got it. I have money now. I guess that's what I'll do. I'll, um, get on a plane. But you're in Kentucky."

"We're going home tomorrow. We'll be back at night."

"Tomorrow?" So soon? Was this it? Was this really her chance? Would Demetri find her?

"Tomorrow. Get on the next flight out of there, even if it's a red eye or whatever. Get out of there now, Candy, and go to the track or wait at the airport. I can meet you when we get back. Get out of there."

Candy paused. This is it. I'm going to do it. "I will."

"Do you promise me? You wouldn't go back on your word to your best friend, would you?"

"I promise, Rach."

"Do you have my phone number at the track? Or at my house? Do you remember?"

"No. I forgot. Give them to me, quick. I have to get off here before… Go ahead, Rach."

Candy took down the phone numbers the best way she knew how. She wrote them on her stomach with black magic marker.

Her instincts had been good to her. Having her money wired down to Florida was probably the smartest thing she had ever done. "Thanks, street smarts," she muttered as she scanned the living room from the kitchen. She wondered how much she might be able to stuff into her suitcase as she wiped the tears from her cheeks.

However, the suitcase, along with all of her clothes and other possessions, namely, the magic box, were in the bedroom where Demetri lay in a drunken slumber. She most certainly did not want to go in there. Could she leave all her things behind? Start over in New York? Of course, Rachel would help her. But the box…

She found herself padding with small steps down the hallway toward his room. It was also her room, but not anymore. This was it. No more. It was time to –

"Can," she heard from behind the closed door. Her heart almost stopped and she slapped her hand over her mouth to keep in a whimper. Her breathing quickened as nervousness set in, making her sick to her stomach. Leave now, run away, or go in there, face him, maybe get him back to sleep and take a chance at grabbing things she wanted to take with her. That box. She had to have that box.

She was in front of the door when he moaned again. "Can? I, Oh, God…" Then, she heard the sound of him vomiting. She closed her eyes with dread. While part of her hoped he might choke to death on his own vomit, part of her couldn't bear to see him suffer, though she wasn't sure why she felt that way.

Her hand, with a mind of its own, had opened the door, and now she had a narrow view inside. Fortunately, he had grabbed the trashcan, and it wasn't all over the carpet. Throwing open the door, she ran to the bathroom and grabbed a towel for him. He moaned as she rushed back with it, and then handed it to him. "Oh, thank you," he groaned as he wiped his face with the towel.

"Here, I'll take that," she found herself saying, and then took the trashcan from him. She pulled her shirt up over her nose as she made her way back to the bathroom so she wouldn't smell the rum-laced liquid. She was glad he hadn't eaten much, but that was probably by choice. Food would have made the alcohol less potent. She tossed the can into the tub and ran water in it, then peeked into the room. He was out cold again, still holding the towel over his chest.

With the water on, she hoped the sound masked the sounds of her finding her suitcase in the closet, and even throwing things inside. Part of her wanted to make as much noise as she wanted, and if he woke up, she would just…just what? *Get hurt.* So she tried her hardest not to make a sound as she moved back into the room.

The closet door was open, but Demetri was on his side, facing it. If he woke up, she would be in big trouble. Moving inch by inch to avoid making a sound, she slithered to the closet, moved things one by one, still inch by inch, then pulled out the suitcase. She was moving so slowly that the whole process of getting it out took ten whole minutes. Fortunately, Demetri was still snoring as he lay in the bed, the sweet yet sickening smell of his breath polluting the air.

She began to feel a little braver as she grabbed things and tossed them inside the open suitcase. When Demetri moved slightly, she jumped and grabbed her chest, but thankfully, he stayed asleep. Then, on her knees, she crawled to the bed again, reached underneath, and pulled out a long, flat cardboard box covered in flowered contact paper. She opened the lid to find her magic box, and she pulled it out and placed it gently in the suitcase among the clothes. Then she put the lid back on and slid it back under the bed as silently as possible.

Jumping to her feet, more anxious to get out of the nauseating smell and away from him, she ran to the bathroom for her toothbrush and whatever else she could grab in one trip. Within seconds, she had thrown her things into the suitcase and then peeked at him one last time. He was still asleep.

The water was still on.

Leave it on? Or turn it off and take a chance that he would wake up with the change in sound?

She opted for leaving it on, not caring what his water bill was going to be. She wasn't going to be here, anyway. So she closed her suitcase, picked it up, and with one more look at her hunk of a boyfriend, she blew out a breath of air and left the room. Then she grabbed her purse and his car keys and left, not caring if he ever found his car.

Chapter Twenty-Three

She had no idea how she managed to get herself on the plane. The Eastern Airlines 727 was the first flight to LaGuardia, which was closest to Belmont Park. The plane had to make a stop in Washington, D.C., but she told herself not to so much as glance out the window. As the plane descended and landed at National Airport, she kept her eyes in her magazine and refused to lift them. She had to move to allow a man to leave the seat next to her as he deplaned, but otherwise, she hardly moved.

Then, back in the sky and not even an hour later, the pilot announced that they were going to be landing soon. She bit her tongue, hoping not to cry in front of the other passengers. Another man had taken the initial man's place next to her in first class. She had told herself that she deserved to sit in first class for a change, and the cost didn't matter. She may never have this chance again, and besides, she was soon going to have another job anyway. She hoped to work for Julia again and to spend time with Rachel. It was all going to be worth it.

"Please fasten your seatbelts and return your seats to their upright positions," the stewardess said with her smooth, husky voice as they neared New York City. Candy looked out the window from her aisle seat. The man next to her glanced at her for one moment with a polite smile, then gazed out the window. Candy's eyes were huge and eager, and she was trying desperately to control her emotions. Everything inside her wanted to laugh, cry, jump up and down, and run around. Despite this, she sat with her legs crossed and was poised and proper like anyone else in first class.

"This home for you?" the man next to her asked.

Candy's heart jumped for joy at the mention of the word *home,* and tears finally fell as she nodded. She couldn't speak, but she hoped he understood. He seemed to because he smiled again and looked out the window, making sure to sit back far enough so she was still able to see.

The minutes crawled by as the plane descended into New York City. Finally, they landed and it was time to deplane. Fortunately, Candy was near the front of the plane and found her way out and up the ramp quickly. She was practically running into the airport.

Now what?

She had to wait for Rachel. Or maybe get a cab to Belmont.

Candy stood at the baggage claim carousel, watching suitcase after suitcase slip by. Just when she thought hers was not there, she saw it. It was a hard, brown case with metal clasps on top, and she had locked them with a tiny key. She hoped the hard case had kept her magic box safe.

The suitcase was heavy, and a man helped her pick it up. She thanked him but was unable to meet his gaze. Her initial reaction was one of terror as she wondered if Demetri had woken up and figured out where she was. Maybe he sent someone to get her and bring her back.

Fortunately, the man walked away without a word. Candy chewed on a short fingernail as she searched the area for anyone suspicious, but she saw no one out of the ordinary. In fact, the scene was calming to her. Even as the hurried New Yorkers yelled at each other and speed-walked from place to place, she felt relieved. This was home. It was everything she had ever known up until last year, aside from a few side trips to Saratoga and Pimlico. They had never stayed long at those tracks and never left the backside. Before this past year, she had only really seen this city. Her city.

Dragging her heavy suitcase toward the huge glass doors, she found cars with New York plates. The old familiar smog filled her nostrils. Cars were honking, and many contained people who were anxious to get home, maybe to their families. The scene made her smile, but then she realized something.

She had no family. Don? What had happened to him? She wished she knew. Again, she was only able to hope that he had ended up in prison for his own good.

Lifting her arm, she signaled for a cab. Instantly, one stopped for her. The driver rushed over to her, eager for the chance to help a pretty girl. His eyes were huge as he scurried around, and Candy grinned as she tried to come across as sophisticated. She was wearing one of her nicer dresses and good shoes. After all, she was flying in first class. She had to look the part.

Soon, they were at Belmont Park, just a few miles away from the airport. The driver helped her with her suitcase. As she was thanking him and paying, she heard her name.

"Candy? Is that you?"

She turned to find Pete, the security guard at the main gate to the backstretch. Often, he was the one who let Rachel and her in as they walked together from Rachel's house or the diner.

"Pete," she cried with her arms out, running toward him. She wasn't sure why, but she cried as if seeing a best friend again. She hadn't known him all that well. Just a few words here or there. But she was too happy to contain herself, and tears flooded her face.

"What are you doing here? Are you back?"

Candy nodded as she tried to control herself. Pete handed her a handkerchief. "Thanks," she whispered, then took a breath in and blew it out. "I'm back, Pete. I'm really back."

"Did you hear? Did you hear about Rachel and Julia?"

"Yes." Candy jumped as she shouted her reply. "Pete, I thought she was dead after she was kidnapped, and I left, I ran away. But then I saw her on TV yesterday and finally found out she was alive."

"Yup. She's right as rain."

"I talked to her last night. She said they're coming back tonight. Oh, I still have my pass." She began searching in her purse, but Pete held up his hand.

"Not necessary, young lady. Let me help you with that. It looks heavy." Pete went right for her suitcase. It was strange to be treated so kindly.

Pete had someone carry the suitcase for her as she cried and cried, hardly able to thank everybody for all of their help. Old friends recognized her, talked to her, told her she looked great, that she looked so much better and healthier. Her dress had sleeves long enough to cover bruises, aside from one on her forearm. One was a normal occurrence for most people, so she hoped it would not attract too much attention.

Once she made it to the Hanover barn, her home away from home, and sometimes just home, she greeted everyone and eventually changed her clothes to something more barn appropriate. Without being asked, she dove into helping and working, doing anything possible to stay busy.

The work and the people helped the day fly by. As the sun set, Candy felt a twinge of nervousness. It was more of an excited nervousness, though, as she could not wait to see Rachel and meet her adorable husband. *She's married. I can't believe it.*

Candy sat in a circle with a group of track workers from Panama and other Latin American countries as they played drums and sang. Some danced. Whenever they tried to pick her up to dance, she refused as she felt out of place. She understood a little of what they were saying, but not enough to join in like the others. Still, she was glad for the distraction, as it kept her focused on the music and not the time.

It was getting darker, and people left one by one, leaving only a few. By nine in the evening, Candy began to worry about Rachel and her crew. Where were they? How long did it take to drive from Louisville, anyway? She paced the area, wishing she had a horse to walk between the barns, as it would have given her an excuse to be up and around and not relaxing like everyone else.

Finally, she heard the rumbling of a truck. She faced the direction of the sound, and several men near her stood up as they waited for the truck. Candy did not see anything at first, but then a silhouette began emerging from the darkness. She couldn't take her eyes off of the dark pickup truck pulling a long horse trailer. The men around her cheered and jogged up to walk with the truck and help them park near the barn.

Candy stood frozen in place, though she wanted to jump up and down. She covered her face with both hands, trying to hold in her excitement, but it came out in tears instead. Then when Rachel shot out of the truck like a bullet, Candy was still frozen and stood there until Rachel slammed her tiny frame against her friend's tall and not-so-thin-anymore body.

They made quite a scene as they squeezed each other and cried loudly for a few minutes. Soon, Julia approached, followed by Billy, Willy, and then Erick, on his crutches. Rachel introduced her to Erick, who shook her hand and smiled. Sure enough, he was just as adorable in person as he had been on television.

Finally able to calm herself, Candy helped everyone unpack. Anxious to meet the Derby winner, Candy begged to walk Chivalry for a bit to loosen him from his long trip. Willy, Chivalry's groom, allowed it, although he was quite possessive of his horse.

Chivalry eyed Willy, confused, as Willy walked away from him to help unload things instead of walk him. Rachel patted her horse and walked next to Candy as she stared at and admired their Derby winner.

Erick helped where he was able, although everyone continually told him to sit down and allow his leg to heal.

Rachel and Candy, with their tears finally dried, walked together and talked.

"Candy, please tell me what happened to you. What happened? Where were you?"

"Very long story. But first I have to know what happened to you."

It was hard, but Rachel managed to tell the whole story. Rachel hadn't been able to talk to anybody about her kidnapping and the horrific events to anyone for several months just after it happened. She had had nightmares and flashbacks bad enough to interrupt ordinary conversations at the mention of a trigger word, smell, or sight. But Erick had encouraged her to talk about it, and each time she told the story, it got easier and she felt better. Her nightmares and flashbacks decreased down to almost nothing a year later. Erick had saved her life by helping her this way because Rachel hadn't wanted to live with the pain.

By the time Rachel's story was over, Chivalry was ready for bed, and they handed him back to Willy.

Candy then told her story. The entire story was a series of misunderstandings and bad timing. It was a story full of "if onlys" and "I should haves." Candy tried to apologize for not staying and for overreacting, but she swore she wasn't thinking clearly. All she had thought about was getting away from everything. She wanted to start over and somehow find a better life. With Dylan, and then Demetri, she had thought each time she had found the answer, but it turned out to be the wrong answer. These events made her not trust herself or her own decisions because she had made so many poor choices. Everything seemed right at the time but then turned out to be very wrong. She was scared to death now to make any decisions for herself.

Nevertheless, the fact of the matter was, she was here, she was home, and she was away from Demetri. For now.

Rachel insisted Candy stay at her house, but there wasn't much room. They had decided Candy deserved a good night's sleep. So Candy decided to stay in a nearby hotel until she found another place to stay.

Rachel walked with Candy to her room and then went inside to talk. They stayed up all night long catching up. Candy showed her her modeling portfolio, and Rachel's reaction made Candy snort with laughter. Rachel couldn't believe how perfect Candy looked and insisted she try modeling again sometime, but Candy refused. There was no way modeling would ever work again. She didn't fit in. She fit in at the track, and it was the only place she felt truly comfortable.

Candy also showed Rachel the evidence of Demetri's abuse – bruises, scrapes, even scars from burns. There was no way to show Rachel the scars on the inside, though. Words were not enough to describe the horror of her life with him for the past year. But since Rachel had gone through such a tough time, too, Candy knew that Rachel understood. Unfortunately, it was something they now had in common, but it was only going to make their friendship stronger.

"What's this?" Rachel asked as she rose from the bed and headed for Candy's suitcase.

Candy groaned slightly but watched as Rachel carefully lifted the box from its resting place and brought it to the bed. Rachel sat down facing Candy while still holding the box. Candy wanted to take it from her, but she did not want to seem silly. The truth was, though, she was feeling anxious and possessive.

Rachel recognized the emotion and handed the box to her friend. Candy breathed a sigh of relief. "Thanks."

"So? What is it? Is that your parents' ashes?"

Candy laughed. "Why does everybody ask me that?"

Rachel smiled and waited patiently for Candy to continue. She raised an eyebrow when Candy did not speak for a few moments. Candy shrugged one shoulder, then spoke. "It's just a box. It was my mom's. That's all."

"Oh, nice. You put jewelry in it?"

"Nothing right now, actually."

"Nothing?"

Candy nodded. "Can I tell you something?"

"Of course. You can tell me anything." Rachel set her hand on Candy's knee for a second.

"Well, it was my mom's. And she used to keep it under the bed. I think she was hiding it from my dad because he pawned stuff sometimes for drug money. I don't know why, but I used to sneak in there every once in a while just to see what was inside the box. Every time I looked, it was something different. Sometimes I waited just a few days, sometimes I waited a month. Every time, it was something new inside. I wondered if it was a game, or was it that she was hiding things from my father? Or was it that she hid them, and he found them, and pawned them?" Candy shrugged as she stared at her box. "Guess I'll never know. But I'm keeping it as a reminder of her, of my childhood, of what not to do with my children, if I ever have any."

Rachel's eyes filled with tears, and her bottom lip protruded slightly as it normally did whenever she was sad.

"Don't start the tears, missy. I won't be able to stop. Let's be positive. Let's just say that I'm going to be a good mother. Period."

Rachel took a breath and composed herself. Then she tapped Candy's knee. "Solid."

"Groovy."

"Copasetic."

"Don used to say that one a lot," Candy said, effectively killing Rachel's attempt at lightening the mood. "Sorry."

"It's okay."

"Have you been by my old house at all?" Candy asked as Rachel moved to sit next to her, leaning against the headboard of Candy's hotel bed.

"Yeah. We tried to see if you were there, but it was empty. Don wasn't even there."

"I wonder if I should check the jail for him. Or the morgue." Strangely, Candy couldn't cry about this. Her own brother might be dead. She hated herself for not feeling worse. It was almost as if she hardly knew him and he was just another guy on the street. And she felt the same way about Demetri.

Just the thought of Demetri's name set her stomach on fire with fear. "What if he finds me, Rachel?"

"Don?"

"No. Demetri."

"How? How could he know where you are?"

"He knows I used to live up here. He'll probably figure it out."

Rachel wiggled her feet back and forth as she thought, then stopped when she came up with something. "We'll just hide you. We'll protect you, Candy. He can't get onto the backstretch. We'll just –"

"No, Rach, he can. He's a trainer."

Rachel muttered a curse word under her breath. She never used those words unless it was really bad. And this was really bad.

Epilogue

Birds chirped, the warm Florida sun shone through the curtains, and there was the sound of a waterfall. What more could a guy ask for?

Wait. Waterfall?

"Candy?" Demetri groaned as he struggled to sit up. A dirty towel fell from his chest to his lap, but he did not notice. As he held his head with both hands, he tried again. "Candy?" No answer. Glancing at the clock, he saw that it was nine. *Nine?* "Shit. That bitch. Why didn't she wake me up?"

His sudden fury gave him the strength to stand up, but it gave way to confusion as he heard where the waterfall was – in his bathroom. His first thought was that she had killed herself in the tub and was running water to muffle the sound of her cries or perhaps to wash away her blood. He sprinted into the bathroom to find the tub empty, except for a trash can. Water overflowed and drained, making it look like the fountain at Hialeah. He turned it off.

He knit his eyebrows as he scanned the yellow-tiled bathroom. Her toothbrush was gone. *What the hell?* Running back into the bedroom, he searched for her clothes. Some were there, but many were missing. His suitcase? Gone. The stupid little box on top of her dresser? Gone.

"Candy!" He did not expect an answer, and he searched the house, knowing damned well she wasn't there. From room to room, he barreled through like a buffalo, smashing doors open and poking holes in the walls behind them with the doorknobs, knocking over lamps, hurling trinkets that she had bought across the room, smashing them into a million pieces. The lamp by the front bay window beckoned him. He snatched it up, ripped the cord from the wall, and –

Wait a minute.

First, he peeked outside to see if anyone was there. He knew everyone was at work at this time of day and hoped the coast was clear. He carried the lamp outside and then hurled it with tremendous force through the window. The large bay window shattered, leaving glass spewed across his living room.

Well, shit. That wasn't smart. Who breaks a window from the outside using a lamp from the inside? Quickly, he went to the garage and searched frantically for something big. Something heavy. Shop Vac? No. Pool chemicals? No. Car battery. Yes. With a loud grunt, he picked it up with both hands, staggered to the front window again, lifted it above his head like a weight lifter, and hurled it through the window. It nicked a leftover icicle-shaped piece of glass, sending it into the house as well.

Then, satisfied with his crime scene, he went to the kitchen and called the police. They were there soon after.

"Mr. Kaya, I'm very sorry for your loss. Do you have any pictures of her we might be able to give to the news? Or perhaps for the paper?"

"Huh? Oh. Yeah. I guess." He rubbed his unshaven face as he went to the bedroom and tried to find one. But as he searched through his things, then hers, he saw no pictures of her. Him, yes. Her, no. Muttering under his breath, he went to the living room and searched there. No pictures, not even her modeling portfolio. "Um, officer? I don't have any pictures of her."

"Does anybody else?"

"I…I don't know. I'll have to ask at work. I have to call in anyway. They're probably wondering where I am."

"Yes, sir. If you could find us something to use, it would be very beneficial to us."

Demetri nodded, grunted slightly in reply, then went to the kitchen to use the phone. A black magic marker sat on the counter, and he stared at it, hoping it would tell him what she had written and where. But it did not say a word, so he dialed the office at his barn.

"Hey, um, Bart." Demetri found a fellow trainer in the stands at Hialeah.

"Yeah." Bart continued to watch his working horse through his binoculars.

"Hey, I was just wondering if you talked to my girl before she was…taken. Like maybe there was some clue or something that would help me figure out who took her or where she might be."

"Naw, man. I don't know anything about it. I probably only said two words to her the whole time she was here. You working with police on this?"

"Yeah. Getting nowhere, though." Demetri blew out a breath of air as he leaned on the rail next to Bart. Bart's horse galloped by, and Bart lowered his binoculars as the horse neared them, then passed.

Demetri couldn't get anything out of Bart or anyone else he had asked. It seemed she had vanished into thin air. As he headed back to his office, something hit him. He remembered his cousin in New York. Candy was from New York, too. *Maybe she went back there. Maybe she's working at Belmont again.*

He hurried into his office, shut the door behind him, and slid into his desk chair. He picked up the phone and searched his Rolodex for his cousin Tony. Tony had connections.

"Yo, TO-ny," Demetri shouted into the phone as he did his best Long Island accent.

Tony laughed. "Man, you need to give that shit up. You're from Florida, not New York."

"Hey, I need a favor."

"What can I do you for?"

"I'm looking for someone."

"Not again."

"Yes. Again. But this time, I'm really in love. Last time it wasn't love. This time it was. Is. I don't even know if she's still alive. But I think she might have gone back to New York."

"Back? She's from here?"

"Yeah. She said she worked at Belmont for a while, for a female trainer. Maybe she went back there. The trainer's daughter was her best friend, but she died. Candy had no parents, and this friend's mother was like a mother to her. I bet anything she went back there. Anything you could do for me? Can you check into it?"

"Do you mean the trainer who just won the Kentucky Derby? With her daughter riding?"

"What?" Demetri screamed as he stood to his feet. "That's the same woman? Did she lie to me? That bitch. She lied. That friend isn't really dead?"

"Well, if it's the same friend, no. This is the only female trainer I know of in New York, though. And a daughter who died…well, she almost died. But she's alive and kickin'."

Demetri's blood boiled. "That's where she is, then. I'm sure of it. I need to get up there. Dammit."

"Well, they'll be at Pimlico soon."

Demetri nodded as he formulated a plan.

Candy drifted in a vast sea of nothing. There was no time. She saw nothing, felt nothing, but she heard something – voices. They were faint, as if she were listening in on a long-distance phone call between New York and Alaska. Or maybe they were echoes, as they came from no particular direction, and the words were unintelligible.

There was nothing but white. It was bright, but not blinding. *This must be it,* she thought. *I'm dead. Where do I go now? I thought I was supposed to head into the light, but I seem to be in it already.*

She was so relieved for the pain to be over that she could have cried. Or, maybe not, because as she looked down at herself, she realized she had no self. She had no body, so she must not have eyes. Or ears? So, how could she hear those voices? Were they the voices of hell? Was she headed that way? They were getting louder, though ever so gradually. She could tell she was floating closer to something, but she saw nothing off in the distance. Everything was just... white.

At least I'm not burning in a lake of fire. Yet. Will I be soon? Candy wondered if she could somehow avoid it by holding on to a root hanging from the ground. Would her form of hell be to watch her parents burn beneath her as she clung to the root for all eternity? Did she not take good enough care of them? Was that her sin?

Wait a minute. Parents are supposed to take care of their kids, not the other way around. Ha. Two drug addicts who ignored their kids... I'd send them to hell if I had the choice. They deserved it. Or did they? Did anyone? Was I so bad that I deserved to be sent there? Was I so horrible to people?

Maybe. Candy remembered praying to God for forgiveness, yet not knowing if there was such a thing as God or even forgiveness. *Just in case,* she had thought. And so far, she could not tell if it had worked. She seemed to be in between. *Maybe this was that Purgatory the Catholics talk about.* She didn't see anybody, though. No relatives, no animals, no other people either. No Jesus, no Satan. *What the hell?* she wondered, then tried to slap her hand over her mouth to censor herself, but remembered again that she was just a soul now. No body.

At least the pain was over. No more thirst, hunger, or back pain, which she had thought odd. It was all gone, and she was forever grateful to whoever brought her soul into this white light.

Suddenly there was a loud motor, and she felt vibrations. It was as if the entire sea she had been floating in became tumultuous and dangerous. She was scared. This was it. She hadn't spent enough time in Purgatory or wherever that was. *No,* she tried to say, but it would not sound. She could not cry though she was deathly afraid.

Strangely, only minutes later, it stopped.

The sea was serene and smooth again. Had she had lungs, she might have breathed a sigh of relief.

"Hold on, baby," she heard in her ear. *What? Who was that? It sounded like... Was it? Was he here, too? Couldn't be. No.* She didn't want him to be here. She couldn't have him suffer. Though leaving her behind was the worst thing he had ever done to her, it didn't warrant him a visit to hell.

She heard more voices now, women shouting orders to each other. She heard them loudly and clearly, but she did not understand a word of their language. She could tell, though, that they were taking her somewhere. Were they angels of death, perhaps?

The shouting continued, but she felt like she had stopped moving again. She could not see anyone, only hear them, and still could not make out their words.

Then, all was quiet, and the light dimmed into darkness.

About the Author

Raised in Southern Maryland, Kristie Higgins grew up as a horse lover, riding friends' horses whenever possible. Short stories written as a horse-obsessed teenager have stuck with her and are now emerging as novels.

She is a graduate of Indiana University, Bloomington, and a retired instrumental music teacher. She taught in various elementary schools in Maryland for twelve years before retiring. No musician can ever give up music, so she plays keyboard in her church, with her two teenage sons playing guitar and bass alongside. At the end of the day, she relaxes by watching horseracing, crocheting, and writing with the help of her two cats, Shadow and Cookie.

63833362R00191

Made in the USA
Lexington, KY
19 May 2017